Trapper Tom

FuzionPress

TRAPPER TOM

PAUL VERNON BRUCE

First Printing: September 2024
First Edition

Paperback ISBN: 978-1-955541-59-6
eBook ISBN: 978-1-955541-60-2
Hardcover ISBN: 978-1-955541-61-9
LCCN: 2024918830

Interior and cover design by Ann Aubitz

Published by FuzionPress
1250 E 115th Street
Burnsville, MN 55337
Fuzionpress.com
612-781-2815

Chapter 1

TOM AWOKE IN HIS SMALL, one-room cabin at the first glimmer of light. Looks like it might be a clear day, he thought. Finally, the days were getting longer, and his calendar—assuming he had marked it correctly—said it was late February, a week or so after Valentine's Day. Is that still a thing? He laughed to himself. Certainly he wasn't that disconnected, was he? Almost eight weeks into the 1980s and he hadn't talked to another human. His hunger was growing with the light, and knowing he had another day of work—checking his trapline—he rolled out of bed, added some wood to the stove, then dug through a cooler and grabbed a section of venison sausage. He looked into one of his three metal canisters for some flour, hoping for his usual breakfast of venison and biscuits. Not to his surprise, he was very low on flour—just enough to make a couple of small biscuits. He checked one of the other two canisters, and the cornmeal was also low. No need to check the dried bean canister—that'd been empty for days.

He usually would have made his midwinter trip into Purdy by now, the closest town, with all the services he needed, but a few weeks of great bounty from his traplines had made him not want to take a break. Then, as the traplines had settled into a more normal pattern, the weather had taken a turn for the worse. Extended snowstorms and cold snaps had gone on for a couple of weeks. With the weather now settled down for the time being, he had gone as long as he could without replenishing his supplies.

As he mixed the biscuit dough in the slowly warming cabin, he started planning his trip to town. He needed most of a day to make the trek each way. He didn't want to take a chance that bad weather would cause him to have to spend a night in the open. With all the new snow, the journey would be difficult, so he had to plan carefully: one day down, sell the furs that were ready to go, buy the supplies he needed for the rest of the winter, then some leisure and rest time. He always rented a room in the motel, enjoyed a long, cleansing shower, took a trip to the barbershop, and had a meal or two at the diner, then a day to hike back. He always tried to do a Saturday–Sunday trek in order to attend a church service and keep his promise to his mother: "Yes, Mom, I go to church whenever I can."

He always enjoyed a church service. It allowed him a chance to "socialize" in a structured way and let people see he was still alive and okay. Purdy was a small town, much like the ones where his parents had grown up. But it was the county seat and the only real town in the county of the same name, so it had the K–12 school. That, along with a handful of businesses, including the fur dealer, a department store that also served as an outfitter for people venturing into the area for outdoor activities such as hunting, fishing, and hiking, and a specialty lumber mill, meant the town had some staying power.

While Tom preferred his life in the woods and his traplines provided a comfortable living, he wasn't a complete recluse. He had to admit he enjoyed some of the amenities of "city" life. He did like a nice shower and a chance to clean up. He liked to let someone else cook a meal or two, with luxuries like eggs and bacon or a chicken pot pie. While the trek into town and back was rigorous, he actually didn't mind a midwinter respite from the solitude. Once he'd sold his furs and bought his supplies, there was money left over, which he would leave in the bank and be able to use when he went down in the spring to sell the last of his winter's furs and get his gardening and other supplies.

It took six to seven hours to make the hike each way, and he was glad the days were longer. It was no fun to be out in the woods after dark. It was easy to lose your way, though he was so familiar with the area he'd be unlikely to ever get truly lost.

The land where he lived and trapped, as well as the land that he would traverse most of the way to town, was heavily wooded, with ridgelines, streams, small lakes, and swamps—virtually inaccessible except on foot. There once had been some logging trails, but this far out of town, even those had grown over. Even snowmobiles had limited available range, due to the extremely rugged terrain. He stayed very much at home through the winter, as his living consisted of running a trap line, and checking it every other day. It took a full day to check and reset, with the intervening day spent cleaning and curing the furs he collected, so his life developed into a steady, comfortable rhythm. He had been living this way for quite a few years now and found he enjoyed it more all the time.

Tom had a family, though his dad had passed away, and his brother had moved to Chicago to work as a financial analyst. His sister had stayed close to home in the suburbs near his mom, and she was his one regular contact. In fact, if he didn't go into town soon and send his annual midwinter letter, she'd worry. The motel had stationery and would sell him a stamp. Every chance she got, she told him how she worried as the winter went on. There weren't many such opportunities. She was always harping at him to buy a radio so she could—via local broadcasting—send word to him if she needed to reach him. So far, he had ignored her pleas, using the excuse that the service was spotty where he lived, which was true. Besides, he treasured his solitude, and a radio and batteries were just more stuff he had to pack in. Maybe someday he would do it, especially as his mom aged. He really noticed it each year when he made his annual visit home. It was strange how he could be so uncomfortable in the very suburbs where he had grown up.

As the biscuits baked, Tom began his shopping list: flour, cornmeal, and beans, of course, but also some toiletries. His scissors had broken, and while he didn't shave, he did try to keep his beard trimmed so it stayed out of his way. He also didn't want to look like the Unabomber when he did have to go to town. His goal was to not attract attention. He didn't want to be a sidewalk curiosity. Adding to his list, he also enjoyed such amenities as toilet paper and toothpaste. Some candles and a few trapping supplies rounded it out, and just like that, the venison sausage was sizzling in the pan and the biscuits were ready. The water was also hot, so he poured some into his cup with a spoonful of instant coffee grounds, and breakfast was ready.

As Tom ate, he looked again at his calendar. It was Wednesday, so if he worked his trapline as normal today, he would also work Friday as usual, then not reset the traps until he returned on Monday, and continue his normal routine for the rest of the winter. Trapping season was almost over, but he had a month or so to give it one last good run.

Breakfast eaten, he put his plate and silverware in the wash basin and prepared to go out into the cold. With the days a bit longer, he would be back well before dark as long as all went well. It would also be good to look for a rabbit or grouse so he'd have something fresh for supper.

The weather cooperated over the next few days, and just as he planned, Tom began his walk down to Purdy at first light Saturday morning.

Chapter 2

TOM WOKE ABRUPTLY TO A NOISE in the motel room next door to his—shouts, scuffling, a scream, then a gunshot, then another. Pulling on his pants and shoes, Tom stepped quickly to the door of his room. Looking out, he saw a man running to a car parked across the lot in the dark. The door of the room next to his was open, the light on, and a girl, perhaps only in her teens, lay on the floor bleeding profusely. She looked at Tom as he entered, then her eyes went blank.

In that instant, he recognized her from the motel office when he had checked in the afternoon before. She had seemed angry and had been sharing words with Phil, the motel owner. That conversation had abruptly stopped when Tom walked in. She had taken her key and walked quickly past Tom and out the office door. Her mannerisms seemed odd for Purdy, but Tom hadn't given it much more thought. Now here she was dying right in front of him.

Tom turned back to look out the door, heard a shot, and simultaneously felt pain welling in his upper arm. The man in the car sped away. The driver's window was open, and Tom managed to get the briefest of looks at the driver as the car passed under a light. A handgun was aimed out the open window. This time Tom saw the flash from the end of the barrel and heard the shot. Yet another shot was taken in his direction, so Tom dove back into the room, nearly on top of the now obviously dead girl.

As Tom stood up, Phil appeared in the doorway, cursed loudly, bent to take a good look at the girl, then picked up the phone in the room and dialed 911. As the phone rang, he looked over at Tom, almost smiled a bit, then asked , "Are you ok? What the heck happened here?"

Tom couldn't answer any of those questions. Instead, he sat down on the end of the bed, staring at the girl, trying to sort out the events of the last few seconds. Who was she, and who would shoot her and why? What if Tom had just stayed in his room, minding his own business? He felt like he was in a trance or having a bad dream.

Phil hung up the phone, and within minutes, a deputy sheriff—Bobby somebody, if Tom recalled correctly—arrived, followed by an ambulance. The town had a small hospital as well as a clinic and an urgent care. The EMTs quickly pronounced the girl dead, then the sheriff rolled in. Tom struggled to remember the sheriff's name. He had seen him around town a few times, but it was only Bobby he had visited with. Bobby was quite the outdoorsman and was always interested in what Tom knew about hunting and fishing.

Bobby was clearly at home investigating a crime scene, which surprised Tom. He must have some background Tom was unaware of. Bobby took pictures from every angle, including several of Tom, who was by now sitting in the corner on the only chair in the room. Bobby also photographed the bullet holes in the wall opposite the door.

The EMTs turned their attention to Tom, who, in the shock of the events, had all but forgotten he'd been shot in the left upper arm. One of the EMTs noticed the blood flowing freely from the open wound and began irrigating and bandaging it.

The sheriff ordered the ambulance crew, over their protest, to take both Tom and the dead girl to the hospital.

"We need this guy treated and Doc Bradford needs to do a preliminary evaluation on the girl before we send her in for an autopsy. Get some ID on her if you can."

"But Doug…"

Ah, that was the sheriff's name. The EMT continued. "We're not a hearse. We're not supposed to haul dead bodies."

"Understand, but this is a murder. We need to get her in to start an autopsy exam, which has to take place in a clinic, not a funeral home. Doc Bradford knows the steps to start. So both she and this guy…"

"Tom," Bobby chimed in.

"Tom, then, need to go to the same place—for very different reasons. Consider it a law enforcement order and put that in your report if you wish. In fact, I'll phone the state crime lab from here to let them know to expect her tomorrow. Let Doc know I did that. It will help him know what steps to take."

The sheriff then turned to Tom and said, "Make sure you know you are in custody. If I had another deputy, I'd send him along with you, but I don't. Go in the ambulance, and Bobby or I will be by as soon as we can to get your statement."

The sheriff then turned to Bobby and continued, "Bobby, stay here as long as you need to in order to document the crime scene—pictures, measurements, everything. Then seal off both this room and the room next door, where Tom was. I'm going to go to the office to get the info Phil has on the girl who rented this room, then died here."

Only then did Tom notice that Phil had disappeared.

Through all this conversation, the pain in Tom's upper arm was increasing.

Going out the motel room door, the sheriff looked over at Tom. "Go with these guys now. As I said, you're in custody, but I can't deny you treatment for your wound."

Then to the EMTs: "Make sure the doctor knows he's supposed to stay there. I won't be long."

"Can I go back to my room and get my stuff?" Tom directed his question to the sheriff.

"No. Bobby, go over and grab him a shirt. Leave everything else. All of this is a crime scene, so we can't let you go back in your room. Sorry."

"How is my room part of the crime scene?"

"There might be something there that connects you to our victim."

"I never saw her until I saw her in the office when I checked in here yesterday."

"Sorry, Tom. As Bobby can tell you, we need to follow police crime scene investigation protocols, and since you are here with the victim, your room is part of the crime scene."

Tom was almost as shocked at that as he was with the crime itself. He took the flannel shirt Bobby handed him and tied it around his waist. No need to get it all bloody.

The ambulance pulled into the urgent care, and Tom was allowed to get out before they unloaded the body. A nurse met him and walked him into a curtained area, where she took over the treatment begun by the EMTs. She looked at the wound and said,

"You were very lucky. This is just a graze, though it is pretty deep. An inch closer to the center of your arm and you may have had a bullet lodged in your arm or even a broken bone. Or worse yet, it could have severed an artery."

Tom, in a feeble effort to be glib, replied, "And I think my t-shirt is salvageable ."

The nurse looked at him. "Always with the brave, pithy comment. You outdoors types are all the same. I guess it's better than crying and fainting."

"Here, take these—they'll help with the general pain. Also, I'm going to have to put some Novocain in this arm so I can trim off some of the hanging skin before I bandage you up. It'll take a few minutes to work, so sit tight. I'll be right back. Once I'm done, I'm sure the doctor will want to see you and most likely stitch you up."

No matter how much skill and experience a nurse has, the doctor always has to make sure he earns a few dollars, Tom thought.

The nurse injected the Novocain and stepped out, coming back in a few minutes to complete her work on his arm. She cleaned, trimmed, and covered the wound with a bandage to control the bleeding, then left again.

A moment later, the doctor walked in. Tom, still a little groggy from pain, the pain pills, shock, exhaustion, and the Novocain, barely looked up. To Tom's surprise, it wasn't Doc Edwards, who had treated him for a few minor injuries over the years. This must be the Doc Bradford the sheriff had mentioned in his conversations with the EMTs. This doctor was dressed in scrubs, including a mask and cap. That struck Tom as unusual, and he struggled to focus. The doctor carefully unwrapped the temporary dressing, then said,

"As usual, my nurse has gotten a good start on your treatment. But I do need to do some more trimming, then sew it up, and get a good bandage on it. Because of the extent of the trauma, I think I'll override her Novocain and give you a more general anesthetic."

Tom's vision and thinking are now rapidly clearing up. Despite the mask, Tom recognizes the doctor's eyes, size, and mannerism—but mostly the eyes. Suddenly he realizes it could be the shooter. He was not an expert in human behavior, but he was an expert on identifying animals, including any danger. His instinctive alarms were going off.

As the doctor prepared the syringe for a shot, Tom asked, "When will the nurse be back?"

The doctor ignored the question and continued to concentrate on the syringe.

Tom tried a different tack. "Just for the heck of it, what exactly is in that shot?"

Again the question was ignored, and as the doctor turned back toward him, Tom knew he was the shooter. He mustered all his strength, pushed the doctor away, and ran out the door—through an emergency exit and out into the cold.

Chapter 3

HE WAS WEARING ONLY A T-SHIRT, with his boots and pants, so the cold he ran into was jarring. For a second, it took his breath away. Luckily, he still had his flannel shirt around his waist. That was still not enough clothing for this midwinter cold. He quickly found his way to complete darkness, and, stopping to catch his breath, he put on his flannel shirt, the pain of pulling it over his wounded shoulder almost causing him to lose consciousness. He had to stay awake and focused. He could see the doctor outlined in the urgent care door. Tom worked his way further into the darkness, knowing he needed to keep moving and that he wouldn't last long without warmer clothing.

Fighting through the pain, Tom considered the entirety of his situation. If the doctor is—or even might be—the shooter, can he trust the sheriff? Too risky. In small towns, doctors are godlike. No matter what the circumstances, the sheriff would almost certainly believe the doctor's word over his.

Given that, he considered his options for survival. There are precious few. It's way too risky to go back to the motel. Or was it? His gear and outerwear may mean the difference between life or death. His room was a crime scene, locked, and the sheriff had the key. He'd have to break in. That created another set of risks. Did he overreact to the doctor? Why did the doctor not answer any of his questions? That in itself was unusual. He may have overreacted, but maybe what was in the syringe was lethal. Then there'd be no second-guessing.

Tom was pretty sure this guy was the only doctor in the county, so he was likely the coroner as well. Or at least could influence a coroner. Even if the injection wasn't lethal, it could probably incapacitate him long enough to plant some evidence, then give the doctor time to talk to the sheriff and frame Tom for the murder. Suspect dead or compromised, evidence managed—either way, the case would be solved. Nice and neat. If it hadn't been for the mystery shot the doctor wanted to give him, he might have taken his time with the sheriff, making his statement, trusting the justice system. But the syringe had changed all that. Too big a chance to take.

Tom's thoughts were swirling. Way too many stressful events in way too short a time. How did this all start? Who was the girl? Why kill her? Especially in such a sloppy way? Drug runner? Prostitute? Pregnant? Didn't trust her local doctor to do a back-room abortion? Were the rooms on either side of the murder scene usually vacant? The whole motel was usually more or less vacant in the dead of winter. The county was sparsely populated and too far from any major city to be readily accessible to winter fun seekers in any volume.

Tom kept working his way away from the urgent care, sticking to the alleys. He saw county sheriff department cars a couple of times, so he was very careful to stay out of sight.

From time to time a dog barked, and he either stood still or, if the barking continued, moved away. Lucky for him, all the dogs seemed to be indoors and no porch lights came on. Sticking to the alleys and crossing the dimly lit side streets as rapidly as he could, he worked his way away from the hospital.

He was definitely getting colder. He didn't really know anyone in the town, certainly not well enough to trust them in his current situation. He had always kept his visits to town brief: the motel, the diner, the church—where he tried to just come and go. Maybe he should have stayed after church for coffee a few times instead of declining in order to get his stuff and head back to his cabin. The fur dealer, who Tom had never visited with much. And he didn't know where he lived. Maybe he should have taken the time and effort to make some friends here. He had visited the most with Bobby, over a meal in the diner, and that wasn't much. Bobby would have no choice but to turn him in, and from there it would be back to the hospital and the doctor would have another crack at him, probably with Bobby or Doug standing watch.

He moved to where he could see the motel. There was yellow tape over his room door and the room next door. It was way too well lit to break in.

Focus, Tom thought to himself. *What are the next essential steps? I cannot go back to the motel. I need to get home to get shelter and supplies.* He also needed to make sure his arm didn't bleed badly, making him easy to track. He knew the sheriff knew vaguely where his cabin was and would show up as soon as he could get there. He would be able to snowmobile part of the way but would have to hike after that. Right now, Tom needed warmer clothes—preferably a coat, hat, and mittens. He would not survive the night without those basic items. Or a really good shelter, which was pretty unlikely. He needed to stick with plan A: get some warm clothes and get back out into the woods.

If he broke into the outfitter's store, he'd be able to get everything he needed, but that would certainly attract the police and would be an actual crime. It would make him look even more desperate. His chances of getting away would actually go down.

The church! It collected clothes for the poor. There should be something there he could wear. In this small town, it may even be unlocked.

His watch was on his motel nightstand, but Tom figured it had to be close to 2 a.m.

Tom stayed in the alleys, moving very carefully, working his way toward the church. He tried the back door. Locked. Tom tried the side door. It was locked but loose. Tom gave it a push—the latch gave way and he was in. He closed the door behind him and found his way to the charity mission room. He was profoundly lucky: not just a heavy outer shirt, but a decent parka a couple of sizes too big. Also an old pair of choppers, complete with wool liners and sturdy leather outers.

Somebody had probably donated them after getting some more modern mittens. A standard red and black winter hat with heavy earflaps. That fit okay.

He also needed matches. Tom worked his way back to the sacristy. Sure enough, he found a few books of matches. Also, in a plastic bag, the communion bread for the service that would take place in a few hours. Take it? Mortal sin? No, it was just bread until it was blessed. The altar guild was a resourceful group. They'd figure out a replacement. With the matches in his parka pocket and the bread in hand, he worked his way back to the side door. He closed it again. There was no need to tip off his presence any earlier than necessary.

Now, how to get out of town, into the woods where he was on his own turf. His place was north, so he headed out from a dead-end street that ran to the southwest. The sheriff was smart. At first light he'd be looking for tracks to the north, toward Tom's cabin. Tom hoped to find an empty hunting shack where he could warm up and get some sleep. His arm ached a lot. He should have stolen some aspirin!

He walked for an hour, so he was maybe two miles from town, down an old logging trail headed mostly west. No cabin in sight. He made out a downed pine—lots of cover. He had no knife or gun, so he hoped it was unoccupied. Dim moonlight let him see shapes, so he approached cautiously but not quietly. He heard some scurrying away, so it was only rabbits or squirrels. The presence of rabbits or squirrels made it unlikely to be a home for any larger predators.

Tom went around to the side away from the trail, broke one branch, and worked his way in. He did his best to make the branch look whole again. In his years as a trapper, he had been stuck out on a trapline more than once, and this experience helped him now. He was not warm, but he was out of the wind. He broke off a few more branches to make some room and used them to insulate himself against the cold of the ground. He cleared a small area down to the dirt and made a small fire. Not much heat, but it made him feel better. Curled up in his oversized parka, he could get his legs inside. He felt a little warmer. He tried some bread. It was quite good and helped him feel even better.

He tried to think of a good plan to exonerate himself and return to his comfortable life in his cabin. Instead, he kept reflecting: How did he even get here? How did he figure out that little cabin was his home? What kept him there, and will his solitude now be ended? With these thoughts circling in his head, and despite the pain, exhaustion overtook him and he got some much-needed sleep.

Chapter 4

TOM WAS BORN AND RAISED in the suburbs just like millions of other kids in the 1960s. He went to school, tried playing a band instrument—trombone, actually. He found he enjoyed singing, so he stayed with choir. He liked the kids better too—a little less uptight.

He had played all the usual youth sports but found that fall sports interfered with his love for hunting, and spring sports interfered with his love for fishing. So he stuck with basketball and was good enough to play all through high school, becoming a starter his senior year.

His parents were good, solid, everyday suburban people. They had moved to the metro area from smaller towns, very much like this small town. His parents had met at a technical training school near where they had grown up. There they had both learned their professions, his mom becoming a nurse and his dad an electrician.

For them, the suburbs beckoned—lots of work opportunities, with good enough pay and benefits, and they carved out a good life for Tom and his older brother and sister. A life in the suburbs. And like many other transplants, they enjoyed their visits back to their small hometowns to visit parents and other relatives. For all of them, that meant time in the woods or on the lakes: hiking, fishing, small-game hunting, and, of course, the annual fall deer hunt.

Tom enjoyed the circle of friends and relatives who gathered for a weekend or two to hunt deer, but year by year, he found he enjoyed his solitary bow hunting time even more. When his dad passed away unexpectedly when Tom was in college, the friends-and-family hunts and trips to the woods gradually went away. But for Tom, his love of the outdoors became even stronger. It reminded him of the best of the times he had spent with his dad.

Over time, he spent more and more time in the woods. As he worked his way through college, which was expected of him, he selected majors in biology and zoology. His natural scholastic ability, along with his love and knowledge of the wilderness, helped him excel in his studies. So when he was offered a graduate teaching position in zoology and a chance for a master's degree, he took it. With that degree in his pocket, he spent a summer working for the state fish and game department, which simply increased his love of the wild, though not the bureaucracy of a government job.

He'd even started on some doctorate work, but "ran out of gas." He soon tired of the rules, requirements, and the university politics, not to mention the hours of study. He was simply drawn to the wild. So, after one year of study, he took a personal sabbatical, moving into the woods for the summer and that fall, just didn't bother to go back to school. He had learned he could readily sustain himself by hunting and fishing. He tried teaching in a community college and enjoyed the work and the students, but none of them had his passion for living off the land. They wanted all the answers and then an hourly job.

While holding this teaching position in Thompson Falls, he had stumbled across the chunk of land he'd eventually purchased—deeper in the woods than any of his family hunting expeditions had taken him. A carveout the lumber companies didn't want because of inaccessibility and poor lumber—some big trees, but lots of brush: extremely rugged. It was 640 acres, some of it swampy, some of it hilly, and not even a logging trail remained to get there. With no access road, the price was dirt cheap, and no bureaucrat cared enough to walk in and see if he was building his cabin to comply with any code. He had spent the summer building the cabin. He grew a small garden for his staples, and the small game he trapped and shot, and fish he caught, rounded out his diet. In the fall, he bagged a deer, so he had a basic meat supply for the winter.

Then, as the ground and water froze, he started setting out traplines, which provided the cash he needed for the food and other supplies he could not produce for himself. His only interaction with society were his trips to Purdy, an annual visit back to see his mom and the rest of his family, and making sure he kept his hunting, trapping, and fishing licenses up to date.

Chapter 5

TOM WOKE ABRUPTLY. Cold, confused. *Where am I? Why?* It all came flooding back, driven largely by the pain in his arm. He should have stolen some pain meds. He worked through an overwhelming desire to get moving. *Think, Tom, think. What do I need to do? Get my story to the sheriff? Turn myself in? No, the doctor is too influential, and all the circumstantial evidence is against me. I was in the room when the girl died. I had the room next door. Amazing that my circumstantial guilt took so long to form in my own mind.*

The sheriff told me to wait at the urgent care to take my statement. Instead I ran. All based on my belief that the doctor is the actual shooter and was going to give me some injection he refused to describe. Why was he in my treatment room with a mask and hat? The gun may have been wiped and left in my motel room or at some other easy-to-find spot. My wound was only a graze, so no bullet. That had to be in the wall opposite the door, as well as the other bullets shot from the car. Bobby took a lot of pictures and has to have documented that. How do they explain his wound? Self-inflicted to create doubt? Sloppy gun work? It all boils down to the doctor. If he was the shooter, it was just too risky to let him administer that shot. It could be lethal or it could just knock Tom out long enough to plant the evidence and sway the sheriff.

Who was the girl? Why kill her? That was the real root of the problem. He had no answer. Right now, his focus had to be on survival. His best solution seemed to be to work his way to his cabin and wait for the sheriff, but not allow himself to be trapped or be confrontational. As he thought, he cleaned the small branches off a five-foot length of pine to use as a walking stick. It may help him balance, and he felt a little bit armed.

He worked his way out of his pine shelter. It was barely light out, but he immediately noted one lucky break: it was snowing. Not hard, but enough to cover his tracks. It would take him most of the day to get home, and he needed to do it unseen. There may be people out in the woods since it was a Sunday—snowmobilers, cross-country skiers, snowshoers. He would have to proceed cautiously.

Tom decided to work his way home very methodically, not in a beeline, so any tracks he might leave would reveal a direction. He would have to stop every half hour or so to rest and nibble on the bread—communing with nature and what was supposed to be communion bread. Ironic somehow. West, north, east, north. He heard snowmobiles in the distance a few times. They were not a risk, but snowshoers and cross-country skiers were. They didn't make much noise and sometimes went further off the known trails, especially the snowshoers.

The snow continued, and now, about midday, Tom guessed, he came across a spot along his trapline. He could easily follow that home. He still proceeded quietly, cautiously, slowly. There was no need to get careless now, though he was definitely tired and hungry. The only control he had over his situation was not to be caught by surprise. A couple of hours later, he knew he was well within a mile of his cabin. He had to develop an approach plan in case the sheriff or someone else was watching his place.

The usual path from town was between two long, winding ridges, and a snowmobile could make all but the last few miles without risking getting stuck or hitting a snow-covered deadfall, or driving off or into a ledge. He worked his way to where he could overlook that last stretch of trail. Just as his tracks were covered by the snow, he could see no tracks on the trail. Sticking to a hillside overlooking the trail, he worked his way back to the end of the snowmobile trail. There sat a snowmobile. The sheriff, or someone, was likely in or around his cabin. His arm really ached and he was out of bread. Using snow as water all day had not helped his ability to stay warm. Staying mostly to the ridges, he made his way to where he could see the back of his cabin. He could feel his strength ebbing. Whatever his plan, it had to work—he couldn't run again. His mind now racing, he forced himself to focus through the exhaustion, cold, hunger, and pain. He also knew he might not last another night in the open, so getting into his cabin was vital.

He approached the cabin from behind to get a better look. Smoke was coming from the chimney. Whoever was waiting for him had moved in. He worked his way up the east hill and looked in. A deputy—in fact, the deputy who had worked the crime scene, Bobby—was sitting in a chair, staring into the fire. Bobby was not overly smart, but a decent guy. From their handful of conversations, Tom knew he had a wife and a couple kids. He was almost as comfortable in the woods as Tom. He might be hard to bluff, and there was no way Tom could overpower him in a fight, especially now. He knew Bobby would have to step outside at some point to relieve himself and get some fresh air. It was well into the afternoon, but Tom waited and then—his sketchy plan worked!

Bobby went to the door and stepped outside. He walked a few steps from the door and unzipped his pants. This was Tom's chance. He quickly and quietly worked his way up behind Bobby, poked him in the back with his walking stick, and said, "Don't turn around—you know who I am. Carefully hand me your gun and the radio." Bobby complied, probably thinking of his family.

With the gun in hand and the police radio in his parka pocket, Tom said, "Now back into the cabin. Nice and slow ."

He knew there wasn't much time before Bobby would either have to radio in to the station or head back to town, or he would just get a call for an update from the sheriff, so he had limited time and limited options. He didn't need the whole department and maybe the state police coming up here. "Bobby, what are your orders?"

Rather than answer, Bobby said, "Tom, where's your gun ?"

Tom smiled. "Your gun is my gun."

"No, the gun you stuck in my back." Tom showed him the walking stick.

"Oh Lord," Bobby said. "I will never live this down."

"No," said Tom, "you were expecting a ruthless killer escaped from justice. You had every reason to believe I'd be armed and desperate." Not leaving any time for Bobby to take the conversational lead, Tom continued , "Bobby, we need to talk. You need to tell me what's going on in town and I need to tell you what really happened."

Bobby began, "Apparently, you murdered a runaway in the motel, got shot in the process, and ran away before the doctor could finish treating your gunshot wound. Not sure why you came back here or what you want with me."

"Well, Bobby, most of that is not true. I did run from the ER, but only because I am pretty sure the new doctor is the one who actually murdered the girl. But let's back up. Who is the girl, and does anybody know why she was killed?"

Bobby looked stunned. "Doc Bradford killed the girl? Nonsense!"

"Listen, Bobby—I am going to tell you everything I saw and did. I need you to just remember it and tell the sheriff when you are all alone with him. Can you do that? Will you do that?"

"Sure, I guess. Since you have my gun."

"Smart guy."

With that, Tom, using the gun as a pointer, directed Bobby to get a chunk of venison sausage from the cooler, put it in the pan, and get it cooking on the stove.

Tom held up the radio. "Will the sheriff call you, or do you have a call-in time?"

"If I don't hear from him, I'm supposed to call in at five. If he finds you, he'll call me. I figure that's unlikely now."

"I think you're right. Let's settle in and have a bit to eat. Sorry I don't have more food to offer you. That's why I was in town. I left my bag of flour and a bag of cornmeal in my motel room, along with my other supplies. You could open a can of peas and carrots from that shelf over there. We'll kind of have a stir-fry. I think there may be a couple of crackers in that last tin on the end of the shelf.

"Next question, Bobby," Tom just had to ask. "How did you even find my place?"

Bobby replied, "I wondered if you'd ask. I spend a lot of my free time in the woods. I actually came across it one other time on a hike with my kids. I have to admit, though, without that, I'm not sure I could have located it, especially in winter. That knowledge is why Doug gave me the assignment of coming up here."

"Just my luck," thought Tom. "Not as secluded as I thought."

As the food was cooking, Tom went through all the details as he remembered them: from hearing the shot, what he saw in the parking lot, and his escape from the ER. He even confessed to breaking into the church and taking the clothes, matches, and communion bread. Tom knew that sharing this detailed litany with Bobby was risky, but it was the only thing he could think of to give himself a chance. The memories were quite vivid for Tom, and he wanted to make sure he recounted them all while they were still fresh in his mind.

Tom reiterated that he was quite sure the ER doctor was the same person he saw at the motel and who had taken a shot at him. All the time he was talking, he was trying to be as sequential as he could, not sure how well Bobby was tracking. At the same time, he was thinking, "Though I have chosen a very solitary life, I need to brush off whatever persuasive skills I once had."

Even if Bobby might not have been his first choice for someone to work with, right now Bobby was his only choice. He decided that he needed to do all he could to get Bobby to trust that his story was the truth and be sympathetic with Tom's situation. It wasn't like Tom wasn't naturally friendly, but he sure was out of practice.

Tom was thinking hard about how to set up the whole situation for Bobby and hope he carried out at least some of it.

Time was of the essence, so he needed to buy himself some time.

"Bobby, you know I've never hurt anyone, right?"

"I guess—not that I know of."

"In fact, I go out of my way to stick to my own business, right?"

"You sure do. I only see you a few times a year."

Satisfied, Tom continued. "I don't want you to do anything to jeopardize your job or the sheriff's trust, but I really need to ask you to do me a huge favor. Remember, once I got your gun, I could have shot you and easily disposed of your body. Yet here we are, talking like old friends."

Bobby looked at Tom with one eyebrow clearly raised.

"I don't know about old friends, but I do appreciate being alive ."

Tom saw he was pushing a little too hard on the friendship thing. Back off! Need to get this right. Maybe a different approach.

"Bobby, I need your help. And to start, I need some time. When you call in, can you tell the sheriff that you haven't seen me and that it's too dark to work your way back to your snowmobile, so you need to stay the night out here? Tell him I might show up yet. So, one truth and one half lie. I do have the upper hand and am trying to deal with you as fairly as I can. But I really do need your help."

Keeping Bobby here created a number of advantages: one fewer guy out looking for his trail, and a guy who was good in the woods at that; the sheriff and others believing he wasn't at his cabin; a meal and a night in a bed; and a chance to pack up for an unknown time of living in the woods, which also was a big help. And, mostly, a chance to get Bobby to raise some of the investigation questions that he needed to make sure somebody raised.

Bobby's reply was just what Tom expected. "Tom, why not just turn yourself in and trust the sheriff to do the investigating? He'll listen to your side, and if you're innocent, it will all work out."

"I appreciate that, Bobby. I do. But here's the rub: I know the new doctor killed that girl. I also know he shot me to try to cover it up, and I am pretty sure that if he had given me that injection in the ER last night, I wouldn't be here with you right now. He's probably bright and smooth-talking, and I'm sure he has already done his best to convince the sheriff that I'm the killer. He's a well-respected member of the community because of his position, and I'm a trapper who is considered to be barely civilized. I think you can see the difference. Also, he needs to frame me because he almost certainly knows who the girl is and why she was there, as well as why he had to kill her. The big question in my mind is why he was so sloppy about it. Was it her gun and he took it away? Did they have some kind of arrangement that she broke? You can see there are lots of questions."

Bobby stared at Tom. "Either you are creating an elaborate alibi in your head, or you have really given this some thought."

"Bobby, as you might imagine, I've thought of nothing else since I got rousted from my motel room early this morning. That and surviving."

Tom tried yet another questioning tactic. "Bobby, what did you do before you became the deputy here?"

"I always wanted to be in law enforcement, so I went to a junior college to study criminology, and even played a little football. However, I never really liked school so dropped out and joined the Air Force, where I was lucky enough to get assigned to MP training. It's mostly dealing with drunk, ornery kids who think they're proving they are men, but the training and my size got me through ok. I did my four years and a two year re-up, then switched to the reserves and went to a tech school and took a law enforcement course. I was hired directly from there by the Thompson Falls Police. I stayed there a few years before this deputy position opened up. I came up here to be able to hunt and fish more. Also, less crime, or so I thought."

This is huge, Tom thought. If Bobby was willing to open up and essentially recite a verbal resume, then some trust must be building. It also gave Tom his next big opening.

"Bobby," Tom said, being sure to say Bobby's name as often as he could, "when you were in Thompson Falls, did you ever work with the detectives or watch them work?"

"A number of times . Why?"

"I figured you had because you seemed to know what you were doing at the motel. But more importantly, you know then that a good detective has good instincts. When they look at a crime, they often have a very good idea what happened and who did what, almost right away. But they know that to get a conviction, they still have to take all the appropriate steps, follow the process in order to rule out other possible scenarios, and build their case block by block, so it holds up in court."

"How do you know that?"

"Am I wrong ?"

"No, but that's a lot to know for someone who says he's as clean and honest as you."

"Bobby, it's as simple as calling it a scientific process, whether it's biology, chemistry, or crime. Besides, before I moved up here, I used to watch too much TV. You worked that crime scene, Bobby, and you took lots of pictures. Is there anything that you recall that didn't seem right, if I in fact killed the girl?"

"You're right. I did examine the crime scene. That's one of the reasons Doug hired me. And I did take lots of pictures. That always helps to remember and to figure things out. But I got sent up here before I got a chance to do anything but put it all in a file."

Tom was making progress, so he moved on to his next question. "The bullet that grazed me went somewhere. Did you look for that?"

"No, as I said, once we were told you'd run from the ER, we all got sent out to search for you. But you're right. That bullet had to end up in a wall or someplace in that room. It would have to be in the pictures I took."

"I know you work for the sheriff, but please be sure when you get back to ask the sheriff to let you revisit that motel room and see if anything else turns up. You can even mention that bullet as well as the missed shots. They should be lined up where they had to be taken through the door. The sheriff has to know they're important to find."

This was going well. Tom had actually developed a rapport with Bobby. However, the clock was moving rapidly toward 5:00.

Time to close the sale? Make the vital request?

Bobby jumped in before Tom could go for the close. "Tom, I love my job and I love living here. Sheriff Jones is 58 years old. I'm 38. I am the only full-time deputy in the county. If you're so smart, I think you can see where this is headed. My wife teaches at the school and between the two of us, we do okay. But I am first in line for being the next county sheriff, and I can't do anything that would interfere with that."

"Absolutely. But what I am suggesting would help you get that job." Tom knew he had to make his pitch now, or things with Bobby might turn confrontational. "Let me know if you can make this work."

"First, someone needs to make sure the sheriff conducts a thorough investigation—a step-by-step investigation so that when I am brought in, he has an ironclad case. Rule out any other possible crime scenarios. Don't take any shortcuts. Make sure he follows all the rules of evidence. You know the process. Second, convince him that you have examined this cabin and the woods around and know this area well, so you have the best chance to bring me in. Then, when you and the sheriff have the case all figured out and it's time for me to come in, you bring me in, and you look great. Make sense?"

"It does, but how do we explain the 'half lie' that I haven't seen you?"

"Bobby, only you can make that decision, but maybe this will help. It has started snowing again and it's getting dark pretty fast. It would really be treacherous for you to start back down to your snowmobile and work your way back to town. Whether I am here or not hardly matters, since you couldn't bring me in right now if you wanted to."

Tom decided to quit talking and let that soak in. His battery-powered wall clock showed 4:57. Then it clicked over to 4:58. It also might be off by a couple of minutes. Tom didn't need to know time all that precisely, so he didn't worry about exact minutes.

Bobby stared into the dying fire. In all their talking, the food had warmed up, and the fire needed more wood. Tom was woozy with hunger and the aching of his wounded arm but decided that putting some wood on the fire would make the cabin more inviting and make him seem more in control.

He stood, wobbled a little, but recovered, and took a big gamble. He left Bobby's gun on the table next to him, walked over, and nonchalantly placed a couple of logs in the stove. He was careful to never take his eye off the gun, but Bobby was captivated by the fire and the new life it now showed. Tom went back to the table, repossessing the gun. Then he got a couple of plates and put out the food for each of them.

"Hungry?" Tom asked.

Chapter 6

BOBBY PERKED UP. "Yeah, I could eat."

The police radio beeped. Tom looked at Bobby. Bobby looked at the radio. It beeped again. Bobby picked it up. Tom could hear both ends of the conversation. The sheriff's voice crackled in.

"How you doin', Bobby? Still at Tom's cabin?"

"I'm fine, sir. Still at Tom's cabin." 'Sir' must have been a leftover from his years in the military. "We should have thought a little more about the check-in time, though. It's getting dark up here. Not sure I want to work my way back yet tonight. How about I spend the night up here and work my way back in the morning? I can also look around for any tracks as I work my way back."

The sheriff hesitated, then said, "You ok there for the night?"

"Yeah, I've got a good fire going and there's food here. I'll be ok. No indoor plumbing though. TP is hanging on a peg by the door. Maybe I won't eat too much ."

"Ok by me. I'll call your wife, ok? And no overtime—we're on a tight budget, you know."

"Not what I wanted to hear but I understand."

Tom motioned to Bobby to keep the line open. It was risky but could prove beneficial.

"Ask him what he's learned," Tom whispered to Bobby.

"Any news on the investigation, Sheriff?"

"It all points to Tom. I have no idea why he would have done it. He was in a different room, we can't find any connection to the girl, but he sure acted guilty when he ran from the ER. If you find him, see if you can just talk him into coming in to the station so we can sort this out. But if he gives you any trouble, you have all the authority you need to do what's necessary, in particular to protect yourself."

"Got it. See you in the morning."

Tom dug into his food. He was as elated as his weariness, hunger, and sore arm would allow. The meager meal really hit the spot. Bobby hadn't had to directly answer the question of whether he'd seen Tom, so was "home free" on his concern about lying. Tom had the evening to coach Bobby on his line of investigation, and he could get some food, some sleep, redress his wound, and pack for some unknown time of roughing it in the dead of winter.

Tom wanted to keep Bobby engaged. "Thanks, Bobby, for a chance to hear me out and thanks for asking the sheriff about the investigation. It gives you the opening to pursue the process we discussed. They have me as their prime suspect, but no motive or any of the other pieces that would wrap up the case for them."

Tom continued, "How's the food?"

"I've had better, but it's not bad."

"Thanks for not ratting me out."

Bobby laughed. That was a good sign. "Tom, if I wanted to take you in, I'd have grabbed the gun when you were putting wood on the fire. Now I have to trust you enough to believe I'll still be alive in the morning."

Tom laughed. "I guess I had to take that chance, so thanks. You should be alive in the morning unless you have a heart attack in the night. That would be really bad luck for both of us."

"No problem. I know that I really can't cuff you and get you out of here in the dark. We are stuck here together and I have to trust you not to shoot me and you have to trust me not to shoot you or tie you up in your sleep."

Tom smiled a bit, then said, "Thanks. That isn't exactly reassuring, but I'll take it. I do need to step outside, though, so I'll take the radio, just in case you have a change of heart.

"While we eat this first course, I'll throw a small venison roast into the pot. That way we'll have a head start on breakfast."

Tom thought how nice it was to deal with people who had a reason to live.

He covered the venison with more snow. The room filled with steam, making it feel a little warmer.

"Bobby," Tom restarted the conversation, "We need to know everything we can about the dead girl. Start with the motel owner. What name is on the register for that room? Who paid for it? Has she been there before? Have other girls booked rooms recently?"

"Slow down, slow down," Bobby said. "I just realized I'm really hungry, and that's a lot of questions all at once. We've got time, and I need to make sure I've got everything well placed in my brain."

Though Bobby was listening, Tom had no way to be sure he wasn't just buying time and that Bobby didn't really believe any of his story. Tom had to be sure he stuck to questions rather than trying to convince Bobby he was innocent.

Tom waited a few moments, then turned the focus to Doc Bradford. "I don't ever recall seeing him before, Bobby. Is he new in town?"

"Yeah, he came here last fall. Just out of med school. Old Doc Edwards had been wanting to retire for a while, so getting a doctor to replace him was really good news. Surprised you hadn't run into him - he spends a lot of his free time fishing. He's out on the lakes a lot. He also comes and goes a lot. I wish he'd stay put in Purdy more. Emergencies don't wait for a doctor."

"Explains why he can't shoot ."

"What?"

Tom continued, "Never mind. Do you know anything else about him? Wife, girlfriend, other hobbies? Where does he go on his days off? Who subs for him?"

"Whoa! Whoa! Whoa! That's a lot of questions, and I'm not sure I'm the right guy to go that deep into his personality or even his lifestyle."

"I'm sorry, Bobby, that all just came flooding out. Let's slow it down and break it down."

They worked through all Tom's questions about Doc Bradford as they ate. Working through it, for the first time, Bobby seemed to fully engage with Tom's line of questioning. He even added several questions of his own. Besides fishing, what would attract a young single doctor to this remote town? It was not a great job – little or no support staff, pretty much on call 24/7. Not a lot of eligible girls and certainly no abundance of single gay guys if that was his preference. The big draw is independence. The only doctor in a sparsely populated county has pretty complete autonomy. Not only the medical expert, but almost automatically the county coroner. Any serious illnesses would be transferred to the hospital in Thompson Falls, just over 60 miles away, but all the fishhook injuries, the simpler gunshots, other accidents, and flu epidemics were all his, as well as annual physicals, both for the adults and for the school athletes, and any other health complaints.

Most of the people in the county were natives: they either stayed and ran family businesses or found work with the county or city. The church had a succession of pastors either at the beginning or ending of their careers, but all in all a pretty close-knit bunch of people.

How had this remote place attracted a brand-new MD?

Tom also wanted the sheriff to pay some attention to the motel owner. When Tom had checked in—wow, was that just yesterday?—he had realized the guy behind the desk was new, rather than the older couple who had run the place for years. Letting his attention lapse, he really did like that hot shower a couple of times a winter, and a room where he didn't have to add wood to the fire two to three times overnight.

Then his focus returned. What was the conversation between the motel guy and the dead girl? Why did they end it abruptly when he walked in?

"Are we still solving this crime?" Bobby asked.

"Sorry, Bobby, I drifted off for a minute - I was back at the motel."

"How long has this new guy had the place?" Tom continued.

"Just since this past fall. He bought it from the Rogers when old Ed had some health issues. They moved to Thompson Falls so they could get into a 55+ apartment. I think they have a daughter there, and some grandkids. And the better medical care Ed's condition seemed to dictate."

"Where did he come from? Did anybody know him before he came to town?"

"Not sure where he came from. The word is he knew the Rogers before and he had shown an interest in the hotel before Ed's health issue. It was a quick transition. They left—he took over."

"What's his name - besides Phil?"

Bobby looked confused. "Not sure. Why?"

"Your boss has been sheriff here for a lot of years. You don't get and keep that job if you don't know what's going on with just about everything and everyone."

Tom continued, "Also, when I checked in, he and the victim were having some kind of heated conversation that they cut off the minute I walked in. Doug may find that interesting."

Bobby laughed a bit. "Maybe she needed more towels. You may be stretching your investigation a bit."

"You could be right, but she didn't leave with towels. She just left, kind of in a huff, and now she's dead. Again, Doug may find that noteworthy."

Tom didn't share that alternative, which was that you could also keep the job by ignoring everything going on. If that was the case, Tom was in a lot of trouble. People like that took the easy route at every opportunity, and right now, that would be believing Doc Bradford.

"And you're thinking that if Phil is running any kind of shady operation—drugs, prostitutes, or both—that Doug would know about it?"

"I would like to think so. Did he ever suggest to you that he knew Phil any more than just in passing, or that he had done any kind of background check on who was taking over one of the most visible businesses in town—the only motel in the county?"

Bobby thought for a second. "I don't recall any such info. I think once the Rogers sold to him so quickly, it was almost like they were recommending him. Of course, they really wanted to sell. I have no idea how they knew Phil."

"So over the past few months, we have a new motel owner and a new doctor, and now we have a really visible murder. Interesting development in such a quiet town."

Tom continued. "Obvious question: Have you had any other incidents or calls to the motel since the new owner took over?"

"Yeah, now that you mention it. We had a really minor drug bust there just after Phil took over. Phil acted as shocked as anyone—even more shocked, if I recall his reaction. Some kids—a guy in his early twenties and two underage girls. Charged with intent to distribute—we turned it all over to the state police and haven't heard anything since. You know how long those things take in the court system. I wasn't involved, but I'm sure Phil will get called to testify, since he was right there when we made the bust."

"Bobby, I need to ask you for my first favor that's an actual task. I really appreciate all the info and the conversation, but I really have to question the roles of both Phil and Doc Bradford in this murder. It may be nothing, but as a part of your detective work—you, meaning you and Doug—need to do criminal and credit background checks on both of them. You can do that quietly without alerting them because you are law enforcement. Or better yet, have your state police contact do it."

Bobby was intrigued. "Do you think that will clear you"?

"It may help, but the real line of work here is, as the police on TV say, to clear them from any suspicion. Just routine. I'm not so sure it will clear them, but we need to know. From my perspective, any suspicion we can put on Doc Bradford in particular helps me. This is one of the steps that needs to happen before I can turn myself in.”

Just then the radio beeped. Tom nodded, and Bobby answered, “Deputy Osterman .”

“Doug here—just one last check-in before I turn in for the night. No sign of Tom yet?”

Bobby looked hard at Tom. “Doug, if he shows up, I’ll try to talk him into turning himself in. I don’t think a gun battle in the woods with him is a good tactic. By the way, do you have the murder weapon?”

“No, haven’t found it.”

Bobby continued, “Any ID on the girl?”

“She had an ID, but it was the kind that comes with cheap wallets where you fill in your name and address. Not likely valid or accurate.”

“Did Phil recognize her?”

“No, but you are sure asking a lot of questions.”

Bobby looked at Tom desperately. “I’ve had a lot of time to think just sitting up here—no TV or radio. Trying to piece things together in my head .”

“Sounds like you’re running for sheriff!”

“Just trying to learn and help out where I can. Anything else, boss?”

“No, but keep thinking. I sure can’t figure out why Tom would kill someone. Doesn’t seem the type, though Doc Bradford seems to have it all figured out.”

With his eyes still on Tom, Bobby asked, “What is he saying?”

“The obvious. Was at home in bed, got a call to come to the ER, and there was Tom, getting treated for a bullet wound. Tom ran before I could come in and get his statement. Pretty suspicious to him. It all fits, but still not sure of any motive or anything that links Tom to the girl.”

Doug continued, “I’ll start with Phil in the morning. Checking the register, anything suspicious, etc.”

Bobby replied, "Sounds like the right process. Do you know anything about Phil before he came to town? Remember the girls in that drug bust last fall? We never had that when the Rogers ran the place."

"Bobby, are you sure you didn't bring a stack of detective novels up to Tom's place with you? Or are you always this suspicious and I never noticed?"

Bobby replied, "No, no novels, but I was, as Johnny Carson used to say, 'harking back' to my time on the force in Thompson Falls, when I occasionally worked with the detectives. Just trying to recall their processes. If Tom did it and we prosecute, we need to cover all these questions or his lawyers will. The first thing any detective will tell you is that it sucks to get surprised in court. If he didn't do it and we drag him in to court, that would be the biggest surprise."

"Wow, Bobby—sounds like I need to give you more time to think! Like I said, I'll start fresh in the morning and the first thing I'll do is check in with you. You know, in case you've thought some more."

"Over. Good night"

Tom could have hugged Bobby. He really was listening. But Tom was also really tired and had to pray that Bobby didn't think so hard that he'd change his mind and conclude Tom really was the murderer. It was probably time for both of them to get some rest. He had to figure out the next angle for Bobby and make sure there was no backtracking. Also, he hadn't been in a bed for a long time. He was used to roughing it, but never without food or while trying to cope with a gunshot wound. Apparently "just a graze" meant something different if the bullet just grazed somebody else. It was also good to hear Doug say that Tom didn't seem the type to kill someone, though the new doctor was sure trying to make it look that way. Even a sliver of an open mind was better than nothing.

"OK, Bobby - I really appreciate your questions for Doug. Great discussion. Next question is, what kind of gentlemen's agreement can we make about sleeping arrangements? First of all, truce until sunup?"

"I guess. Even if I got the drop on you, I'm not sure I could get you out of here. I need one thing from you."

"What?"

"You promise me that if we get this investigation on a solid track, you will come with me and turn yourself in, and not double-cross me."

Tom nodded. "Agreed."

Chapter 7

TOM AWOKE AT FIRST LIGHT, mostly due to the throbbing in his shoulder. A night in his own bed had felt really good. He saw Bobby in the rocker, along with the gun and the radio on the table. No indication of any betrayal of their truce. With day breaking, Bobby had had time to think and no longer had the excuse of not wanting to work his way back to town in the dark.

This morning was therefore a decision point for both of them. Tom got up slowly, got some water from the bucket of snow that had melted overnight, and took a couple of aspirin. He put some water on the stove to heat up for coffee—instant had become his way of life. He put the venison back on top of the stove. Good thing there was a little bit of cornmeal left.

He sat back down on the bed and pulled his boots on. Although it was just starting to get light, it was after 7 a.m.

He looked over at Bobby, and it was apparent Bobby had been watching him.

"Coffee?"

"Sure, why not. Is it any good?"

"Not really - but it's hot and has some caffeine. You may have noticed by now this isn't exactly a four-star hotel."

"Says the guy who got the only bed."

"I only wash the sheets once a month in the winter, and that month is about up. I was going to wash them when I came back from town all cleaned up. Figured I was doing you a favor."

"I am deeply appreciative. Should we step outside and take our morning pee?"

"Sounds good to me. You bring the radio, I'll bring the gun."

"Is the truce over?"

"Not unless you want it to be, but if your boss calls, he might get worried if you don't answer. This way we each have one free hand."

Tom followed Bobby out the door. When Bobby turned left, Tom turned right.

"Don't pee on the house, OK?"

"Gotcha ."

Tom waited a few seconds, then started back up with his train of thought from last evening.

"Bobby, the more I think about it, the more I wonder about Phil and Doc Bradford. I really want to figure out where they both came from and if there's any history, or if there's some other relationship."

"I agree, but the short-term problem is how we deal with today. If I go back to town and claim I haven't seen you, that puts me in a really tough spot. If I stay out here, I'll bet you a million dollars that Doug starts snooping around out here at some point during the day to see if he can find your place for himself and see what I'm up to. If he sees you or any clue that you've been here, I'm probably out of a job. Maybe even in line for an accessory charge."

"You're right. I think we need you back in town working the angles we figured out last night and I need to make myself scarce. Let's go back in and get a bite and see if Doug radios you. If not, you call in and tell him you're coming in for a shower and some clean clothes. While you're gone, I will pack up for a few days of camping out. If Doug comes up to take a look, our story will have to be that I must have showed up here after you cleared out. I'm sneaky that way. That clears up our story for last night and today. You stayed overnight. Slept in the rocker because the bed looked dirty. Helped yourself to food and cof-fee.The bigger problem is how to stay in contact every few days to keep up on case developments. And I am serious when I say I'll turn myself in as soon as I believe I won't get railroaded. You have to be real loose with any statements about having seen me. Noncommittal. You don't want to lie, you just don't want to say anything. If it comes out, you'll have to say I surprised you and kept you at gunpoint overnight and when you woke up this morning I was gone. That way you don't look too bright but you don't look dishonest."

"Maybe we should just go with that story, Tom. I've been known to doze off, and it is as close to the truth as we can get. I can handle the 'not too bright' accusation as long as I'm the one who does find you and bring you in. That makes me whole in the deal. Kind of evens things out."

"That makes sense, Bobby. Now how do we communicate?"

"First, we have some coffee and eat. My thinking stops with that. I may even doze off!"

Tom poured some of the hot water into a kettle and added the last of the cornmeal. He cut the venison roast into pieces and put it in a skillet. Then he put a spoonful of instant coffee in each of two cups and added the boiling water. He handed one to Bobby and turned his attention to the cornmeal and venison. The radio crackled.

Both men started, alert to the potential danger. Bobby answered by saying, "Bobby here ."

"Doug here. How you doing? Any sign of Tom ?"

Tom waited breathlessly for Bobby's response. This was a crucial moment in the situation.

"Yup ."

"You got him?" Doug sounded excited.

"No. He came in late last night after I fell asleep and got the jump on me. When I woke up this morning, he was gone."

"What ??"

"I'm really sorry, Doug. He treated me okay. Told me he didn't kill the girl but got scared and ran. He left me tied to his rocker and packed up a few things and left again. I just got loose and was waiting for enough light to come back into town."

"You should have called me the second he left."

"Like I said, I just got loose."

"How long ago did he leave?"

"An hour or so."

"What did he take with him?"

"His rifle, a tent, sleeping bag, and some food."

"So he's armed?"

"Yup."

"Did he say anything about where he was going?"

"Not a word."

"Well, get your ass in here. This needs to go in my report."

"I figured. So sorry. We'll get him. I think I can track him down."

"But can you capture him? So far not so good."

"I know, I know. I'll get him next time."

"See you in a few hours."

"You bet, boss."

The cornmeal and venison were ready to eat. Tom put them on the table.

"Thanks, Bobby."

"Well, that didn't go too bad, did it?"

"Not too bad at all. Here, take this rope and rub it really well around your wrists, so it looks like you worked your way out of being tied up. Then leave the rope on the floor by the chair. We need to eat and get out of here."

"Yeah, Doug will have checked his watch when we hung up and figure a time that I should be back in town."

"Before you go, let's plan to meet again at the cabin at noon, Thursday. You can tell Doug that you need to go check things out again, to see if I've been here again. That work for you? If I can't make it or if someone insists on coming with you, I'll leave any notes I have in the fork of the big oak tree about a hundred feet straight back from the cabin. Hopefully you can do a walk around by yourself, looking for tracks. OK?"

"Sounds good ."

The only remaining sounds were those of two hungry men enjoying their meal.

As soon as Bobby walked out the door, Tom rinsed out the dishes he and Bobby had used and put them in the wash basin, thinking they looked timeless—assuming anyone who came in would think he was just a bad housekeeper. He then grabbed his rifle, his sleeping bag, and tent and put them on the table. He had had to let Bobby take his radio and gun, and while he trusted Bobby for now, he also knew he had to leave the warmth and comfort of his home in case Bobby got turned around—mentally or physically—by his boss or anyone or anything else that popped into his head.

He then grabbed his trapline backpack and added the few scraps of food in the tins, the rest of the venison roast, some cereal bars, and a canteen, as well as his smallest kettle and his machete. He made sure he had all of his aspirin. He double-checked his matches and ammo, then loaded his pack and looked carefully out the door. He always had to be prepared to spend a night or two out on his trapline, so he had his checklist memorized. As he left the cabin, he grabbed the snowshoes he kept hung up next to the door.

He followed Bobby's tracks for a few hundred yards. Then, in the smallest break in the pines he could find, he slid through and went up the hill for another hundred yards. Turning toward town, he stuck to high ground until he could see that Bobby was dutifully trudging down the trail toward his snowmobile.

Satisfied that Bobby was on his way, Tom turned back on his trail and, sticking to the ridge, worked his way north and east to the far east end of his trap line. As focused as he was on this murder case, he felt bad missing out on resetting his trapline. Without the supplies he'd had to leave at the motel, he knew he'd have no way to last the rest of the winter up here. This was indeed a bit of a quagmire. With that negative thought, some doubt crept back into his mind. While he knew he was as innocent as he could possibly be, he also knew it would take some work to clear himself. And some help from others. While Bobby was willing to help him for now, he was not sure about Phil, the motel owner, and certainly the new doctor had other plans. He still had no idea how hard the sheriff would work on the case. Though he'd had Bobby make sure to raise the "rules of evidence" argument, he knew it would be really difficult for Bobby or the sheriff to work hard on what looked like an open-and-shut case. Trading this level of freedom for a prison cell would be a harsh end to his years of independence.

It was good to be out in the fresh air, on his own terms, and doing what he did best. It allowed him to settle into a comfortable routine and freed his mind to think. So far, he'd had a few big breaks that had kept him alive and out of jail: recognizing the doctor before the injection—whatever that might have been; finding the parka, hat, mittens, and matches at the church, which had kept him alive that first night in the woods. Who knows how long it would have taken to find his frozen body? Then it would have been really simple to pin the murder on him and close the case.

Getting the drop on Bobby and establishing a relationship with him that kept them both safe. Bobby was in Doug's doghouse right now, but that should work itself out, and it was minor in comparison to the fate that Tom faced if he couldn't keep working on a plan to prove his innocence.

Now he caught another break. It was starting to snow again, which could be enough to cover his tracks. He kept on his planned trek and it was snowing harder and harder. He could hear the wind screaming through the treetops, and Tom was glad he was in the shelter of the forest. Hopefully Bobby was getting back to town alright.

The doctor's role in this escapade was pretty clearly fixed in his mind. The question was how he came to be at the motel and who the girl was. What the heck went so wrong that caused him to shoot her? Did she try to shoot him and he got the upper hand? Clearly, whatever was supposed to happen had spun out of control. And then for the doctor to take a shot at him was really out of line. Something so serious that caused the need to kill the only witness? Or was that just a panicked reaction? How was that supposed to not attract attention from the sheriff? Make it look like Tom and the girl had killed each other, or better yet, that some third party had killed them both and gotten away? When the doc couldn't kill Tom right on the spot, that story unraveled and a new plan had to be hatched. Tom still needed to die, or be doped up enough for the frame-up to take shape. Either way was not a rosy picture for Tom.

What about Phil? Why was the motel sold to him so quietly and quickly? How was or is he connected to the Rogers? The motel did okay in spring, summer, and fall when the woods and lakes filled with fishermen, tourists, and hunters, but was a definite money loser through the winter. The land was too rugged for hardcore snowmobiling and most of the lakes were too remote in the winter to drag in ice fishing houses or even temporary shelters for ice fishing. The whole place was just too far away from any populated area to make it an easy weekend trip. Just heating the place had to be a sizable expense.

In fact, Mrs. Rogers had told him once that after deer hunting season they shut down half of the twelve rooms, drained the pipes, and turned the heat off to save money. The place was never much of a family place; most of the clients were men—hunting and fishing mostly. You could use the word rustic. Just like the town and, in fact, the whole county.

Was there a connection between Phil and the doctor? If so, Phil would be helping Doc Bradford concoct his frame-up of Tom. That was not a good thought. It was interesting that so many little things he'd never had to question before suddenly loomed in front of him. Phil buying the motel. Tom had thought the Rogers had wanted to sell and move away. A new doctor willing to come to such a small, remote town and county. Another good thing on the surface.

Now, it either all smelled a little fishy or Tom was turning cynical due to his current circumstances.

He had given Bobby all the leads he had thought of. What else was there? What could Tom do to help himself out of this jam? For now, he had to look to his own survival and focus on finding a place to set up a camp for at least a few days. He needed a spot that was out of sight and protected from the weather as much as possible. To succeed and stay alive even a short time, he had to quit recycling his thoughts on the crime and focus on the task at hand. However, that was not so easy.

As he walked, his thoughts turned to the one area, so far, that he didn't want to consider. Was the sheriff somehow in on whatever was going on at the motel? If so, did he have an active role, or was he just willing to turn a blind eye? No sense shutting down one of the county's handful of long-term businesses, even if some parts of that business were less savory. Or patently illegal.

If the sheriff was actively involved, Tom may have put Bobby in some danger. Too bad that didn't cross his mind last night. Or was it? Maybe keeping Bobby blithely unaware was the safest plan. Bobby was such a mild-mannered guy—innocence just kind of poured from him. He'd already played the victim in this case and could certainly continue to do so.

Tom finally turned his full attention to the task at hand, continued his journey, stopping as he crossed every rise to see if anyone was following and how well his tracks were covering. Suddenly he had a horrible thought—even with his snow-covered trail, a good dog might be able to track him. As far as he knew, the county didn't own any tracking dogs, but some of the people in town might. Doug could maybe talk them into helping out, or at least lending him a dog or two. Most good dog owners didn't like the lending part, and if the word got out that Tom was desperate and had a rifle, the interest in joining a posse might be pretty low. Besides, with this snow, on top of old snow, it would be a hard scent to follow. Also, with the new snow, it was dangerous to head out into these woods. If you were the least bit unfamiliar and unable to track yourself home, it would be pretty easy to get lost or even take a fall. It was no fun to slip and slide down a steep hill. Hopefully the dog risk was minimal.

So, as Tom took a breather on the top of a ridge, his brain decided to recap the cast of characters.

The victim—who was she and why was she in town?

Phil—was he simply an innocent motel owner caught up in a bad scene, or was he somehow involved?

Doc Bradford—clearly involved, Tom thought. Once you shoot people and shoot at other people, you are the crux of the matter. If the doctor didn't shoot the girl, then nothing else that has happened makes any sense. Have to keep that as the operating theory for now.

Doug—again, was he completely in the dark, passively involved, or actively involved? Hard to believe he was completely in the dark. He'd been sheriff for years and had a reputation for knowing who was who and what was what in the county. If he was actively or even passively involved, that created danger for Tom. And there had already been one drug bust at the motel since Phil took over.

Bobby—if he was somehow involved, he'd have shot Tom in his sleep and brought him in dead, solved the crime, and been the hero. Not Bobby's style, but it would have made him a shoo-in for sheriff. The fact he was willing to spend an evening thinking through the crime with Tom indicated that he had no thoughts of his own or any skin in the game.

The Rogers—they owned the motel, then suddenly sold it and moved to Thompson Falls. Seems innocent enough: it was no secret that they were aging and that Mr. Rogers had had a health setback, so would sell for the right price. Tom wondered what that price was. Was there any connection between them and Phil? Hard to believe a single guy would roll into a small town in a small county and put down good money for a small, old motel. What were the terms of the sale? Cash? Contract for deed? The town was off the beaten path, for sure—in fact, it was about 20 miles from the nearest state highway. But that might make it a good place to lay low or do some unsavory business.

Too many thoughts, too many people. Tom needed to focus. *It all comes back to the girl.* Who was she, why was she in town, and what led to her being murdered? It was hard to believe there had ever been a murder in this county before—if there had been, maybe it had been some hunting rights dispute or some domestic problem.

The next time he had a chance to contact Bobby, that would have to be the first topic: What is the investigation revealing about the girl?

After that, sadly, the focus turned to the sheriff. Until it could be determined whether the sheriff was involved in any way at all, turning himself in could prove extremely dangerous. Tom would need a good attorney from outside the county. His sister and her family lived in the suburbs—she could track down someone if it came to that. That is, if he got his one phone call. Was that real or just on TV? Tom laughed to himself. If only he were a more experienced criminal instead of such a novice, then he'd know the ropes and could better defend himself.

A good attorney would look at all of that, but Tom would have to work the rest of his life to pay the legal bills unless some of this background work was already done. Even if his lawyer was really good, Tom would have to provide him with as much detailed background as he could and also clearly explain his theory of the case.

Tom once again topped a rise and scanned all the countryside he could see, limited as that was through the snow and wind—his trackers could be coming from anywhere. He saw nothing and heard nothing. It was good to know a snowmobile couldn't be used to sneak up on anyone.

Continuing down the far side of the slope, Tom was headed for a pine thicket not too far from his trap line that would keep him out of sight and protect him from the wind. He had camped there before when the weather had turned against him. With a small fire, he could heat—or at least thaw—some food and water. With his tent and sleeping bag, he would be fairly comfortable. He would be close to the far east end of his trapline and well away from any well-traveled trails, either snowshoe or snowmobile.

It was getting dark by the time he had his camp set up. He waited until it was fully dark, then used the wood he'd gathered to start a small fire. When he had hot coals, he filled his kettle with snow. When that melted and was hot, he added some cornmeal. He knew he would need some carbs to stay warm. The cornmeal wasn't going to last long. Looks like a pure protein diet was his immediate future.

Chapter 8

TOM AWOKE TO A THROBBING PAIN in his shoulder. This was getting old. But it also meant the past few days hadn't been just a dream. The pain was real and the events that had brought him here had been real.

It wasn't light enough to see anything yet, but he felt around for the small canteen he'd filled last night. It hadn't frozen. He grabbed a couple of aspirin and a cereal bar. For today, he'd stay close to camp and mind his own business, mostly watching to see if anyone was trying to track him. He was sorry he had to give up tending his trapline, at least for the time being. It was his only source of cash income, and if he had to hire a lawyer, he would need cash. He didn't know his exact bank balance, but it was probably no more than a few thousand dollars.

Again, he forced himself to focus on the here and now. Food. He had the venison roast, but that was now mostly gone. If he could shoot and dress a deer, he could eat for today and dry enough meat to last over a week. With that, he could disappear into the woods forever, making his way to Canada or somewhere else where he could build another cabin and just live out his life in peace. No more going into any town— all he needed was ammunition, and occasionally a few other items. He could barter or steal those. He pondered this while it grew light enough to go outside and start his tasks for the day.

"No, I'll put that aside for now," he thought. "My first choice is to clear my name and maybe even become less of a recluse." The value of having some friends was becoming more and more apparent. At some point in his life, he knew he'd need to move into some town or another, just for medical care if nothing else. "I'll only disappear into the woods forever if this turns south and it looks like I am certain to be convicted. Then if I can make a break, I'll be gone forever. Prison is not an option."

Tom realized he was talking to himself, which wasn't all that unusual. But this was different than talking about the best spot for a trap or how to plant his garden. This was much more urgent and important. He had made his lifestyle decision long ago, and living his life in freedom had been too conscious a choice. He couldn't let it go now.

The day was uneventful, which was good. It had stopped snowing, so Tom was careful not to leave any more tracks than he had to. He organized his campsite, securing the food he had brought with him, using his machete to gather more firewood, and taking stock of his meager possessions.

Tom reconsidered his deer-slaying plan. The does would all be pregnant by now, and it was clearly not hunting season. He'd better try his hand at some small game. If they did bring him in, he didn't need a deer poaching charge added to whatever the sheriff had already lined up against him.

Tom followed his tracks back to where he could move down toward a creek. From there, he found a tree with a fork in it just off what looked like a deer trail, and just high enough to be out of grazing sight of any game, all of which used deer trails. Even the animals knew it made no sense making your own tracks through the deep snow this time of year. Taking his position in early afternoon, he continued to think and plan but kept an eye out for any game. His luck continued. Within an hour, some grouse flew in, and as they picked their way in and out of the nearby thicket, he dropped one, listening and watching to see if the shot had attracted any attention. Even this deep in the woods, one shot would likely be dismissed by anyone close enough to hear it, but multiple shots might attract some attention. Then, just as dusk began to settle in, a large rabbit warily worked his way down the trail. He drew a bead on the rabbit, which was now stock still. He knew he once again had to make a kill shot to avoid any attention. That and the approaching cover of darkness should prevent anyone from pursuing him yet tonight.

He pulled the trigger, the rabbit jumped, then fell. Clean shot. Bobby began his work. He field-dressed the rabbit and the grouse as quickly as he could and carried both back to his camp. The wolves would be thankful for the free meal he had left beneath his hunting spot. He just had to be ready if they tracked him back to his campsite.

It did not take him long to finish dressing the rabbit and get it cooking over his small fire, still hoping the wolves wouldn't find him to be a second free meal. The familiar work was a relief from the idleness, especially when he could think of nothing new and recycling his old thoughts was getting frustrating. As the strips of meat were fully roasted, he enjoyed eating his fill for the first time all day. He continued to roast the grouse, then package it and the leftover rabbit in snow so it would cool quickly and be ready to eat, like jerky.

The next step was to construct a note to take back to the oak tree to communicate with Bobby. He had to be careful what he wrote in the note, fully aware that it would end up as an exhibit in any trial. Given the likely scarcity of any other written evidence, this note would get a lot of attention. Best to keep it brief and to the point. It also occurred to Tom that he couldn't implicate Bobby in any way or implicate anyone else for that matter, so this note had to make a very few key points.

First, make it clear that Tom had nothing to do with the murder. Second, stick to the facts that everyone already knew, and third, focus on the girl, making it clear he did not know her and certainly didn't know why she was shot. Finally, ask straight out if anyone knew why he was shot. By someone he was quite sure wasn't Bobby, Doug, or any member of law enforcement. He knew it was the doctor, but he couldn't put that in writing. Or could he?

Maybe it would be best to hand the sheriff what Tom thought was the smoking gun and see if he could force the investigation to move in that direction. He'd already told Bobby he was sure that was the real situation. For now, however, that would have to be enough. Tom didn't know enough about the sheriff or how things worked in court to know if such a bold accusation would work for him or against him.

Maybe he could provide a description of the car and the driver and let the sheriff work from that. Or provide the same to his new lawyer or some other investigator he might retain. A description of the car he saw. That would be enough to at least give his story some credibility, and if they found a bullet or two in the wall that could have come through the open motel room door, grazed him or missed him and then hit the wall, that would be helpful to his case. Tom chuckled to himself, which was a relief in his current situation. What if there was a bullet in the wall with traces of his blood on it? Would that prove his story, or would it just be used to aid the claim that he had winged himself to try to eliminate suspicion of his crime.

By firelight, Tom got those thoughts transferred to his piece of paper, then set about working on a plan to deliver it back to the oak tree where he had told Bobby to look for any communication. He'd need to pack up his camp and take it with him, in case he was followed and needed to change locations. Hopefully he could elude whoever tried to follow him, and he couldn't count on 6 inches of fresh snow to fall every time he needed to travel through the woods. It felt good to organize his thoughts in writing, and it would hopefully leave a record no matter what happened to him.

He laid down and enjoyed a reasonably restful sleep.

With the calm in the copse - sounds like a good name for a book - Tom thought. The sunshine breaking through the trees the next morning, he undressed enough to examine his shoulder wound. He took the dressing off and used some of his canteen water to wash it. There was no new bleeding, which was good, but it sure did hurt. Tom left it open for a bit and turned it toward the sun to dry. Since he had no new bandages, he would have to leave it undressed and hope it didn't get infected. His undershirt would have to serve to keep it clean and dry.

A day of rest, he decided to stay in his little camp and enjoy the woods he had grown to love so much. It truly was his home. It was quiet and peaceful, and he spent the day taking care of his few possessions. He double-checked all the webbing and straps on his snowshoes. He wiped down his rifle and carefully examined and cleaned his other camping supplies. He didn't know how long they would have to support him, so he wanted them in good shape.

As soon as it was dark, he started his small fire and warmed up the last of the rabbit strips, then put the grouse on to roast. Again, food felt good in his stomach.

Chapter 9

TOM APPROACHED THE FORKED OAK TREE from the northwest - from behind his cabin and from the opposite direction of his campsite in the pines. He set down his pack and worked his way to the tree. Seeing no tracks, he proceeded cautiously. He put the note in the main fork, about eye level. Turning to retreat, he saw some movement in the woods to his right. He stopped, then from that direction he heard Bobby's voice.

"Just stay right there, Tom, and keep your hands where we can see them ."

"We?"

"Yup, Doug is with me. He insisted on coming along. Can't argue with your boss."

The sheriff emerged from behind the trees on the left, shotgun pointed at Tom. Bobby emerged from Tom's right, similarly armed. While the cover of the trees left Tom an escape route, and his rifle was in his left hand, there was a good chance he'd get shot in the process. Tom knew Bobby spent enough time in the woods to be a good shot and had to assume the same for Doug. He also knew that with shotguns, they didn't even have to be good shots. More than that, he knew he had nothing to gain by gunning them down, no matter how much he wanted to be free in the woods again. He had to remember that was plan B, not plan A. He would only take that route if the wheels of justice ground the wrong way. The best way to keep Plan B on the table was to be fully cooperative all the way through whatever process this was going to follow.

He had told Bobby he'd turn himself in, but thought he'd have more time. This was a good time to remain calm, hoping it would give him a little control over the situation.

"No problem, men. I have no desire to get shot. Am I actually under arrest?"

Doug replied. "You are, Tom - for the murder of Sarah Thompson. Now put the rifle down and take a few steps away from it."

Tom spoke as he did as directed with his rifle.

"I assume that's the girl who was shot in the motel last weekend?"

"It is. Are you saying you didn't know that?"

"I had no idea. I never knew her."

"So you're claiming you didn't shoot her?"

"Of course I didn't. Why would I?"

"Maybe some mix-up between the two of you."

"We were in different rooms, as you may recall. I didn't even know she was in the next room until I heard the shooting."

"So that's your story?"

"That's the start of it. I can make a written statement when I get to your offices."

"Then why did you run?"

"That'll be in my statement. I want to be sure it's all clear and concise before we discuss any more. I'll also need to make my one phone call to my sister. That's still within my rights, eh? Just like on the TV police shows?"

"It is - didn't figure you for a TV watcher."

"Not for a long time, Sheriff, but I still remember the old cop and robber shows. I was hoping the one phone call was still on the table."

Tom was very careful to say all of this with Bobby as a witness. It might just help keep the sheriff honest.

"Bobby, did you see where I left my pack?"

"I did."

"Would you please get it and put it in my cabin? No sense in just leaving it in the woods."

"Now that's real reasonable, Tom." Doug sounded a little relieved. He probably didn't relish a chase through the woods at his age, and the county probably didn't require him to keep in Marine Corps shape.

"No problem, Sheriff. I always planned to turn myself in, but don't forget the note I just left. I would really like some answers to those questions. As I said, I didn't shoot the girl. Don't know who she is. But from here on out, I need to make sure I get treated fairly under the law, so I can make my case."

"I figured you'd head out. I was glad Bobby told me about your plans to leave him a note or two. Just didn't want to pass up a chance to bring you in. As sheriff, I think we're all safer with you in jail."

"You're all safe no matter where I am. I'm no criminal and you know it."

"I don't know it, and you stole from the church!"

"I did, and I will admit to that. Though it was stuff from their charity box, and I sure did need some charity. On the other hand, I hope you have my own parka and other stuff. Or is that in the goodwill box at the church now?"

"No, we have it at the office. Once you're in jail, you won't need a parka. You can give this one back to the church. In fact, you can thank the pastor—new one in town from right after Christmas. Young woman. Never thought I'd see that. At least not in this town."

Doug continued. "You can apologize for breaking in when you get a chance to talk to her. You have a right to some spiritual counsel. We're real old-fashioned that way ."

Tom's spirits lifted a bit. Of course! Another ally in this nightmare—or at least a potential ally. He'd have to proceed cautiously, but then he always did.

"She's dating the new doctor in town, but I'm sure she can find time to do a jail visit."

Tom's spirits fell as rapidly as they had risen. She may not be willing to save him. Still, it might help to talk to her. He had a real shortage of friends to start with and wasn't currently making any new ones. He would have to kind of feel her out as he went, building his story carefully. That should at least keep her from testifying against him, in case the doctor had already told her some version of events.

"I'll come in with you, as long as Bobby gets the note and can put my stuff inside."

"Sounds good, Tom, but I will keep a gun on you. You know I can't get you down out of these hills with handcuffs on, so if you don't behave yourself, I will have to shoot you."

"Sheriff, I got his pack and rifle. It's loaded."

"Put the pack in his cabin as he said and bring the rifle with us. We'll keep it locked up in case he talks you into letting him out of jail. Make sure the door is shut and latched. No need to let a bear or other ransacker in."

Bobby looked down, then did what he was told. Maybe Doug had seen through Bobby's story and assumed a little more collusion than was merited.

"Let's get going. Bobby, you go first, then Tom, I'll go last so I can keep an eye on both of you."

Tom cringed a bit. He sure hoped Bobby wasn't in any serious trouble. When he wrote his statement, he'd have to make sure he made Bobby look as good as he could. He also hoped that Doug wasn't so far in the weeds on this deal that he would see fit to shoot both Tom and Bobby. If he was going to do that, it would have to happen real quickly, while they were still well back in the hills. Tom made sure he'd stop frequently to check back. Bobby wasn't naturally suspicious, so Tom would have to try to be wary enough for the both of them. Bobby also didn't have as much at risk, or at least Tom thought that Bobby didn't think he was at risk. Trusting your boss too much can be a bad thing.

Then Tom laughed a bit at himself. If Doug was going to stage the double-shooting escape attempt scenario, he'd have to shoot Bobby with Tom's rifle, then shoot Tom with his shotgun, and the story would be complete. It was a little scary how good Tom was getting at this game. He needed to settle down.

Chapter 10

THE THREE OF THEM WOUND their way down through the hills. Tom used every switchback to keep an eye on the sheriff, who was having trouble keeping up. Between the snow and the terrain, it was tough going. The sun had come out, and while it wasn't warm, the snow was giving way a bit. Each of them lost their footing several times, and they had to pause every 10 to 15 minutes to catch their breath. The tough going gave Tom time to think, and using that time, he very carefully prodded the sheriff on how exactly he had the case figured.

"How did you figure I killed the –girl—Sarah, you said?"

"Mostly because you got shot in the process and then you ran. I watched those cop-and-robber shows, too. But then I got elected sheriff and have some real-life experience. I also have had some training and worked a little in a big-city police department before I decided I didn't like big-city police work. Or even living there."

"Do you have a murder weapon?"

"No. I figure you dumped it in the woods somehow."

"When would I have had a chance to do that?"

No response.

"What kind of gun was it?"

"Just how innocent do you plan to play, Tom?"

"I told you I am innocent. My question is simple enough. Semi or revolver. If it was a semi, there would be some shell casings around. I counted five shots, including the one that hit me."

"No shell casings. Slugs we found in the girl were from a .38 Special, and the gun was most likely a revolver. And there were six shots total. Somehow you counted wrong."

That was interesting. Doug was not just answering questions; he was volunteering information. That might be good news, or maybe Doug was just a talker.

"Maybe it was the first shot that woke me up."

When they reached the snowmobiles, Doug was prepared. He had a waist chain he put on Bobby, then handcuffed Tom to the back of that waist chain.

"Take it easy now, Bobby. No need to rush. We'll be back in town within the hour, regardless," Doug said, as he mounted the second snowmobile. "You go first, Bobby. I'll follow."

From his current situation, Tom had no view of the sheriff as they worked their way the rest of the way into town—then right down Main Street to the sheriff's office. Doug didn't remove the handcuffs or Bobby's chain until they were in the jail cell. He undid the waist chain and let Bobby out, and finally, he undid Tom's handcuffs before he closed the cell door. After that, he collected all of Tom's clothes and his handful of belongings, including a reload for his rifle, careful to put the personal items in a bag in Tom's view and the clothing in a laundry bag. The parka and other items he hung on a peg on the wall by the jailhouse door.

"Now, take a shower before we put you in your jail coveralls. We want you clean and to make sure you're hiding nothing before we let you dress again." Doug handed Tom some clean underwear and a pair of orange coveralls through the bars, with 'Thompson Falls City Jail' stamped on the back.

"Nice touch, sheriff—'Thompson Falls.' How'd you come by these?"

"We have a small budget, Tom. The Thompson Falls County sheriff is an old friend. When their coveralls are too faded or worn, he ships them up to me, and to some of the other smaller counties around. Fact of life. Most people are happy to know their tax dollars are being well utilized."

Tom stepped into the shower. He noticed Doug staring at his wounded shoulder.

"Tom, I'm sorry, but I forgot about your wound. We do need to have the doctor or a nurse come in and treat it. Once again, I am not allowed to neglect an injury."

"Having the nurse clean it and dress it wouldn't be a bad idea."

"I'll call her so she can be here by the time you are done with your shower."

Once Tom was dressed in his orange coveralls, Doug fingerprinted him through the jail bars, while Bobby watched.

"This may not be a standard way to take fingerprints, but over the years, I found it works pretty well. These will be sent to the state crime lab to be tested against the crime scene, and to see if you have any criminal history. You wouldn't be the first guy to go live deep in the woods to avoid outstanding warrants."

"Rest assured that is not the case for me, but I don't doubt you are right."

Tom was in one of just two cells. A lot of small towns had quit keeping prisoners overnight due to cost and liability issues, renting the service from a bigger county nearby. Only in this county there was no other service nearby. It was at least an hour in good conditions to the next nearest county seat, and they had little more to offer than here. The only town of any size, Thompson Falls, was about 60 miles away, all on two-lane roads. In summer, the trip wasn't bad, but in winter it could be impassable at times.

The cell was as basic as it could be: cot along the back wall, shower, toilet, and sink along one side—all in plain view of the office desk. Luckily not the front door or the window. This would be interesting.

"Bobby, can you call over to the diner and order us three of the dinner specials? I'll start a pot of coffee. I know I'm hungry and I bet Tom is too. And I've never seen you turn down a meal. After that, I need you to follow up on a report of a car break-in over on Johnson Lake Road. That call came in while we were out."

Tom became even more convinced that the best thing to do now was to cooperate as much as possible.

"Thanks, Sheriff. I am hungry. I'll try to keep my requests and your expenses to a minimum, though I do need a phone to make my one phone call. And if you let the pastor know I'm here, I'd like to give her the parka and stuff back and personally thank her."

"You can call your sister, and you are entitled to legal counsel. Tomorrow morning, we'll walk you over to the courthouse for your arraignment."

The sheriff continued, "Tom, while we wait for Bobby to bring dinner, how about you sit down at the desk here and write out your statement. I'll keep a close eye on you to prevent any funny business. We do need a statement for the files."

The sheriff handcuffed the two of them together and walked him to the desk, cuffing Tom's left hand to the chair before disconnecting the cuffs they shared. Tom then did as he had been told, relating everything from seeing the victim at check-in to escaping the ER and helping himself to the charity items from the church, even the communion bread. As he did, he felt better, knowing that whatever happened, his statement was now part of the proceedings.

When he was done, Doug reversed the handcuffing process and walked him back to the jail cell. Once inside, he uncuffed him.

"We'll take care of the phone call and the pastor right after we eat. And along with the cost of meals, I'll need to have Marilyn start working a full shift again. She's been part-time for the winter. With a prisoner, I have to have someone here 24 hours by regulation, and Bobby and I need some help covering those hours. I hope you don't give her a hard time. If you do, I'll bring in her husband. He may be harder on you than the justice system. He's the high school phys ed teacher and he coaches football and wrestling. Ex-Marine. Kind of a fitness nut."

"I'll keep that in mind."

The food was good, especially since it was Tom's first real meal in quite a while: a hot turkey sandwich with peas and carrots. He felt healthier already.

"Thanks for the meal. That was good."

Chapter 11

TOM SAT DOWN ON THE COT and had some time to think. If only he hadn't been so careless going back to the cabin with the note. He thought he'd be earlier than Bobby and could take control of the scene.

Now he really needed to talk to his sister and hope she could round up a good criminal defense attorney. There may be a local public defender, or one from another town in the area, but Tom knew his case required a better lawyer than that. The frame-up may be too tight.

Tom couldn't see the door to the sheriff's office, but he heard it open and two women's voices. They were already talking and both said hello to Bobby.

All three came back to his cell.

"This is Marilyn," Bobby said, "and I think you already met Judy the other night in the ER."

"Hello, ladies. Nice to meet you, Marilyn, and sorry I ran out on you the other night, Judy. It was nothing you did. The reason will all come out later."

"No offense," Judy replied. "I've seen a lot of big tough guys who don't like needles."

Tom smiled. That was a good story to go with for now.

Marilyn said, "I'll be here to keep an eye on you for your stay. I hope you won't be any trouble. I like to have things real quiet."

"Understood. I've had little time in an actual bed the last few days, so I mostly hope my snoring doesn't bother you."

Judy spoke next.

"Well, let's take a look at that arm. I hope you took care of it, so I don't have to worry about infection."

Tom had to slip the coveralls down around his waist and pull off his T-shirt for Judy to get a good look at his arm. He simply put his shoulder out between the bars so Judy could reach it easily. Marilyn watched. When Tom looked her way, she said, "No one is ever left alone with a prisoner, no matter who it is."

"Makes sense."

Judy treated his arm professionally but with some level of tenderness, then applied a salve and taped on some gauze.

"Looks pretty clean ."

Tom replied, "Your first dressing lasted a couple of days, then I was careful to clean it out, but I had no bandages, so I tried to use my T-shirt sleeve to keep it clean. The biggest issue for me was the pain. It hurt quite a bit."

"You did fine. I cleaned out some lint and I don't see any infection, so it should heal okay, though you will have a heck of a scar. Another inch to the left and you'd have a bullet in you. Another half inch and you'd have a badly broken arm."

"I think you mentioned that in the ER the other night."

"I probably did. It's still true. As it is, you should heal up just fine, except for the scar. Now that you're in jail, we can actually treat it correctly."

"I guess that's the upside to being captured then. Did you work at the clinic when Doctor Edwards was here?"

"I did. I miss him. He was really slowing down, though. I'm glad he will get some time to enjoy his retirement."

"Where did he go?"

"He moved to Thompson Falls. He has a couple of kids there and a couple more a little further away, as well as a handful of grandkids. Now they'll get the benefit of his medical skills."

"Does he ever come back up here?"

"Not in the winter. He may come back for a visit this summer if he's up to it. He has a lot of friends here."

"I only saw him a few times. I remember he treated me for a bad fishhook injury one time and another time when I'd cut myself chopping wood and the wound just wouldn't close without stitches. Seemed like a nice guy and was always so calm."

"He sure was. Nothing fazed him. I sometimes wondered if he understood the seriousness of an injury when he was working, but he always got people patched up. Not like the new doctor."

And there it was, the opening Tom was looking for—and Judy provided it. Now to try to draw it out.

"How long has Doc Bradford been here?"

"He started about Thanksgiving time. Doc Edwards had set that as his retirement goal. He wanted to have Thanksgiving with his family for the first time in years. You know how hard it was for him to get away, the only doctor and all…"

"I'm sure it really kept him tied down. How about the new guy? Does he get away at all?"

"Not so far. He's stayed pretty close, except for a few weekends here and there. Has made a few friends."

"Such as…" Tom hoped he wasn't pressing too hard. Judy was happy to talk, however.

"Well, Phil, who bought the motel. He's a little older than Doc Bradford, but they both came to town about the same time, so that created a bit of a bond. We've also got a new pastor in town. Have you met her? She is a breath of fresh air in this stodgy old place. She came right after Christmas. Just out of seminary. I guess that's what a small town gets these days. But she is great. She's added a lot of energy to that old church."

Tom figured he could circle back to the pastor. "Where did Phil come from? I knew that the Rogers wanted to retire, but it still seems rather sudden."

"It was a shock to all of us, too. Right after Doctor Bradford started, Ed Rogers came in for a routine checkup, and Doc Bradford found some serious issue that Doc Edwards must have missed. Told him he needed to take it easy, retire if he could."

"That must have been a shock."

"It was for all of us. Doc Edwards was a good doctor, and we all respected him. Hard to believe he missed something so serious."

"What exactly was it?"

"It had a long name, something I wasn't familiar with. Some kind of circulation problem. The Rogers put the motel up for sale within the week, and Phil answered the ad almost immediately. He said he'd been helping run a motel in the Chicago area and was looking for a place of his own in a smaller town. We sure meet that requirement. They made the deal, and the Rogers were gone inside of a month."

Tom paused to take that all in. That was quite a sequence of events. He would need to have his lawyer, if he ever got one, talk to the Rogers and see how the health situation was. Also, to do a background check on Phil. Those two transitions fit together a little too nicely.

"So you like the new doctor? Seems to know his stuff?"

"Well, he sure spooked you, didn't he? He's good. Handles the routine stuff, sends people to Thompson Falls for anything serious. He's not as cool, calm, and collected as Doc Edwards, but he settles down if any of the rest of us old-timers try to make clear that we're wondering what the rush is. Hopefully he'll get more comfortable as he gets used to the place. He's pretty young."

Tom wanted to ask if he'd sent Mr. Rogers to Thompson Falls, but figured he'd better leave that alone. However, he did circle back to the new pastor. "So the new doctor and the new pastor are getting along pretty well?"

"Oh, they've gone to a movie, once that I'm aware of, and only because I had to page him and she came along. I don't really track either of them outside of work. No idea if they'd say they were going out or not."

Tom just nodded and took that info in. Judy continued.

"I'm done here and have taken enough time. The clinic will send out a posse if I don't make it back soon."

"And I need to make my one phone call. Thanks for visiting. As you may have observed, I'm a little out of practice."

"You did quite well. I'll check back on you in a couple of days."

"Thanks."

With that as her cue, Marilyn told Tom to step to the back of the cell, and she and Judy nodded to each other as Judy went out the door.

"So my phone call?"

"As soon as Bobby or Doug get back, so I don't have to manage you alone. Shouldn't be long."

Tom sat back down on the cot and contemplated all that Judy had told him. There was a lot going on in this little town—too much to be a string of coincidences.

Chapter 12

TOM WOKE TO THE SOUND OF A VOICE. He instantly recognized the jail cell, but it was fully dark out now. As his eyes adjusted, he saw Doug just outside the bars of his cell.

"Sorry I took so long to get back, Tom, but you can sure make your phone call now."

"Thanks, Doug. Any rules or time limits? I need to call my sister. What if she doesn't answer?"

"Tom, this isn't the big city. We'll make sure you get to talk to her. The last thing I need is to lose a case just because we didn't provide a prisoner his rights."

"Thanks. I'm new at this, and on TV the person always answers on the first ring."

"Phone is in the hall. I have to cuff you again, using a waist chain so you'll have room to operate your hands. There's a ring embedded in the wall next to the phone. I'll connect you to that, then I'll stand between you and the main office door so you'd have to run over me to make a break for it. Clear?"

"Yup." Tom dialed his sister's number.

"Marci, is that you? This is Tom."

"Tom, what's up? Did you finally get a phone? Or return to civilization? I had you marked down to call me in April."

"I wish it was a simple, friendly call, but instead I'm calling because I need your help. Please listen. I need to be brief, but I'm hoping to fill in the blanks later."

"Now you're scaring me ."

"Don't mean to, but I do need your help, and for now, your full attention."

"Ok. Go ahead."

"I'm calling from jail, here in Purdy."

"What?"

"I will explain. Please just listen."

"Ok."

"I have been arrested for a murder I didn't commit. When I came into town for supplies on Saturday, a girl in the room next to mine at the motel was shot and killed. I did not do it, but since I was right next door and went over to her room when I heard the shots, I was the easiest suspect. I need a lawyer, a good one. A lot of the evidence makes it look like I did it. I don't want to trust my case to any local public defender. Can you find an attorney who can help me? Also, I need you to help with the retainer or other up-front costs. I have a little money in the bank here, but it's not much. I never needed much until now. I just sold some furs, so I also have a little cash, but that's even less than the bank account."

"Wow, Tom, that's a lot to take in. This sounds serious, and I will absolutely help you. Randy does some IT work for a big law firm, and they should be able to get someone to help you. And don't worry about the money—Mom and I can both front that. And if you go to prison for life, you can pay us back working in the laundry."

"Very funny."

"What should I tell Mom?"

"Can you and a lawyer get up here without her knowing?"

"I think so."

"Then I'd prefer you told her nothing until you come up here and get the whole story and the lawyer has started his work. Ok?" He waited for Marci to agree, but when she didn't reply, he continued.

"I'm being arraigned tomorrow morning, so I'd like to at least talk to a lawyer before that so I don't mess anything up. Clearly I'll plead innocent, but some legal advice would be appreciated."

"Tom, we'll find a lawyer and come up as soon as we can get on the road."

"Thanks much. Hope to see you soon."

"Love you. Can't believe this has happened to you after you worked so hard to be all on your own."

"Me either. Makes me hate civilization even more. But so far the sheriff and his staff have treated me just fine."

"I'll get back to you as soon as I can locate an attorney. Randy is sitting right here, so I'll put him to work right away."

"Thanks a lot. I'm so glad I caught you. Give my best to Randy and the boys."

"No problem. Just to be clear, it may be tomorrow morning before we can track down a lawyer."

"I figured as much. Thanks again. Oh, by the way, just so you don't get another shock, I was shot in the arm by the guy I believe is the actual killer. Nothing serious, just a graze."

"Again, wow! Sounds like you had a nightmare experience!"

"I'd have to agree. There's more, but that can wait. Please just see what you can do to get me a really good lawyer. And make sure he or she knows I'm innocent."

"Will do. Love you and will see you soon."

Tom hung up. Usually when he finished a conversation or a visit with his sister, mom, brother, or any family member, he was glad it was over. Now he wished he could stay on the phone just to hear a friendly voice and see how things were going. Maybe complete isolation from his family wasn't the right lifestyle after all.

Doug and Marilyn were both keeping a close eye on Tom throughout the whole conversation. As soon as Tom hung up, Doug spoke.

"Looks like you're done. Back to your cell. Need anything else before you turn in? I can't offer you a nightcap, but you're allowed a midnight snack. Marilyn can go back to the diner before she goes home. I'll take the first shift here tonight, then we'll try to get on a regular schedule."

"No, I'm good. I seem to keep falling asleep, so I think I'll just turn in. Just for the heck of it, what time is it?"

"About quarter to nine. If you look out the cell bars hard left, there's a clock on the wall behind the desk that you should be able to see. There used to be a wall and a door between the cells and the office, but to keep our ability to house prisoners, we had to remove that so we can see you at all times. Not much for privacy, but I understand the rules. Don't want you chiseling or filing your way out. Or hanging yourself."

"Don't worry, Sheriff. I am probably as good as anybody at living in the open, but won't adopt it as a lifestyle. I'll stay put."

"Good. I'll be here the night. Then Bobby will walk you over to the courthouse at nine tomorrow morning for your arraignment. I hope you don't give him any trouble."

"I won't. You have both treated me okay so far, so I can work with that."

Tom didn't want to use the word 'appreciate,' though that was his true sentiment. He knew much of the decent treatment he had received was required by law, and he wasn't sure where the line was. He laid down on his cot, trying to focus on his plan, but quickly fell asleep.

The next thing he knew, he was hearing Doug's voice: "Tom, Tom, wake up. You've got a phone call."

Tom tried to get up quickly, but in doing so, rolled right onto his bad arm. The pain quickly finished waking him. Doug had him back up to the cell bars and put the waist chain back on him, then cuffed each hand to the waist chain.

"Step back while I open the door."

Tom did as he was directed, then the sheriff walked him to the phone, cuffing him again to the ring in the wall. Tom glanced at the clock: 8:15. He must have really slept. He picked up the phone. "Hello?"

"Tom, this is Marci. I'm here with a lawyer who says he'll represent you at least initially to get you through arraignment. After that, he needs to understand your case better. And now I have to leave because he needs this conversation to be privileged. Ok?"

"Sounds good. Thanks for lining him up so quickly."

Tom sensed a bit of hesitation in Marci's voice. "Bye, and good luck. I'll talk to you a bit more when you've finished your conversation with the lawyer."

"Thanks again. Love you."

A new voice came on the line. "Tom, this is Lionel Levitt, of Levitt, Roberts and Stone. I am the lead litigation attorney here, so I will help you through this initial phase of the proceedings, then either keep your case or refer it to an associate, depending on a variety of things, including the specifics of the case, the schedule, and my availability.

"Now please listen, and don't volunteer any more information about what happened beyond answering the exact questions I'm about to ask you. Give me only short answers so whoever is near you can't get any details they don't already have, okay?"

Tom already liked Lionel's no-nonsense demeanor and approach to his situation. "Okay. Go ahead."

"I understand you're being arraigned this morning. Correct?"

"Yes, about 9 o'clock as I understand it."

"Do you know what an arraignment is?"

"Only from TV. I guess it's where they enter the charges and ask me how I plead."

"Pretty close. The other thing is to set bail."

"Well, I have no…"

Levitt cut him off. "I said don't talk ."

"Sorry."

After a brief pause, Levitt continued, "Just listen to me. I assume you plan to plead not guilty, is that right?"

"Yes ."

"Very good. Do that. Then the prosecutor will request bail, and for murder, that is likely either no bail allowed or some ridiculous number like $1 million."

"Okay."

"I assume you will have no representation with you in court. Is that correct?"

"Correct."

"Then enter your plea—nice and clear: 'Not Guilty.' Then, when the prosecutor makes his bail request, state that you are in the process of retaining counsel, so will not oppose the initial bail decision, but retain the right to argue appropriate bail once you are fully represented. If you want to nuance it, make it sound like that since you have been rushed to arraignment, there has been no opportunity for you to be adequately represented. In most of these cases, whether small town or big city, they will have a public defender present in the court to offer to represent you for initial pleadings like these, but their job is to make a few bucks and take the easy way out, most likely by going directly to some kind of plea deal. If you didn't commit the crime, you don't want that. Right?"

"Right."

"Any questions ?"

"No ."

"Good. I have my own court business already scheduled for this morning. In the meantime, my assistant is making arrangements for me to travel to Purdy, is it? To meet with you in person. Your sister says you are smart and observant, and I hope she's right. Be ready to tell me all you have observed: mannerisms of the judge, prosecutor, everyone and everything. We won't walk through the whole story until we meet in person, but the tone in the courtroom is good to know. When I come up, is there a place there where we can meet in private?"

"I don't know; I can check."

"Please do that. Good luck. I need to step out, so Marci will pick up and talk to you."

Chapter 13

TOM WAS RELIEVED to hear his sister's voice again. "Tom, you still there?"

"Yes. He sounded a bit gruff."

"He's a litigator. Lots of experience. Lots of moxie."

Marci continued, "Randy and I plan to come up with him and show him the way. We can visit when you're not with him."

"Good, it will be nice to see you. What about the boys?"

"They can stay with Randy's sister and her family. They have a couple of kids, and they all get along."

Tom's conversation with Levitt had buoyed his spirits a bit. Having a good lawyer gave him some hope. Maybe this whole misunderstanding would be cleared up in relatively short order.

"Well, thanks again. Will I see you tomorrow?"

"That's what we're planning; should be there early afternoon. How's the jail?"

"Not bad. Decent cot, shower, people are professional. In fact, breakfast is waiting and I'd like to eat before I go to court."

"I understand. Love you. Good luck."

"Love you. See you tomorrow."

"Bye."

Marci sounded like she may be near tears, another reason to cut off the call. But breakfast was on Marilyn's desk. Doug had left, and Bobby and Marilyn had come in. Bobby walked him back into his cell and undid the shackles. Marilyn slid his breakfast tray through the slot, and

Tom put the tray on his lap and started to eat. Suddenly, he realized he wasn't all that hungry after all. He ate the toast and a little bit of the egg, then shoved it back. He kept the coffee and sipped on that as the clock moved toward 9 a.m. This was not a situation he had ever thought he would be in.

Marilyn answered the desk phone about five minutes to nine o'clock and said, "He's ready. Okay, Bobby, time to take him over."

Bobby walked over and re-shackled Tom. Sadly enough, this was becoming routine, so both knew how to make it go quickly. Bobby then cuffed his own left arm to the waist chain with a long single chain and wordlessly prodded Tom through the office to a door that took them down a short set of stairs to a tunnel. The tunnel was only about seven feet high and the same wide, with a couple of rows of glass block windows near the ceiling. Not more than 100 feet later, they went up another short set of stairs, through a door, and into a small room with only one other door and another glass block window high up.

"Lucky it's February, Tom. This room gets really hot in the summer."

"Lucky is exactly what I was thinking, Bobby."

"Sorry, I was just trying to make small talk…"

The other door to this little room opened, and a big guy in a blue business suit said, "Bring the prisoner in."

Bobby and Tom walked into the courtroom. Bobby unhooked his shackles and sat behind the rail. Doug stood at the main door to the courtroom. The man in the blue suit went and stood by the door to the judge's chambers, then said, "All rise."

The judge, a middle-aged man with salt-and-pepper hair and dark-rimmed glasses, walked in. When seated behind the bench, he said, "Please be seated."

To Tom, he looked entirely humorless. He turned to the man in the blue suit and said, "What is on our docket this morning ?"

"One matter, Your Honor: an arraignment for murder for one Thomas John Reynolds ."

The judge looked directly at Tom.

"Are you represented by counsel?"

Tom stood as straight as he could, trying to look and sound confident. "I am in the process of retaining counsel."

"Would you like to have a public defender assigned temporarily to assist you in this arraignment?"

"No, thank you, Your Honor. I will represent myself today."

The judge didn't pursue this topic any further. "Let the record reflect the defendant has refused counsel and will represent himself for this proceeding. Please remain standing while the charges against you are presented."

The judge turned his gaze to the man at the other table. "Mr. Zillman, I assume you are here to represent the county."

"Yes , Your Honor."

"Please proceed."

"Your Honor, Purdy County brings a charge of murder against the defendant for the murder of a woman currently identified as Sarah Thompson in the early morning of Sunday, February 22nd. The state charges that the defendant used a revolver to murder the deceased, with the county still to determine premeditation."

"And how do you plead, Mr. Reynolds?"

"Not guilty, Your Honor."

"With any modifications or reservations?"

"I'm not sure what you mean."

"Very well. Do you plan to claim insanity or self-defense or anything like that?"

"No, Your Honor, I simply didn't do it."

"No need to enter arguments here. I'm just trying to give you the opportunity to seek court-ordered counseling or evaluation."

"No, sir."

"Your Honor."

"No, Your Honor."

"Duly noted: a plea of not guilty has been entered."

"Mr. Zillman, does the county have a bail request?"

"Yes, Your Honor. Given that the defendant is accused of murder and has already fled once and has exhibited an extensive ability to disappear into the wilderness, we request that, for the safety of the residents of the county, he be held without bail."

"Does the defendant have a reply?"

"Pending the retention of counsel, I will accept for now the bail terms requested by the county but will reserve the right to argue for appropriate bail once I am fully represented."

Maybe Tom was grasping at straws, but it seemed like maybe the judge was actually a bit impressed with his ability to represent himself in a courtroom. The judge continued.

"Mr. Zillman, your response?"

"Since I hear that the defendant is accepting our no-bail request, I am fine with his response. I doubt that whatever lawyer he lines up will change our position or his situation."

"Mr. Zillman, I just admonished the defendant for arguing his case during an arraignment proceeding. I didn't think I would have to do the same to you."

Turning his attention to Tom, the judge continued.

"Mr. Reynolds, you will have no bail arrangements available to you, which means you will be in custody until that changes, which can only be done via another court appearance. Do you understand?"

"Yes, Your Honor."

"Thank you all for your time and cooperation. Mr. Zillman, do you have a request for the trial to begin?"

"Your Honor, the only thing that prevents us from bringing our case today is the likelihood that Mr. Reynolds will enter a plea agreement once he finds an attorney. We can start in two weeks."

The judge looked surprised. "That would have to be the fastest murder case ever brought. Usually the judge is not the one being railroaded. Barring any intervening necessary court business, we will reconvene in 30 days to rediscuss bail, share any updates on progress on any other front, and establish a trial schedule." Hearing no response from anyone in the court, the judge continued.

"Take the prisoner back to his cell. If there are no further items, we will adjourn."

Everyone rose as the judge returned to his chambers. Immediately after that, Bobby walked around the rail, reconnected himself to the waist chain, and they retraced their steps to Tom's cell. As they walked, Bobby said, "The judge was his usual calm self, but I've never seen the DA so anxious to put someone away. Guess he wants you as a notch in his gun belt. Murder convictions don't come up often here, so he's anxious to have one."

"Thanks, I was thinking the same thing. I thought he was going to ask the judge for a verdict right then and there. Who's the guy in the blue suit?"

"He's the bailiff. Retired sheriff from another county. He serves as the court marshal. Too heavy to wear any of his old uniforms, so he dresses up, looks as official as he can, and has a 9-millimeter under that suit coat. He is not to be trifled with. I've seen him manhandle some teens who thought they were tough. The judge gives him a lot of latitude and respect. I guess that is wise, given this guy protects his life."

Chapter 14

BACK IN HIS CELL, Tom ran the whole court episode through his head over and over again. He didn't want to fail in his first assignment from Levitt. The DA, the judge, the bailiff, Doug appearing and disappearing. Was there anyone else in the courtroom? Yes, a younger woman, by herself. Newspaper reporter? The county had a weekly newspaper, the Purdy Purview. I suppose a murder in Purdy was as close to big news as you could get.

But wait, there was another woman who came in and stood next to Doug for just a couple of minutes, then left with him. Who could that be? The exotic new pastor?

Tom thought it was actually kind of impressive how quietly Doug and the bailiff supported Bobby in securing the safety of the court. Each covered an exit, never said a word or looked hostile. They just made it clear that making a run for it was highly unadvisable.

The judge seemed to want to run a fair hearing and was right to admonish him, Tom thought. He just wanted to be clear that he was on the record as not guilty and didn't realize he had crossed some line in making that clear. But the DA, that was interesting. He also crossed that line and clearly should have known better. His argument for no bail didn't seem out of line, but the hostility was a little over the top. And wanting to rush to trial – I guess the message is that he, like Doug, thinks he has an easy case. Hard to believe he's really done a lot of trial preparation in the five days since the crime. Levitt may find that interesting. At least Doug is treating me okay and even admitted he couldn't figure out why I would kill the girl. That is the heart of the case. Who was the girl and why was she killed? Tom had no motive, but who did?

This brings it all back to Doc Bradford. Tom was sure he had been at the motel at the time of the crime. Tom was pondering that all over again when Doug interrupted his thoughts.

"You have a visitor. Do you want to see her?"

Tom looked through the bars and saw the same young woman he had seen with Doug in the courtroom.

"Sure."

"Hello, Tom. I'm Susan Andrews. I am the pastor at St. Paul's here in Purdy. I hear you have a parka and some other things from our charity room."

Tom couldn't tell if she was joking or being serious. "I do. Is that all you want?"

"Of course not. I was trying to break the ice. Sorry it didn't go over as well as I thought it would. Let me start over. I am here as a pastor and, if possible, just a friendly face. We don't need to talk about what you did or didn't do, assuming your innocence. I can also serve you as a counselor, but only if you want me to fill that role. Is that better?"

"Yes, thanks. I will start over as well. As I have told everyone, including the judge this morning, I didn't kill the girl. Never touched the gun. Don't know who she is; I just happened to be first on the scene, so got myself implicated. When I concluded that I might be the only suspect and was likely to be railroaded, I headed out for the woods, hoping that with some time and thinking, I could clear my name.

"I really needed the items I took from the charity room at church. They likely saved my life. I am not sorry I took them, but you can certainly have them back. I will even pay for any cleaning. I feel worse about the matches and the communion bread. Hope you had more on hand."

"I was surprised to find no communion bread waiting for me on Sunday morning, but we have a resourceful flock, so a phone call was all I needed to make sure we got another loaf in time for church."

"Why did you fear you'd be railroaded?' "

Despite how friendly Susan seemed, Tom decided to be careful how much he shared with the pastor. He knew Lionel Levitt would not be happy to hear of him rolling out his whole theory to anyone before they had had a chance to talk.

"That will all come out. I have retained an attorney who should be here tomorrow. To no one's surprise, he told me not to say anything until we get a chance to go through the case. What I've shared with you is the simple reason I fled, and everything else is, as a TV attorney would say, 'facts not in dispute'—in other words, common knowledge. I do appreciate you taking the time to visit with me."

"Happy to do so. I don't believe I've seen you in church, but I am told you are a trapper, hunter, and fisherman who lives deep in the woods, so I suppose regular churchgoing would be unlikely."

"I would have been in church last Sunday except for the murder. I generally make the trek into town every month or so in the summer, and even go to the city to visit relatives for a week each year. They seem to like to see for themselves that I'm still alive and whole. In the fall I hunt and fish and preserve all that meat for the winter. Then, once I can set up my traplines, about December first, I stay very busy and make just one midwinter trip to town, generally about this time, to replenish supplies, enjoy a couple of hot showers and a visit to the barber. I do also attend church before I head back out for the rest of the winter."

"Sounds like an interesting life. Very unique in our day and age. As far as the murder goes, it's hard to see how or why you'd have killed the girl, unless you left out the female liaison part of your story."

"Again, I really can't discuss the case with you, but the truth is I never even knew she was in the next room. I only went over when I heard the gunshots. Guess I shouldn't have gone to her room to see what was going on."

"Most people run from gunshots or at least take cover. You ran toward the shots, and that alone is suspicious behavior. But as you said, we probably shouldn't be talking about all that."

To himself, Tom thought it was good Susan wanted to understand his side of the story.

"Any time I can create doubt about my motives in the mind of anybody in town, it helps my case," Tom thought.

"I have a lot more personal history I could bore you with, but tell me, how did a nice girl like you end up in a town like this? And I mean that tongue in cheek. What brings you to Purdy?"

"Fair question. And in my short time here, I am finding I really like it. I grew up in a town kind of like this, but more of a farming area. I was raised in a strong church family. I was my class's girl nerd—salutatorian, in fact. The valedictorian had to be a boy, of course. Not just any boy, but my boyfriend, and he was really smart. Except neither of us was smart enough to figure out birth control. Or maybe I'm just trying to say we were quite naïve. I was pregnant when I graduated but nobody knew it. We were married that summer, went to college together, and were raising our little girl, but as we grew up and explored the big city world of a college town, we grew apart. He went one way, enjoying the college party scene, leaving me home with the baby. As I sought some support and meaning in my life, I was lucky enough to fall back on my church roots and had some friends who brought Maggie and me to church in our college town. I knew fairly quickly that I had really found a home. During our sophomore years, we were divorced. After the divorce, I finished my degree as quickly as I could, then went to seminary, did well, and waited for my first pastoral call. Some of the bigger churches weren't interested in a single mom pastor. The pastor here had retired, and after a series of interims, they decided to call me. As the call committee said, they would be happy to be the village that raised Maggie. I knew I had found a home, so had no reservations about accepting this call. You said you attend church when you can, but I don't know how deeply religious you are. In my case, I really feel the Lord found me and carried me when I most needed it, and I am eternally thankful."

"I don't know how deeply religious I am either, though I know I see God in the natural world I live in, and I do enjoy the comfort of a church service. Your story is a lot to share, especially with someone in my situation."

"Believe me, you got the short version. I feel that as a pastor, it is important to be honest and open about my past and hope that it helps to develop better relationships. Besides, in a town this size, it would all come out soon enough anyway. This way I control the message. Maggie gets an age-appropriate version, of course."

"That's a great explanation. I appreciate you sharing. Makes me feel human."

"Thanks for affirming my approach. The elephant in the room, short of why you have been arrested for murder, is what drove you into the woods?"

Tom sighed. She had willingly shared her personal story, so now he felt a bit compelled to share his story as well. The question was how to cover it all but keep it brief enough to not put Susan to sleep.

"My background is different than yours. Bottom line, you found peace in your faith and I found it in the woods."

Tom worked his way through his life story: growing up in the suburbs, including sports, choir, a good family, hunting and fishing trips, a biology degree, a master's degree—hoping he would sound as normal as he could—before sharing the next phase, which was frustration with teaching and society and rules, and just feeling more and more drawn to a solitary life in the woods. "I figured as long as I was self-sufficient and not bothering anybody, I should get to do and live as I chose. By hunting and fishing and raising a garden, I could largely feed myself, and the trapping paid for anything else I needed, so things were going fine. Until now."

Susan smiled. "Well, I know you can't discuss the case, but if I were an FBI profiler, I'd have a hard time pegging you as a murderer. Unless you've been stacking up bodies in the woods all along. I certainly hope that's not the case."

Tom thought it a good sign that Susan seemed to be comfortable joking even a little bit about the situation he was in.

"Thanks, I think. No, no bodies in the woods. Don't even have a juvenile record, or any other criminal record. When the other kids were stealing hubcaps, I was fishing or hunting or playing basketball. But I'm sure the DA will dig deeply into that, if he hasn't already."

"I'm sure he will. He has a reputation for being dedicated to his job. Loves his conviction record."

As much as Tom wanted to probe that, the vision of Lionel Levitt lingered over him, odd for someone he'd never seen. He really didn't want to share any more of the case for that reason, but also, if Susan is spending time with Doc Bradford, he didn't want to open up too much to her, regardless of her position. It was clearly time to lighten the topic again.

"So how old is Maggie, and how does she like it here?"

"Maggie just turned eight and is in second grade. It was hard to change schools over Christmas break, but she is doing well. The smaller classes here helped, but on the other hand, outsiders are unusual, so she's struggling a bit to make close friends. It's hard to cut in on a dance that's been going on since birth."

The outsider comment made Tom want to pursue a discussion about Phil and Doc Bradford, but again he heard Lionel Levitt's voice in his ear.

Almost as if she telepathically understood Tom's thought, Susan stood up.

"I should probably get back to the church. Need to see if anyone has stolen the communion bread."

Tom smiled. "Haha."

"I'm glad you still have a sense humor. I kind of took a chance with that crack. You seem calm given the situation."

"Well, I know I didn't do it and help is on the way. I really do appreciate the chance to meet and visit with you. Thanks for taking the time. Please come back whenever you can. Bring Maggie if you think it would be okay. I do miss my nieces and nephews, and they are growing up fast.”

“Do you mind if we close with a prayer?”

“I would appreciate that and expect nothing less.”

They bowed their heads, and Susan asked for peace, comfort, and truth. Tom thought that was all quite appropriate.

“Don’t forget the parka and stuff. I really did appreciate it.”

Susan nodded and left.

Tom remained sitting on his bunk, thinking about this visit, the arraignment, so many people being new to such a small, isolated town. Were they all interconnected? If Susan was in on some criminal enterprise, she sure was good at covering her tracks. Hardly seemed likely. But if she was seeing Doc Bradford, who knew?

Chapter 15

TOM TOOK HIS TIME with lunch, since the afternoon looked like it might go on forever. As usual, it was good, and Marilyn actually visited a little with him while they ate, chatting through the open wall between the cell and the office. Tom figured he might as well initiate some real conversation.

"Marilyn, are you a native of Purdy?"

"No, but I've been here a long time."

"Where did you come from?"

"Kind of all over, really. I was a Navy brat. Spent a little time overseas, but mostly west coast."

"How did you end up here?"

"I met my husband, Mark, when he was a Marine stationed on the naval base where I lived with my family. I was just finishing high school and he was a little older."

"So your husband was a Marine?"

"Oh yes, and he isn't shy about mentioning it. If you haven't heard, there is no such thing as an ex-Marine. He went to a community college where he played football and wrestled, then got in some trouble—nothing serious, just the typical spring break fooling around. There was a lot of beer involved, according to the standard telling of the story. One of the choices the judge gave him was to enlist in the armed forces. He walked down the hall and picked the Marines. Kind of a self-inflicted atonement for embarrassing himself and his parents. And to show how tough he was.

"I stayed with my parents for a while after high school and did some basic college courses at the community college right outside the base, and Mark and I just stayed together. We went from being madly in love to being very comfortable with each other. We got married when I was 20. When he was discharged, I went off to college with him. I took some classes when I could and got my BA at the same time as Mark. He used the GI Bill to finish his degree. He stayed with the wrestling as a focus for working out. When we graduated, he got a job offer to teach and coach here. We thought it would be a short stay until his coaching career took him to ever-bigger schools in ever-bigger cities. Instead we fell in love with the place and the people here. Mark is the head football and wrestling coach and is the throwing coach for the track team. You know, shot put and discus. He loves getting paid to be constantly working out and feels like he's making a difference for the kids here. Especially the boys, who frequently need some additional direction. He is happy to provide that."

Tom was grateful for Marilyn's easy conversational style. It made him feel a lot more comfortable with his current situation.

"And you ?"

"Spent the first several years here making babies—three boys, one girl. The oldest is 17, born right after Mark's college graduation. The youngest is 8. That's why I enjoy my part-time role here. Doug is pretty flexible with my time, even though I am a deputy. Helps a lot to have me around if we have to lock up a female. I occasionally have to spend a weekend here while a drunk dries out, but other than that, it's a few hours a week. Until now, of course, when I have to monitor an accused murderer."

"Sorry for the inconvenience, but being here isn't exactly my idea."

"I know. Sad situation all around. Obviously really sad for the girl and her family, whoever and wherever they are. Sad for the town and county as well. We thought we were immune from that kind of stuff. We get some domestic disputes and the usual DUIs, but everyone knows the usual suspects."

Tom figured he'd better leave any discussion of the case alone. He wasn't sure if Marilyn could be called to testify or not, but at any rate he had no appetite to walk through any of that again. He went back the usual get-to-know-you line of conversation.

"What is your degree in?"

"Psychology."

"Wow—I guess I should be careful what I say and what I let you observe."

"Don't worry, I can't testify as a psychology expert."

Tom decided to do some buttering up. "But you are a more shrewd observer of people than the average Joe or Jane."

"And that is flattery. How's that for shrewd?"

Tom laughed. It felt good. "Not bad. I guess I'm done with my lunch tray. Now that my arm is getting better and I am facing some time confined here, are there any arrangements for exercise? This cell is pretty small, and I'm eating like a horse. I'm used to being on my feet all day, working my way up and down hills through snow and ice."

"Good question. Don't want you dying of a heart attack before your trial. That would disappoint everybody, especially our DA. Check with Doug. He's the only one who can answer that."

Tom slid the tray out of the cell and stepped to the back of the cell. Marilyn picked it up and stacked it on hers, then set them both on a table by the door. All of this was getting to be more and more routine, which saved time and energy, but it was a sad thing to have as a regular habit.

Marilyn turned her attention back to her desk, and Tom lay down on his bunk. He dozed on and off through the afternoon. Only now, instead of replaying the case in his head, he started thinking about the people he'd been forced to meet in the last few days. Bobby, Doug, Marilyn, the judge, the DA, Susan. Except possibly for the DA, all seemed like really nice, decent people. On the other side of the ledger there was Doc Bradford and maybe Phil. Jury was still out on Phil. *Jury out*. No longer a harmless expression. The jury out could be a very real issue in his immediate future.

For the past half dozen years, his human contact had been limited to the Rogers, and then Phil at the motel, Doc Edwards when he needed some medical care, a church service from time to time when he came in almost late and sat in the back, then left as soon as the pastor walked toward the back of the church at the end of the service, and of course, mandatory annual visits to his family.

Marci and Randy were always nice, and their sons looked at Tom like some kind of Davy Crocket or Daniel Boone. They couldn't get enough of his stories of life in the woods. Marci and Randy had chosen a lifestyle much like their parents. Nice house in the suburbs where the public schools were healthy. College degrees and solid careers.

Tom's brother, Tim, wanted little or nothing to do with Tom, given how widely their paths had diverged. Tim thought he was on top of the world, working high up in a skyscraper in Chicago, managing asset portfolios for wealthy clients both personal and business, wining and dining some client or prospective client every evening. His wife Sadie was nice enough, but she too was happy to be clinging to their golden ring. Big house, nice cars, nice vacations, kids in private schools. It all looked good on paper. And Tim had worked hard to achieve those goals. He had worked hard and gotten what he went after. Both brothers had had the academic ability to achieve much, yet their lives couldn't be more different.

How did Tom end up so far from the mainstream? It wasn't that he didn't like people, he just liked nature more. It had to be some kind of overdeveloped sense of independence. He had fled from nothing or no one, but the forest was more appealing. Maybe it was the over-wrought academic politics of the PhD program he had started. Research was only valued if it produced the answers popular with his professors. Maybe he pushed himself too far down the education rabbit hole. His natural curiosity about nature, biology, and animals had driven him to pursue as much education as possible, only to find that the education was more indoctrination than education.

Tom did think about his mom more and more. She had been a very good parent, not just doing the fundamentals of cooking, cleaning, and chastisement, though she was good at all of that. She really did show her love to her kids in many ways. She always attended their games, concerts and other events, and made sure they were all welcomed home on any holidays. Welcome at any time, in fact. She also made it clear she loved her grandkids and her son and daughter-in-law as much as they let her. It was good that Marci and Randy were so close. Maybe Tom should have stayed closer once his dad died, but everything seemed to be on an even keel, so he charted his own course.

All that aside, none of it mattered now. Despite his innocence, he was in serious trouble. Tomorrow, he'd see how good Lionel Levitt was and how likely he was to be able prove Tom's innocence. Or create, what was that phrase? 'Reasonable doubt?' Or the other TV standard: how often do we say you are innocent until proven guilty? That's certainly not how this felt. After his time with Marci tomorrow, he had to be sure she could convince Mom he was innocent. That was the word. Not just not guilty. He had to clear his name. He also knew he needed all the help he could get.

Too much thinking, now his arm hurt.

"Marilyn?"

"Yes?"

"Sorry to bother you, but do you have an aspirin or something? My arm is starting to ache."

"Sure. Here you go. Two enough?" Tom nodded. Marilyn went on.

"Doug should be in soon, then I need to go. The little ones want me to be there when they get home from school. Bobby will spend the night. He'll likely sleep in the other cell. I'll be back in the morning."

"Have a good evening."

"Thanks."

Chapter 16

DOUG CAME IN a few minutes later, and Marilyn quickly slipped out. Tom didn't want to accost him, so he lay back down on his cot. Bobby popped in with dinner from the diner, and once he and Doug were both eating, Tom raised the questions that had accumulated in his mind since his arraignment.

"Sheriff, when my attorney gets here tomorrow, is there a place we can speak together in private?"

"Yup. We can shackle you up and take you back over to a conference room in the courthouse. It's set up as kind of an interrogation room so we can cuff you to the table."

"Do I really have to be in shackles? With my sister there? And an attorney who is responsible for me?"

"Sorry, but yes, any time you're out of your cell. Otherwise, Bobby or Marilyn or I have to be present, and that isn't proper because Bobby and I for sure will be called to testify, and we can't be there when you are building your defense."

"Makes sense, I guess."

He could see Tom's disappointment but asked, "Anything else?"

"Yeah, as you might imagine, I generally lead a pretty active life physically, trekking all over those hills. Is there any way to get some aerobic exercise while I am in here? Without bail, it will be at least a month."

Tom went on and tried to lighten the mood a bit. "Or else I need to get put on the diner's weight loss plan. Salad plates and dry toast."

Doug didn't laugh but replied, "I know what you're saying. You, me, Bobby, Marilyn - we'll all look like we're ready for hibernation if we keep eating like this. I don't have anything off the top of my head, but let me think a bit. I may be able to come up with something."

"Thanks." Didn't cost anything to be polite, and Tom had nothing but time.

"One more thing. Any chance of getting the paper when it comes out? And maybe a pen to work the crossword?"

"I'll tell Marilyn to give you the paper. It may be a day or two old, but I can't do the pen, unless you're supervised. You'd be surprised how many county jail prisoners attempt suicide, and a pen can be lethal, as you might imagine."

"Understood."

"In the meantime, here's last week's paper. Better than staring at the wall, maybe. And I'll see if there's some way to work things out for you to get some exercise and find some ways to fill the time."

With that, Doug settled in at his desk, and Tom sat down with the paper. Though the days were starting to lengthen, now that spring was approaching, it still got dark fairly early. Today had been cloudy, which made dusk seem even earlier. As the darkness enveloped him, Tom read the paper until he could no longer see, and about that time, Doug offered him an evening snack. "No thanks, Doug. As we discussed, a shortage of food is a long way from my worst problem."

After a bit more trying to read in the growing dusk, Tom dozed off

When he awoke, Doug was gone and Bobby was seated at the desk, reading a magazine. The office clock showed 11 pm. When Tom stirred, Bobby looked over and asked if he needed anything.

"No, Bobby, I'm comfortable. How are you doing? Are you in trouble with Doug?"

"No, he wasn't too happy with me, without really saying it. He's a really fair guy, which is part of why I stay with him, besides the eventual hoped-for promotion. He bought the story you got the drop on me, then made a break for it. Doesn't raise his estimation of me, but I think he still trusts my integrity."

Tom wanted to make the most of this one-on-one time with Bobby. He tried a more controversial question. "Can you tell me anything about the investigation? Is there one? Or is the list of suspects limited to me?"

"Tom, I told Doug the things we discussed, but he, correctly, stated that the investigation belongs to the DA, and we first and foremost must follow his direction. I'm sorry, but those are the rules of the road, so to speak."

"I see. So if I want to raise these questions for investigation, I guess my only chance is with my own attorney, who is supposed to be here tomorrow."

"Guess so."

Tom was disappointed that Bobby didn't seem like he was going to divulge anything else. But he was still grateful for some company.

"Other than that, Bobby, how are you? How's the family?"

"We're all just fine. Ready for winter to be over, but we've got a ways to go. The lengthening days in February give us some hope, but we'll still have at least one more cold spell, and you can't have March without a blizzard."

"Yup. Your kids in sports or music or anything?"

"Yes, both kids are in band, and both are in some sport throughout the year. Keeps us all from going crazy in the wintertime. It's always good to head over to the high school for an evening of some kind of entertainment. Also, the movie theater is still running, but only Friday and Saturday night show and a Sunday matinee. Nothing all that new, but they keep up and when they can't get anything current they run something old that's just fun to see on the big screen."

"That sounds like a good way to keep it open. So, Marilyn's husband coaches wrestling, I hear?"

"Yeah. We've got a really good wrestling program for a small school. We always have a couple of boys make it to regionals. Once in a while, someone goes to state. He's a really good coach—also coaches the football team. We always have a tough football team too."

"What about the other sports?"

"The baseball team is okay. The same guy coaches basketball. Not much success there. They actually should be better than they play. In fact, they just lost in the first round of the playoffs. Their poor record earned them a bad seed, so there was not much hope. Wrestling is our wintertime bright spot for boys' sports. The girls have some good teams, especially volleyball, so that's fun. They happen to have one really good girl basketball player right now, so they are having a good season. My son plays football and wrestles, and my daughter plays volleyball and basketball. Both are on the track team in the spring."

Tom thought about how different that was from his high school days in the suburbs. So many competing entertainment opportunities that even the good high school teams had a hard time filling a gym or stadium with spectators. It had to be good for the kids to get that much support from the whole town.

"Well, I'm sure sorry if I caused you any trouble, Bobby. That was not my intent. I really do need to clear my name, and right now it's looking like a bit of an uphill battle."

"Don't worry—I'm sure things will look better once you talk to your lawyer, and you can lay out your case to a sympathetic ear."

Chapter 17

LIONEL LEVITT WAS 80 YEARS OLD if he was a day—medium height, medium build, with silver hair, wire-rimmed glasses, and bright blue eyes. When he took off his trench coat, Tom saw an oxford shirt, sweater vest, and wool slacks over black wingtips—immaculate.

He and Marci and Randy had shown up right at lunchtime. Doug shackled Tom up and walked them all through the tunnel to the courthouse, shackled Tom to the table, and then reminded Lionel that he was an officer of the court, so he would be held responsible for any escape or other problems. As they engaged in some strained idle chatter, Doug went over to the diner and picked up a family-style array of food he'd ordered. He then stepped to the door and said he'd be outside in the corridor within sight of the door but out of earshot. Levitt indicated that, except for introductions and small talk, there should be no conversation about the case until the sheriff had left the room for good.

Marci couldn't help but stare at Tom in his orange coveralls and shackles. It was as if the seriousness of the situation had finally struck her. His situation had, in her mind, apparently moved from an episode of a TV cop show to a real crime story with real-life repercussions. Her color had drained, and her eyes were tearing up a bit.

With the food in front of them and everyone settled in, the attorney began his spiel.

"As you can guess, I've been doing this a long time. I'm supposed to be retired, but I can't turn down an interesting case. When Randy contacted my firm, I volunteered right away. If I decide we need to add a younger, more energetic attorney, I will do that, but I am, to use the words of one of my recent opponents, 'a tough old buzzard,' so I'm hoping to handle this myself and keep your costs down."

"Thank you for taking my case on," Tom said. "The whole situation looks like I did it, but I did not. My only guilt is helping myself to some items from the church charity room, and I have returned those."

"Slow down," Levitt said. "Let me lay out how we need to approach this. And if you don't follow my directions, you'll find out just how tough an old buzzard I am."

Tom was starting to get the picture of how this was going to go. "Ok. Got it."

"First of all, you are lucky you have a loving, helpful sister and a brother-in-law with some good contacts, despite the fact you have essentially ignored them for the better part of a decade—until now."

Tom winced. Levitt's words didn't exactly leave a mark, but they hurt. He looked at Marci, and she again had the beginnings of tears in her eyes. The look he got from Randy made him glad he couldn't be on the jury.

"So here's what we're going to do. Usually, I don't allow anyone but me, my client, and any support staff I need into the prep room, due to client confidentiality rules. As we plan a defense and consider options, I don't want Marci or Randy to get deposed because they sat in on discussions about admissions you make and approaches we didn't use and then have to testify as to what and why."

"Understand."

"But given the circumstances, I'm going to modify my approach a bit. You might call it bending the rules, but I don't and I won't. We don't bend rules. We follow the rules, but with my experience, we can modify our approach to fit the situation."

Tom nodded, partly because he wanted to keep things moving and partly because he was chewing and didn't want Levitt to chastise him again.

"We are going to start by having you tell us what happened—slowly, step by step, methodically, leaving out nothing. The rest of us are limited to clarifying questions, with no judgment, suggestions, or anything else. That way, you can inform all of us about how you got into this situation. By working through it methodically, you are also practicing for any deposition or trial testimony that may be required. I want to be sure I understand exactly what happened, and I know from our conversation on the drive here that Marci and Randy are also very interested. This way, we are all on the same page. After that, Marci and Randy will leave, and you and I will continue with the more legalistic parts of the discussion—determining a defense approach up to and including a trial strategy. Are we all clear on that?"

They all nodded.

"Very well. After dinner this evening, you can have some family time, but absolutely no discussion of the case—standard run-of-the-mill conversation. How are the kids? How's Mom? How's work? Any new hobbies? Things like that. Got it?"

They all nodded again.

"Then tomorrow, before we leave and I've had time to think, Tom and I will have another working session. Then one more bit of family time before we head out. On Monday, I need to get to work on whatever filings I need to make and initiate any investigative work that is required. I assume Marci and Randy have jobs and kids and all the usual reasons to get back to their home. Keep in mind this is more of a marathon than a sprint. This will take some time to resolve, regardless of how it ultimately ends."

With that comment, Marci not only teared up but also openly sobbed a bit.

Levitt realized he may have gone too far with his litigator speech. "Sorry, Marci. By 'ultimate resolution,' I meant trial or dismissal or one of the various legal outcomes. I didn't mean guilty or innocent, prison or death sentence."

By this time, Marci was actually crying, and Randy said, "I don't think death sentence references are helping the situation."

"I'm sorry. I perhaps shouldn't have used that in my example. Litigators sometimes tend to be a bit more blunt than the average lawyer. I used that reference to mean it is off the table, not part of any outcome."

Marci got her sobbing under control. She turned to Levitt. "Just remember that whatever happens here and throughout this entire case, I am the one who has to carry all the news, good or bad, to our mother and all the rest of our family. I'd rather not be responsible for our mom's sudden decline."

That brought a definite pause in the proceedings. That was the first time Tom had really focused on the impact on his entire family. He would never have committed the crime he was charged with, yet his whole family, to some degree or other, was now dragged into it. This brought on the first real anger he had felt over the entire past week. It was brutally unfair that his unfortunate proximity to what may have been a collection of crimes affected the lives and reputations of his whole family. He looked at Levitt.

Tom took advantage of the opportunity to make sure Levitt understood the enormity of the situation.

"Marci makes a good point, Mr. Levitt. I'm assuming she has shared the short version I told her of what really happened. I was in the wrong place at the wrong time, but the broader impact on my whole family is all the more reason to clear me."

"Nice speech, Tom, and I will coach Marci and Randy on how and what to communicate with your family. Now let's get to work."

Again, everyone nodded. Tom began his story. As he spoke, he noted reactions from all of them. A couple of times Levitt frowned but said nothing and took extensive notes. A few times Marci asked questions, but it was soon clear that Tom was not to answer unless Levitt said it was okay to do so. At one point, he actually said to Marci, "Don't ask that."

When Tom finished, Levitt put down his pen, turned over his notepad, and said, "Let's all take a break. Randy, please go out and tell the sheriff that we all need a restroom break, one at a time, and that he needs to handle Tom as he sees fit—just to the bathroom and back."

Randy left and Doug came in. Apparently, Randy got the first bathroom break. Doug said, "You can all go at the same time if you want. We have pretty big restrooms." They all looked at Levitt. "Thanks, Sheriff, but no, just one at a time. I want complete control over all our current conversations—hallway, urinal, or otherwise."

Randy came back, then Marci left and returned, then Doug took Tom. Levitt said, "I'll go in a bit, Sheriff. I want to dismiss Marci and Randy first." He turned to address the couple directly.

"Before you go, please do not discuss anything you heard here today, especially in any public place. Everyone in a town like this has exceptional hearing. Now do your hugging and crying and leave us alone for a bit. I'll catch up to you at the motel later."

Tom knew his main function at this brief farewell was to reassure Marci and convince both of them that not only was he innocent, but that now, with Levitt's help, he would be readily cleared of all charges. He tried to sound more confident than he actually was. He also wanted to convey how much he appreciated their ability to get Levitt to represent him. Marci seemed to react well to his confidence and thankfulness, while Randy seemed to just take it all in. After the two of them left, Levitt took his break. While he was out, Doug came in for a bit.

"Crusty old guy, isn't he?"

Tom smiled and said, "I can't comment."

Doug smiled back. "Well, it sure looks like he has you trained already."

Levitt returned, and Doug went back to the hallway. Levitt began the next phase of the discussions.

"Your story certainly portrays an innocent bystander caught in the crossfire of some type of situation that went sideways. Can you repeat it under oath?"

"Yes."

"I need you to be absolutely certain. It is a pretty good story, with a couple of points I want to probe, but I need to make sure you weren't dressing things up for Marci. You were watching her reaction the entire time, and I got the sense you really don't want to disappoint her. Or your mother."

"No, Mr. Levitt, it is all absolutely true as accurately as I can remember. I know it seems…"

Levitt cut him off.

"The key to being a good witness is to stop talking when you are done making your point. I have won a number of cases just by letting witnesses continue to verbally wander after they've already answered the direct question I asked. First lesson: when the question is answered, quit talking. If the attorney questioning you thinks there is more information or explanation needed, they'll ask for it."

"Got it. I just…"

"And yet you just did it again. We'll have to work on that some more."

Levitt continued the conversation point by point.

"You broke into the church, right?"

"Technically, yes."

"Why technically?"

"Because it wasn't hard and I didn't have to break anything. I wiggled the door handle on one of the side doors and the door opened."

"I'm not sure 'poorly secured' is a defense. The door was locked, was it not?"

"Yes."

"And you've provided me the entire list of what you took? Nothing else?"

"Correct. Just what I needed to survive in the woods."

"You left all the silver and gold service items and did not even look for a money bag?"

"Not at all. I was focused on getting what I needed to get out of town."

"And now you've talked to the pastor?"

"Yes. I gave her the stuff back that I took, except for the matches and the bread, which I used up."

"Did you admit to breaking and entering?"

"Yes, I did. Orally."

Levitt paused a bit, made more notes, then moved on.

"You've had a pastoral visit in jail and medical treatment, right?"

"Yes."

"Any other visitors?"

"No, just those two and the sheriff department staff: the sheriff, his deputy Bobby, and Marilyn, who is also a deputy, but essentially does paperwork and runs the jail."

"Does Bobby have a full name? And did you and Bobby rediscuss any of the items you and he talked about when you held him captive?"

"Captive?"

"We'll loop back to that. Bottom line: are you being treated well in jail? Accommodations, meals, overall attitude of the staff?"

"I can't complain. People have actually been quite nice. Meals are very good."

"Have you made any requests? And have they been accommodated?"

"Just two. I asked for lighter meals and for some way to exercise. That cell is awfully small."

"And…"

"Doug said he will try to figure out something for both."

"Doug?"

"Sheriff Pitcher. Outside."

"As I said, I've had a lot of litigation experience, most of it criminal. I've never seen such cozy personal relationships. Did you all know each other before?"

"Only in passing. Everybody knows who the sheriff is, and Bobby is well, just Bobby. I had not met Marilyn before."

"Do you have any idea what Doug or Bobby or Marilyn think about your guilt or innocence?"

"No idea. The sheriff has a reputation for being fair and even-handed, and both he and Bobby have a good handle on crime in the county. They deal with people and events as they have to in order to get their job done."

Again, Levitt paused and looked over his growing pages of notes. Finally, he looked up at Tom and said, "Well, it's crunch time." Tom did not verbally respond, so Levitt continued. "Meaning the two big issues: your ability to identify the doctor and your treatment of Bobby at your cabin. I'll be right back."

Chapter 18

TOM SAT SHACKLED to the conference table for just a few minutes before Levitt returned. He sat down and paged back through his notes. "Let's start with your incarceration of the duly appointed deputy of this county."

"That's putting it harshly."

"How do you think the DA will ask the question? Will he be kind and gentle in his treatment of you, who he is being paid to put behind bars for the cold-blooded murder of an innocent young woman?"

"I guess not."

"How was the DA's demeanor at the arraignment?"

"Pretty gruff, actually. Said he wanted to go to trial in a couple of weeks and said that to let me post bail would risk the safety of the community, besides my already exhibited ability to disappear at will."

"So then let's go back to you and the deputy at your cabin. Why did you detain him?"

"Well, I felt I did what I had to do to prevent Bobby from taking me in and to give my side of the story to someone trustworthy."

"You need to be much more concise."

"Well, I was kind of winging it and hoping for the best. I'm not very good at this. Lack of experience, I guess."

Levitt stared at Tom. "Two quick points: One, be sure to always maintain your composure; you were getting a little heated just now. Two, it is okay to make sure the judge, jury, family, DA—whomever is listening—understands that you are not a hardened criminal and that everything you did was in the sole interest of clearing your name."

"Three—and remember, I have a law degree and not a math degree. You are a fairly laconic speaker, and that can work to your advantage. No matter who is asking the questions, even me, or the tone of their voice, always take time to think before you speak and ask for clarification if you need it. Some attorneys are either notoriously bad at asking a straight question or purposely bad at asking a clear question. Don't answer a question if you don't understand it perfectly.

"I understand what you did and why, but it looks like you held a civil servant at gunpoint overnight and coerced him to lie to his boss, the sheriff. That is not only bad conduct, it is a crime. I believe you didn't kill the girl, but I don't know what to do about charges that could be brought by the church or for your treatment of the deputy. The fact he came out unscathed helps a lot. But it was still a crime.

"Let's move to the doctor. Bottom line, if I understand correctly, you bolted from the ER because you believed the doctor was the same person who murdered the girl and that you thought he might do you harm. Correct?"

"Yes."

"So here's the million-dollar question: Can you identify him positively at the motel and/or at the ER?"

Tom took his time. He took a long time and really thought hard.

"I believe I can. I got a pretty good look at him through the open window of his car, which I can describe, and at the ER, he was wearing a surgical mask, but I went by his eyes. When he pointed that gun at me at the motel, I was looking directly into his eyes, and I am sure they were the same eyes I saw in the ER."

"That's a tough sell, Tom. Most people duck or blank out or pass out when they are facing the wrong end of a gun. Why are you so certain?"

Tom paused again. His next answer may not help him.

"I work as a trapper, and I hunt for my food. I look into the eyes of a lot of animals I have to kill. You never forget that. I was lucky the doctor was a bad shot, though maybe a pistol shot from a car window at that distance isn't an easy trick either."

This time Levitt paused. Tom wondered what would come next, but the silence was a welcome relief.

"Hunter. Hunted. Interesting juxtaposition."

Tom was not sure what to make of that. He knew he was tired of the questions and he could see the shadows lengthening across the room.

Levitt said, "I think that's enough for today. We will pick this up tomorrow after breakfast. What time do they feed you?"

"So far it's been about 8 a.m. Not sure what they'll do on a Sunday."

"Ok. Tom, just to be clear, I am glad to take this case and will do my best to represent you. I have a lot of materials I need to request from the court, such as your arraignment record, the actual charges, and any investigation materials they've gathered thus far. I also want to meet some of the players, but there's plenty of time for that.

"Next question for you to ponder: Do you want me to plead for bail? It's unlikely in this situation, but if you really need out, I can take a swing at it."

Again, Tom took his time to reply. "I can't imagine they're going to let me go home, then try to track me down again, but it would be good to get a chance to go up to my place and finish curing and bring my furs down to sell. It's only half a month of furs, but no sense letting them go to waste. And I'd feel better if I had some money to pay you. Also, it would be nice to kind of close up the cabin and secure everything."

Levitt nodded. "You've made that sound like a reasonable request. I will try to work out a petition for perhaps a brief, accompanied trip. Can't guarantee anything, but I can try."

Levitt went to the door. "We're done in here."

Doug came to the door and said, "Mr. Levitt, do you want me to arrange a ride to your motel room?"

Levitt replied, "No, just point me and I can walk. Don't mind stretching my legs. I've done a lot of sitting today."

Levitt nodded to both Doug and Tom, then headed down the steps to the main door of the courthouse. Doug shackled Tom, then walked him back through the tunnel, into his cell, and unshackled him.

Chapter 19

TOM SAT DOWN on his cot and thought through the day. He hadn't fully anticipated how hard this would be on Marci, and now she had to tell their mom what was going on. The questions from Levitt were intense and starkly defined his situation. He thought he'd feel better after this visit; instead, he felt worse. Having people this involved in your life was exhausting.

"You alive in there?" Doug called from the office.

Tom replied weakly, "Not sure."

Doug chuckled. "Attorneys are always tiring. Your sister and her husband seem real nice. That will help you a lot. Good family overall, I take it?"

"Definitely. We all kind of went off to do our own thing, but our childhood was as normal as you get. No serial killers in the making anywhere in sight."

Tom regretted that last comment even as he was saying it. No need to plant that seed anywhere, especially here and now. Again, he was not used to being mentally exhausted.

"I'm going to take off as soon as Marilyn gets here with your dinner. Bobby had to go out on a call with a conservation officer—apparently some people think deer hunting season never ends. Marilyn's husband and kids are not happy with her Saturday night plans, so please be extra nice to her. We're getting spread pretty thin, and I really don't have any choice but to put her on extra duty."

Tom lay down, and all the events of the day raced through his head. Maybe running deeper into the woods would have been the right approach after all. A lot of people were having their lives disrupted by his unfortunate situation. It took just a moment to know he couldn't have committed the crime at all, let alone put his mom, Marci, or any of his family through this. And what would she tell her kids and Tim and Sadie and their kids? Kind of like having the Unabomber as an uncle.

Levitt had raised the right questions, though. He was still his own best chance to work his way out of this. Deep in thought, he heard Doug greet Marilyn. Then he smelled the food. It smelled great. Eating like this could be a really bad habit.

Marilyn set up a small table against the bars and laid out the food. On another tray, well out of his reach and well within hers, she laid down an unholstered semiautomatic pistol.

"If we're stuck together tonight, we might as well dine like civilized people, and I brought a couple of board games for after dinner. But if you so much as look at me wrong, I will shoot you dead without a second thought. Are we clear?"

Tom had to smile. "That's pretty clear."

"Good. I have invited another mystery guest who will be by in an hour or so."

"Can't wait."

"Yes, you will."

Tom was very much relieved to not have to spend an evening alone with his tormented thoughts. What if, despite his actual innocence and his best efforts and all the skill and experience of Lionel Levitt, he actually was convicted and sent to prison? That couldn't be more different than his life in the woods. But for right now, he was lucky enough to have a dinner partner and some good food.

"This doesn't seem to be in the usual diner containers. What's up?"

"I made this myself and brought it from home. I'll add the cost to my overtime bill."

Tom wasn't sure how to read Marilyn's mood. Was she really angry about the situation, or was she just giving him a hard time? Maybe just stay focused on eating and not try to talk too much.

It wasn't hard to focus on the food. It was superb: pot roast with potatoes, carrots, onions, and peas. Tom couldn't get over how good it was. It was probably the best meal he'd had in years.

"You made this from scratch?"

"Yes, I took advantage of a quiet Saturday at home to put something good together. Then Doug called. There's plenty for Mark and the kids, so I'm glad I went to the effort. Doug will pay, though."

Tom took a chance. "Maybe the county should just let me go to avoid the cost of housing me."

Marilyn looked at him but did not reply directly to his ridiculous request. Rather, she looked at him and soberly said, "Some compliments on the food would be in order now."

"That's easy. It is excellent. Your family is lucky to have you cooking for them. Are you teaching your kids to cook like this?"

"I'm trying. One of the good parts of living in a small town is the lack of fast food. There's the diner and the supper club out on Deer Lake south of town. Eating at home is still the norm, and lucky for me, I enjoy cooking. I also appreciate that Mark and the kids enjoy my cooking."

"Sounds like a good thing all around. My mom was a good cook, but her career made it hard for her to keep regular hours, so meals like this were not all that routine. We did all enjoy them though."

"What did your mom do?"

"She was a nurse. Lots of shift variations, but she tried to be home with us kids when she could."

"Sounds like you had a pretty normal upbringing. How did you end up living alone in the woods ?"

"I've asked myself that question a lot in the past week. I was pursuing a doctorate in biology and conservation but got tired of the academic politics. Took some time off and found I liked the solitude and the work I chose as well as living as close as I could to nature."

"So academic work was easy for you?"

"I managed it okay."

"We should probably move on from talking about you. At some point, our conversation will likely stumble onto your current situation, and I know we can't discuss that. By the way, I need to make a note to have Judy come back in and check your wound again on Monday."

Tom's radar went up. "Judy again, no doctor visit?"

"No, Doc Bradford has been in and out of town a lot. Not sure what he's up to. Probably some training. It's hard to keep up in that field anymore."

"I suppose. Not to be too much of a beggar, but is there dessert?"

"Saving that for later. I brought three, so there's one for our mystery guest."

As long as the mystery guest wasn't Doc Bradford, he figured he was okay to wait and see who it was. Probably not Judy either, and Bobby wasn't much of a mystery.

"Scrabble, Clue, or checkers? I also have a deck of cards if we just want to play some rummy game. Wait, Clue isn't much fun for two people. We'll save that. How about Scrabble?"

That wasn't much of a decision, Tom thought. "Scrabble is fine."

"Now, just so you know, I have to count all the dice and tiles when I pack the games back up. I'm not sure how you'd use a Scrabble tile to escape, but I can't leave anything in your cell. Make sure you don't drop anything, or we'll have to do a full search."

"I'll be careful."

There was a knock on the office door. Marilyn moved the table out of Tom's reach and holstered her gun, moving quickly to the door.

"Oh, hi! Come on in. I was about to torture your brother with a no-holds-barred game of Scrabble."

Marci, Randy, and Lionel came around the corner and into view.

Marci spoke first. "Wow! Smells good in here."

"Marilyn made dinner and brought it over. She's in charge of keeping me locked up tonight. I guess she wants to make sure I won't fit between the bars."

"We just finished dinner at the diner and thought we'd stop over and say good night. Lionel came along to make sure that's all we said."

Levitt stayed back a few steps and looked a little confused but said nothing.

Marilyn gave them all some orders. "No hugging—in fact, no touching. I need to be able to see space between you at all times, but I will clear away the dinner items while you say good night."

Marci started to cry again. "It just hurts to see you behind bars. And shackled the way you were today."

Tom felt a well of sympathy. Again, he felt so bad that his family had to see him in custody.

"Don't cry. They're all just following the rules. It would create a real mess for everyone if I got away, or worse, hurt anyone. Everyone's very respectful, if not downright nice. Marilyn was assigned my overnight watch and was kind enough to bring me a homecooked meal and eat with me. She did promise to shoot me if I tried anything, but that seemed to me to be the reasonable thing to do."

Tom again looked at Levitt, who just seemed to be taking it all in, as did Randy, who seemed less convinced of Tom's innocence than either Levitt or Marci.

Marci composed herself and said, "Well, I guess I don't have to ask how you're being treated, Tom. Marilyn, I really appreciate you showing him all this kindness."

"Yeah, he's stuck here, I'm stuck here, there's no point in being mean as long as he behaves himself."

"Well, thanks again. Tom, do you need anything? I could pick up a few things if you need them."

"No, all I need now is dessert, and Marilyn is holding that back for now."

Levitt finally chimed in. "I'd have a hard time arguing that that constitutes cruel punishment. Unusual, maybe."

Everyone smiled, but no one laughed.

"There's a movie at the Roxy tonight if you'd like something to do. My husband and kids will be there. With no high school sports tonight, there's not much else to do in town."

Tom chimed in. "Why don't you do that, Marci? Better than sitting in that motel room. Last time I was at the motel, I had no fun at all."

Levitt shot Tom a hard glance. "Movie it is. We need to cut this conversation off before it derails."

Chapter 20

AS SOON AS HIS VISITORS had filed out, Marilyn reset the table for Scrabble and unholstered her gun, putting it again in reach if she needed it.

Marilyn easily beat Tom at the first game, but Tom insisted they play again. He held his own the second game, pulling out all his knowledge of esoteric scientific terms—terms he hadn't thought of in years. Marilyn kept threatening to protest, but with no Scrabble dictionary, it was pointless. She still won, but it was a more competitive game.

"Want to switch to something else, Tom? A card game, perhaps?" As she spoke, she actually did count all the tiles and made sure nothing was missing.

At that moment, there was another knock at the door. Marilyn once again pulled the table away from the bars, holstered her gun, and went to the door.

"Oh, hi, Pastor. I kept Tom in suspense about the identity of his next guest. Come on in. Now we can play Clue!"

"I love Clue! And now I get to play with an actual criminal!"

"Alleged," Tom and Marilyn said simultaneously.

Marilyn slid the table back in place and replaced the gun on the table. "Keep your distance, Susan. I don't want to create a hostage situation."

Susan slid her chair to the corner of the table, with Marilyn on the other far corner.

"This time, Tom, I need you to be fully committed to your good faith. I don't want you to be telling the judge I gave you a gun or a knife or a lead pipe or any of the other weapons in the game. Promise?"

"I do, and I assume you have to account for all of them before you pack it away. With the Pastor as witness."

"Susan is fine. No need to call me Pastor, though I am officially here on a pastoral wellness check."

"You don't need to be at the church putting the finishing touches on your sermon?"

"No, I did that this afternoon."

Tom was grateful she had taken the time to visit. "Thank you very much for coming over. I know you don't need to, so I really appreciate it. This is more social time than I've had in the past five years combined."

"And me?" Marilyn chimed in.

"I know you have to be here, but I do thank you for the food and for spending some friendly time with me."

"Don't mention it. Especially to my husband." Both women laughed.

The Clue games went much better for Tom; in fact, he won all three.

"You might just be a better criminal than you claim," Susan finally said, over dessert.

Tom felt relaxed for the first time all day. "No, I'd rather think of it as being a better detective. I hope I don't think like a criminal."

"Sometimes the best detectives are the best because they can think like a criminal," Marilyn offered.

Tom took that in. It made good sense. He thought of the old saying, 'It takes a thief.' Again they were brushing up against the one taboo topic they had to avoid, so he changed the subject.

Directing his comments to Marilyn, he said, "This is the best dessert I've had in a long time. Thanks again."

"No problem. It's Saturday night in Purdy. I figured we might as well live it up, especially since you are living in an alcohol-free zone."

Susan said, "Yes, and that's why I brought grape juice in my traveling communion set. May I offer you communion, Tom?"

Tom looked intently at Susan. Marilyn was counting cards and weapons, seemingly distracted. This was new. He tried to lighten the mood.

"I would, unless this is a ruse to let me know I just ate my last supper and now the padre is offering me absolution before I'm walked off to the electric chair."

"No electric chair that I know of," Susan replied.

"No," Marilyn said. "We don't have one currently."

"Good one, Marilyn." Susan said. "'Currently.' How long have you been waiting for that opportunity?"

After communion, Susan packed up to go and was putting on her coat when there was another knock at the door. Marilyn looked at the door and said, "I really don't know who that could be. You stand over there," she motioned Susan to the corner away from the door, against the wall with the clock.

"Who is it?"

"It's me," a male voice replied.

Marilyn didn't seem at all concerned. "What are you doing here?"

"The kids wanted to say good night, and Maggie thought her mom might still be here."

"Ok. Come on in. Stay in the office, back from the cell."

Tom sat down on his cot, knowing he had to be away from the front of the cell, definitely wishing he wasn't in jail, wearing faded orange coveralls. He was glad that he had gotten to the barbershop on Saturday when he had arrived in town and gotten his hair and beard trimmed. Hopefully he didn't look like an ax murderer. Once again he was overwhelmed by the sheer volume of people suddenly in his purview. He watched them all come in. Two boys who looked to be teenagers, three younger children, and a man with no neck. That was the first thing Tom noticed—no taller than Tom, but clearly the physique of a bodybuilder.

The older kids hung back, typical of teenagers, Tom thought. The three youngest came forward a bit. One of them looked him over, then said, "He looks pretty normal to me."

They all laughed, but it was a bit forced.

"Maggie, that's an astute observation, but first you should be introduced. Maggie, this is Tom. Tom, this is Maggie."

Tom spoke first. "It is a pleasure to meet you, Maggie. Your mother is very proud of you."

"It's nice to meet you too. It's too bad you couldn't come to the movie. It was good. I think we saw your sister there. At least we saw three people we didn't know, which is unusual here."

"That's enough, Maggie, give the others a chance."

It would appear that the whole town knew his sister and her entourage were in town, or at least these people knew. And if an eight-year-old figured out who they were, it would be common knowledge by the end of church tomorrow.

"I'll go next," the man with no neck said. "I'm Mark, Marilyn's husband. I hope you are being as kind to her as she is to you."

"I'm certainly trying to be. I really appreciate the food and the caring environment. This is my first time in jail, and I can't say it's a pleasure, but she and everyone here have been quite gracious, given the situation."

Marilyn apparently wanted to get the situation under control while she still had a chance. "And now you all need to go. This is no place for the kids, regardless of how kind we all are ."

Susan took quick advantage to take Maggie by the hand and head for the door. "Goodnight, everyone. We need to get home and get some rest. Sunday is a big day for a pastor and her family!"

Marilyn gave each kid a hug while Mark kept an eye on Tom. Then she hugged Mark. As they all filed out, Marilyn said, "Isn't it funny, the ripple effect. We had a crime in this town. No question. A girl is dead.

That has to be horrible for her family. And now you and I and Susan and Maggie and my family and your family and Doug and Bobby and their families are all dragged into it, whether any of us want to be or not."

Tom nodded silently.

Chapter 21

SUNDAY DAWNED but not brightly. Tom could peer out enough to see it was once again lightly snowing.

Yes, he was really in jail. It wasn't just a bad dream. He looked at the cot in the next cell. Marilyn was lying in bed, reading a magazine.

Tom thought he'd start the day with a witty comment. "Well, we're both still here, so I guess that's a success for you, anyway."

"Doesn't feel like it. How do you sleep on that cot?"

"It's no worse than what I'm used to in my cabin. And I don't have to add wood to the fire every couple of hours."

"So you may like living in jail?"

"No, not at all. I like to have a lot more freedom of action. Are you on duty all day?"

"No, Bobby will come in so I can go to church with my family. We'll have to sit in the back so no one notices my bed hair. Bobby usually pulls Sunday morning shifts, though when the jail is empty, he can go to church. He just has to carry his radio. Hopefully he'll bring us a breakfast treat. Can't believe I'm hungry after all we ate last night. Now you'll have a few minutes to freshen up while I use the public restroom in the office to do the same."

A few minutes later, Marilyn emerged, actually looking fresher. She said, "You can shower if you want while Bobby is here. Somehow it all works out."

Marilyn sat down at the desk and began working on her makeup. Tom didn't want to bother her and couldn't really think of anything to say anyway. He was just glad that this was all so civil. Tom watched the clock on the wall. It was about 8:00 a.m. He wondered how many hours, days, weeks he'd spend watching that clock. Right now, it seemed like it wasn't moving. That was probably his life for the foreseeable future.

A knock on the door. Marilyn holstered her gun and walked over. "Who's there?"

"Just me, Marci. Can I see Tom for a bit?"

"Sure. We're just sitting here. Both in jail. Only on different sides of the bars."

Marci came in and took off her coat.

"Tom, I don't really have anything specific to say, but I couldn't sleep, so I took the first shower and then told Randy I was headed over. I know we can't discuss your situation, but I see you so seldom I just wanted to visit a bit before we head back today."

Tom replied, "I know what to say, and I should have asked when you first got here. How's Mom and what does she know so far?"

"She's fine. She always looks forward to your summer visit. She's aging, though. A few more doctor visits each year. She does take good care of herself. I'm glad I'm close to her, with you up here and Tim in Chicago and always so busy. I think his kids are coming for a week this summer to stay with her. They get along with our boys, so it should be fun for all of them."

"And…"

"I told her that you were involved in an incident in town and wanted Randy and me to come up. I tried to be completely vague as to type and severity and did not mention Mr. Levitt. I just told her I'd fill her in when we got back on Sunday. Then I guess I have to come clean. I want to do it in person."

"Be sure to make it clear that I am innocent and a victim of being in the wrong place at the wrong time."

Marilyn chimed in, "Just to remind you that I am hearing all of this, and I can be called to make a statement about anything I hear."

"We know," Tom said. "We're just trying to figure out how to make this as easy as we can on our mom."

Tom continued, "And your kids? And Tim and his family?"

Marci smiled a bit through her tears. Tom then smiled. "This whole deal is good for the mascara industry, isn't it?"

Marilyn looked over. "I don't cry ."

Tom smiled again. "Then what was in your eyes when you said good night to Mark last night?"

Marilyn stared at him. "Just how closely are you watching me?"

This time, Tom actually laughed a bit. "Not at all, if Mark asks. I never mess with guys who don't have necks. I don't want to have to stay in jail just to be safe from him."

"Don't worry, Tom, he's tough but has tremendous self-restraint."

After that interlude, Marci attempted to return to the family questions. "I will tell them all the truth. That you have been charged with a crime you didn't commit and that it will take some time to get to the truth. In the meantime, you have to stay in town. I will tell them we've hired a really good lawyer to make sure the right investigations are completed and that you will eventually be released."

Tom listened carefully and nodded. "I guess that's about as accurate as you can be. What do you think Tim will say?"

"Tim will say two things. One, something like this was bound to happen given your lifestyle choice, and two, he will offer some big dollars to get the best attorney in the country to make sure these hicks pay for their mistake."

"Well, I need you to shut him down on both counts, especially the second one. I am willing to stay with Levitt. He seems to know what he's doing and also seems to be getting his finger on the pulse of this whole situation. He is always watching and listening and reading people. I wouldn't want to play poker with him."

"I'm glad you said that. I was going to ask you what you thought. I was hoping you were comfortable with him. He is old, but very well regarded and very professional. He educated us a great deal on the ride up—nothing specific to your case, but how these types of cases typically play out. Especially not to get anxious because this will likely take a while."

The two of them went on visiting about family members, slowly working their way out from the nucleus to aunts, uncles, cousins—covering a lot of the stuff Tom generally only heard during his annual summer visit. They even branched out to high school friends and neighbors.

The office door opened, and Bobby came in, dusting off the snow from his hat and shoulders and stamping his boots. "Good morning, all! Marilyn, you look ravishing after your night in jail!"

"Haha, Bobby. About time you got here. I need to get going if I'm going to meet Mark and the kids at church. I hope you brought breakfast. Do you have a sweet roll or something I can take with me?"

"Take your pick. Fresh from home. See you later. And you must be Tom's sister."

"Yes, I'm Marci, and I take it you are Bobby."

"Sure am. I'm the one who brought in this desperado."

Marci looked quizzically at Tom. She was still wondering at the familiarity of all these people. It just didn't match the seriousness of the situation. She was going to have to ask Levitt for his thoughts on the drive home.

"Help yourself to a pastry. I hope Marilyn made coffee."

"Tom, I'll put a couple on a plate for you. Coffee?"

"Sounds good, Bobby."

"I'd better get back," Marci said. "Randy will think I'm being held hostage. I told him I wanted some time alone with you, Tom, and we've stretched that by a bit. We'll stop by again before we leave town."

"Ok. Thanks a lot for coming to see me. This is the most social life I've had in years. It's wearing me out!"

Chapter 22

AN HOUR OR SO later, Marci, Randy, and Levitt stepped into the jail-house office. The snow had stopped falling and the sun had come out, so all three were stomping their feet to clear the sticky white snow. Bobby stood up. "You I recognize. Not sure who these two guys are."

"This is my husband, Randy, and Tom's attorney, Lionel Levitt."

"Nice to meet you. Heard you were in town. How was the movie?"

Marci quickly replied, "Movie was great, though some of the people seemed to spend more time watching us than the movie."

"Not surprised," Bobby replied. "Strangers in town are kind of unusual this time of year, especially given the current situation. The town gossips are working overtime."

"I can only imagine."

Levitt spoke next. "Bobby, I assume you are a deputy in the sheriff's office. Is the sheriff available today?"

"He can be if I contact him. May take him a little while to get here."

"Would you please do that? Or, I could ask him my question by phone as well."

"I'll call and see which he prefers."

Bobby picked up his radio. "Sheriff, come in. Tom's attorney wants to talk to you."

The sheriff responded inside of a minute. "I'm out on patrol, Bobby. Do you know what he wants?"

"He didn't say, but said it was a quick question, so a phone call would work as well."

"I'll stop in. I am ready for a quick break anyway. Be there in five."

Bobby turned his attention back to the visitors. "Can I offer you a cup of coffee?"

Levitt and Marci declined. Randy accepted. Bobby poured out some coffee into a white porcelain mug. Randy took a sip and grimaced a bit. Bobby laughed. "I never said it was good coffee. There's some creamers there if you want to try to disguise the flavor."

Randy walked over to the table with the coffee maker and all the accompanying materials. "I'm not that picky, but this is really bad. I'm doing the driving on the way back this afternoon, so I thought I could use the picker-upper."

"Go ahead and drink that if you want. Since Doug is stopping in, I'll make a fresh pot. Have a seat, please. Then we can all get a cup if we want."

The smell of fresh coffee filled the office. Tom found the situation a bit awkward. He couldn't ask Bobby any of the questions he wanted to ask. He and Marci had had a long visit this morning. Levitt was his usual taciturn self. Randy continued to act like he wished he was any-where else on the planet. He and Tom had never been close, but Tom always figured that was just because they hadn't spent any real time together. Maybe Randy thought Tom was capable of murder or, at least, was in the middle of some drug-dealing operation.

Doug walked in, stomping his shoes. "Good morning, everyone. Bobby, why don't you run a patrol around town while I see what we need to discuss. In fact, head out on the gravel road that goes east out of town. I think there are some kids snowmobiling out there. Seeing a pa-trol car may keep them from being too stupid. By the way, thanks for making fresh coffee."

Turning to the others, he said, "I hope you have all accomplished your goals for the trip up here. I hear Tom had a good visit with his sister this morning."

Levitt stood. "Thanks for coming in, Sheriff. I hope this won't take too long. As you know, I have been retained to represent Tom in this matter, but I also, to some degree, represent his family—more specifically, his sister, Marci."

"Understood."

"I understand he's charged with murder, but Marci in particular is deeply concerned about her brother's extended incarceration. As you know, Sheriff, cases like this could go on for months, and while Tom is being, from what I have seen, treated very well, he is in a very confining situation."

Doug just looked at him, so Levitt continued.

"So I really have a two-part question. First, if I stayed over tonight, is there any chance of getting on the judge's Monday morning docket? And if I do, is there any chance at all that we could get Tom out on some form of bail, recognizance, or release?"

Doug continued to look directly at Levitt. Then he looked at Marci. Then over at Randy. Finally he looked at Tom, who had been surprised to hear the question.

"I figured this may be your question, and so I've had some time to think it over. First, the judge does keep an hour open on Monday mornings for initial court hearings. Around here that's usually a DUI or poaching or perhaps a domestic assault charge. We hardly ever need the whole hour. Usually the DA has a stock answer for each such complaint, so there's not a lot of controversy. In this case, however, the DA would probably need to be apprised in advance, which may push this hearing to Monday afternoon or Tuesday morning, depending on whatever he and the judge have on their calendars. I know our DA well enough to know that his initial reaction, unfortunately for you, will be absolutely not."

Levitt now took a moment to case the room. They all waited but he said nothing. Doug proceeded.

"As you said, this is a most serious offense, making bail very difficult to get. The one additional person who will get asked to speak at such a hearing is me. Tom seems to be a decent guy and so far has been a model prisoner, but my position has to be to keep him incarcerated.

He has already proven himself to be extremely elusive, disappearing into the woods in the dark of night in the middle of winter, while injured, and faring well despite bitter cold and snow. He is resourceful beyond anyone I have ever seen. Usually the guys who run into the woods around here come back in a few hours begging to be locked up. Not Tom. He has already put my chief deputy in a very compromising situation, essentially holding him captive overnight. We have not brought charges on that, but if you drag me into court, I can press for that. Finally, for someone like Tom, he is a couple days' walk from Canada or another state, and we'd look like fools. Again."

Another brief pause, then Doug continued.

"Marci, Randy, you, as well as Tom, seem to be honest, decent people who would do everything you could to keep tabs on Tom and bring him back in whenever we needed him here. But I also know people in Tom's situation can get pretty creative and desperate when facing the possibility of life in prison. Finally, I foolishly, in hindsight, trusted Tom to go with the EMTs and stay at the ER, rather than send Bobby along or go with him. We have a small staff, as you've seen, and I figured no one would run away in the middle of the night in the middle of the winter with a gunshot wound. I was wrong. I know Tom has told you why he did that, and all that has to work its way through the investigative process. But yet another reason to deny any type of bail or bond."

Doug paused, took a sip of coffee, and waited for any knee-jerk response. Hearing none, he proceeded.

"I have to do what is in the best interest of the people of this county, my staff, and ultimately Tom. I know this has been hard to hear." Doug looked at Marci. "There's tissues on the desk there if you need more. And I don't want to seem cruel, but I'm afraid I have to dig my heels in on my position."

Levitt asked his one additional question: "Would you argue that Tom is a threat to your community, or the population at large?"

"I don't know. Generally, the only time you see that argument made is for a domestic murder. 'No danger to the general public' is the statement generally cited for that. I personally have a hard time even with that situation. All I have to go on is that on the one hand he is in jail charged with murder, but on the other hand he didn't do any harm to Bobby when he held him overnight. Again, though, I don't want any of that to come out in court, or the DA will immediately charge him with kidnapping and wonder what the hell is wrong with me. Really don't want either of those things."

By now Marci was openly sobbing. Randy put his arm around her. "I just don't know what to tell my mother! Knowing what he's accused of and that he's sitting in jail day and night for who knows how long is just going to break her heart."

Doug looked at her with genuine concern. "I don't doubt that. It will be very hard. But if you have to do it, I would suggest you make sure she knows that Tom swears he's innocent and if you believe that, then you tell her that, too."

Levitt stood in an effort to take control of the situation. "I'm sorry, Marci, but I told you it was a long shot. The sheriff has made his position clear, and I fully understand it."

Again, silence reigned, and Marci slowly regained her composure. Randy still had his arm around her. He stared at Tom like he would murder him if he could.

Tom was surprised at the bluntness of the sheriff's speech, but it was all accurate. "Thanks for trying, guys, but I will be okay here. Maybe I'll even be able to beat Marilyn at Scrabble by the time I get out. Please focus on the case, not on me. I did not commit murder, and I need all of you to help me prove that. Besides, Marci," he continued, "once I'm acquitted, I don't want to spend the rest of my life paying your mascara bill."

Levitt spoke next. "If she wants money, she'll have to get in line after me."

Tom looked over at Levitt. "Ouch ."

Levitt replied, "Don't worry, I'll be reasonable. I don't know what mascara costs, and I want to make sure I have the first lien." This was probably as close to funny as he could get.

Bobby walked back in. "Am I interrupting anything ?"

Doug replied, "No, I think we were just finishing up. Would you go over to the diner and get some cookies? This coffee is too good to not have a snack to go with it."

As Bobby disappeared back out the door, Doug said, "I would never try to be mean. I was just answering the question the way I would have to answer it in court. This way we got to do it privately, and not in public or on the record. And I really don't want to embarrass Bobby about your overnight stay in public or on the record, so I will hold those charges over your head. A full-blown exposure might end his career in law enforcement. There's no need to go down that path. Bobby did help me bring Tom in, so he has redeemed himself somewhat. And he is by all other accounts a really solid deputy. Finally, the local paper will come out on Tuesday evening and this is the biggest story they've had in decades. Lord knows what they are putting together. Going back into court would only give them more to work with. They have a reporter stop in every Monday morning at nine to see if there's anything interesting to cover, so they would not miss this."

Bobby burst back in. "I got the variety pack." He then looked around the room. "Looks like I am not sorry I missed this conversation."

Randy said, "Since I'm the driver and we have a ways to go, we should be heading out."

Levitt nodded, and even Marci nodded, never taking her eyes off Tom.

"It's a long drive, guys, go ahead," Tom said. "You can't know how much it meant to see you, and thanks for all your help, Mr. Levitt. Just don't forget about me."

"Take a cookie with you." Bobby held out the box. Doug rolled his eyes. "Guess who has to explain the department expenses to the county commission. And your first clue is that it's not Bobby."

They all turned to look at Doug. "No, really, help yourself, and pour a coffee to go if you want. I appreciate you bringing this question to me informally, because no one, even me, likes to get blindsided in court."

"Drive safely, and thanks again for being here." Tom thought he'd gotten the last word, but Randy turned to Levitt and Marci. "You guys head over to the motel and check out. Make sure we have everything. I'll be right behind you."

Bobby followed them out, and as the door closed, Randy turned to Tom. "I don't know what kind of life you actually live up here—if you're growing marijuana or trafficking sex workers or killing people right and left, and until now I never really cared. But when you dragged my wife into it, that crossed the line. You should have gone with whatever public defender this county wanted to assign you and left Marci and our kids and your mom and all the rest of us out of it. You chose to live in isolation, and now you come crawling back the minute you need help. The others may rush to save you, but I don't appreciate what you're doing to my wife and her mother."

Tom stared at the door Randy had slammed behind himself.

Doug looked over at Tom. "I've been in this business all my adult life, and I will tell you two things. One, that is a well-rehearsed speech. He's been working on that ever since you called your sister. And he had to get it off his chest. More importantly, I often hear that speech from families in trouble, and the words are spoken in anger. Don't dwell on it. You said the right thing. Focus on the case. I hope that's what Marci took away."

Chapter 23

TOM AWOKE to the beginnings of light flowing across his cell. Must be a clear day, he thought. Amazing how quickly I've gotten used to waking up in a jail cell.

Bobby was sitting at the desk, feet up, snoring. Tom used the toilet, taking advantage of Bobby's closed eyes and snoring to provide some privacy.

Hard to believe he'd only been in jail a few days. It was starting to feel normal. How many more mornings would he wake up here? The weekend had been full of visitors and meetings, ending with Randy's scathing attack. He and Randy had always gotten along, Tom thought, but that speech said otherwise. Apparently, Randy had been only tolerating him all these years. And Tom had been a groomsman in their wedding. Maybe that was only Marci's idea and a family obligation. Randy had a well-paying tech job in a firm that had a large and growing business. He had a steady paycheck, he coached his kids' various sports teams, and he and Marci together had purchased a nice house in the suburbs. He was living the standard American dream. Did Randy think Tom had thrown away a similar opportunity to live in the woods? Was he a bad example to Randy and Marci's kids? Or was it simply a belief that Tom had abandoned his mother and the rest of his family to live out some backwoods survivor-man fantasy? Was it resentment that both he and Tim had gone their separate ways, leaving Marci to deal with their mother as she aged? Dealing with her house, car, doctor visits, and all the time and energy that took?

It was interesting that up until now, Tom had not processed all these thoughts. He picked his lifestyle, and they picked theirs. It was, or had been, simple as that. Now it was all boiling over. It was clear now that he had caused Marci and now their mom a lot of anxiety when he picked up the phone to call and ask for help. He simply did not trust Purdy County to provide him with competent counsel, because he didn't know who was behind the murder and who might have a stake in the outcome. He also knew Marci and Randy would be able to track down a good attorney. And they had. But Randy saw it as an intrusion, and while it hurt to hear it, the main message Randy shared was right. He did run back into the fold when he was in trouble, though this was the first time in almost a decade he had done so. His parents had set aside some money to help him get his bachelor's degree, just like his siblings, but he had been entirely on his own since then. Apparently, being independent and not bothering anybody wasn't the entire goal in life. At least that's what Randy seems to think.

It was Monday. The past three days had been relatively busy. He had been arraigned Friday, enjoyed visits and games with Marilyn and Susan, had spent a lot of time with Marci, Randy, and Levitt, and now that was all over. Sunday had been quiet after Marci and the others had left, but he had needed that time to process the events of the prior few days. He hoped his mom was okay and that Marci had convinced her that he was innocent. He would hate to have his mom believe he could be a murderer. There was nothing he could do about Randy for now. Hopefully that relationship could be resurrected. If there had ever been a relationship. Thinking of resurrection, he wondered if he'd see Susan again, or if her visits were just a product of the novelty of a murder suspect in this little jail.

If the visits were over, he sure hoped Doug had found a way to get him some exercise. The office door opened. Marilyn walked in with a grocery bag. "Good morning, Bobby, Tom."

She continued, "You can take off, Bobby, or have some breakfast. I picked it up at the diner. There's plenty."

"Thanks, Marilyn, but I think I'll take off. I'd like to catch the kids before school. Haven't seen them much lately. Maybe even talk to my wife a bit."

"I understand. Tell them all hello."

"Food, Tom, or do you have to run, too?" Marilyn gave him a wicked glance.

"I'm not sure if that was funny or just cruel."

"Sorry. It was supposed to be funny."

"I'm sorry, too. After all the busyness of the weekend, I am finally facing the prospect of a long time just sitting here. Do you know if Doug figured out any way for me to get some exercise?"

"I think he did, but I'll let him tell you himself. Right now, he's patrolling. Most of the kids walk to school, so he likes to have a presence on the streets to remind people to drive carefully this time of day and to keep the kids on the sidewalks. He'll be here in a bit."

Marilyn set up the table and put a container on it. Tom opened it. French toast! This part of a life of crime was not so bad! He hoped the budget or just disinterest didn't end this part of his stay.

"Thanks, Marilyn. This is really good."

"No problem. Let me know if you want seconds. This is one perk of my extra hours. It is good!"

They ate in silence. Marilyn seemed distracted and Tom just couldn't think of anything to say. Small talk was not his forte. When he was done, he put everything back on the table and retreated to his cot.

"No seconds?"

"No, I'm full. Still not used to eating this well."

Moments later, the phone rang. "Yup. Yup, that would be fine. See you in a bit."

"That was Judy. She is coming over to look at your wound. Should be here in a minute or two."

"Ok. It feels good, so hopefully it's healing okay."

A couple of minutes later, right on cue, Judy came in, with a first aid bag.

"Hi, Marilyn."

"Hi, Judy."

"Well, Tom, let's take a look."

Judy once again asked Tom to pull down his coveralls and take off his T-shirt, then put his shoulder out between the bars. Judy removed the bandage and said nothing, which Tom took as good news. She swabbed it with a wipe, then left it uncovered.

"It's coming along real well, Tom. I'll be back on Wednesday. Don't hesitate to tell Marilyn if it hurts or looks inflamed. I'll leave some salve and a couple of bandages with Marilyn, so you can bandage it after you shower. Which you really, really need. Medical opinion only." Judy gave Tom a big smile to go with the message.

Tom grimaced. With all the activities of the weekend and the lack of privacy, he had not showered since the first time, when he was brought in on Thursday. "Thanks, Judy. I appreciate your candor. I'll add that to my schedule for the day."

"I'm sure Marilyn will appreciate that. Not the shower itself, but having a cleaner prisoner." Both women laughed.

"Shower on Cell Block D. A day in the life of a jailhouse matron." Marilyn could barely get the words out without laughing.

"This is fun, guys, but we're really busy at the clinic, so I need to get back. I always wonder at all the people who manage to get injured or ill over the weekend."

"Understand, Judy. Hope you get things under control. And by the way, Doug will be in shortly, so I'll step out while Tom showers. Don't need you starting any rumors around town about why I'm suddenly at the jail so much."

The timing was perfect. Just as Judy opened the office door, Doug stepped in. Sharing the briefest of greetings, Judy was gone and Doug was taking off his coat.

"He's fed and his medical officer says he desperately needs a shower, so if you can stay a bit, I have an errand to run. Should be back in half an hour."

"Sounds good, Marilyn. See you in a bit. Tom and I need to talk anyway. But you can sit in on that since it involves you, as you know."

"It sure does. I'll be right back."

Marilyn was not even out the door when Doug said, "Go ahead and jump in the shower. Here's some clean clothes for you. Now we even need someone to do laundry regularly. I'm going to grab some coffee and have some of this French toast."

Tom was intrigued by the conversation between Doug and Marilyn but figured he had better get in the shower since this seemed to be his only chance to do it without an audience. He had lived so privately that this was all new—even the shower. In his cabin, he had a washtub and tried to use it once a week because it took a lot of effort to melt enough snow and get the water hot enough to sit in. If it was bitter cold, he sometimes went longer than a week. But there was no one around to complain. The curing hides in his cabin masked any smell he might be giving off anyway.

This showering was quite a luxury, except for the viewing. That was just plain weird. He had gone from complete privacy to none.

The shower felt good, and he let the warm water wash over his wound. When he had dried off, he redressed the wound with the salve and bandages Judy had left, then dressed himself. He was glad to get Judy's opinion on the healing.

"Coffee, Tom?"

"Sure, thanks."

Doug poured two coffees and handed one through the bars to Tom. He pulled up a chair just outside the cell.

"I'm going to get started with our topic. Marilyn will be back anytime. Here's the deal, Tom. Over the weekend, it became apparent that even with Marilyn working full time, we still have a hard time covering the shifts it takes to keep you under state-required watch and still carry out our usual duties. Over the weekend I made some phone calls and arranged an emergency meeting of the county commissioners. They met last night and approved what I proposed. What we are doing is deputizing Marilyn's husband, Mark, so he can help keep an eye on you. We've deputized him before for special situations, so this has some precedent, and he's already approved and fully trained. Now the good news. With winter sports over for our local school teams, Mark runs an after-school open gym program to let the kids blow off steam and stay off the streets. With him deputized, we can bring you over to the gym, and you can also get some gym time. Needless to say, he'll be armed and have a police radio, and will do what is necessary to stop any escape. Bobby or I may also stop by from time to time just to check in on you. I know it's not hiking through the wilderness, but you can jog or run sprints or lift weights, or maybe join in with some basketball or volleyball—whatever is going on that day. I also had to run an additional background check on you to make sure you have no history of being a danger to kids. I could do that without your permission because you are in custody. Obviously, I found nothing or we wouldn't be talking."

Just then Marilyn came back. "Sorry I took so long. Have you broken the news yet?"

"Just starting, Marilyn. I laid out the situation and haven't gotten Tom's response."

Tom looked at both of them, and before he could say anything, Marilyn spoke again. "What this does, Tom, is allow me to be home when the younger kids come home from school, help them with homework, fix supper, and have it ready when Mark gets back from dropping you back here. Bobby or Doug will be here for the evening, then one of the three of us will come spend the night. It's not ideal for my family life, but it does help me quite a bit."

Doug chimed in, "And the county commissioners approved the funding because it's only a couple of extra deputy hours a day, Monday through Friday. Actually just replacing a few of Marilyn's hours with Mark's. On the weekends you'll have to do pushups or something— usual prisoner stuff."

They both looked at Tom. He realized that no response might ruin the deal, and he did want the deal.

"This sounds great. I have just a couple of questions."

"Go ahead."

Tom took a breath and continued. "First question: Do I have to wear my orange coveralls and get walked over to the school in shackles?"

"Good question. 'Walk of shame' type issue. No, we're a little more sensitive than that. Our school colors are sky blue and forest green, so we can't have you wearing those colors. We need to be able to readily identify you in the gym and to stand out a bit on the street. Marilyn just went to the outfitters, which also passes as our little local department store, to get you a non-blue or green wardrobe. Marilyn?"

"Tom, just note, I have a jock husband and three sons, two of which are already high school athletes. So I am well within my wheelhouse picking out athletic gear. Unfortunately, our local store isn't exactly a big-box store. Given Doug's ban on blue or green, I came back with a pair of red sweatpants and a pair of gold sweatpants so I can keep one clean for you each day. Also a couple of similar-colored sweatshirts and a couple of really tacky, bright-colored tourist T-shirts—on clearance. Oh, and some sweat socks and a couple of jock straps. Again, this is not new for me. You can mix or match to your heart's desire. Finally, some Cons. Size 10. Ok? I can run them back if that's wrong.

Tom stared at her. "You really have done this before."

Doug cut in, "And for the shackles, here's what I propose. Marilyn will walk you over, handcuffed to her wrist. She is well trained in physical defense. We can keep the handcuffs pretty well hidden if you cooperate. If you try anything, this will be the end of any decent treatment, and we will expedite your trial and sentencing. Mark will be looking for you, and once you are in the gym, you are his. You've seen Mark; I don't think I need to say any more. Trust me, if you run, he can run you down, and you don't want that. You need to be in your sweats by about 3:15 each day."

Tom looked at them both. "Shoes are fine. And I have no plans to escape. That didn't work the first time, and I know now I need to let my attorney do his job. This is a great answer to my question about exercise.

I used to spend a lot of my winters in a gym, so I'll figure out how to get a good workout in. I really appreciate this."

He looked directly at Marilyn. "Is this why you had Mark stop by on Saturday night?"

"No, that was all on him, but I can see it had an impact. He does that when he wants to see who I'm spending my time with."

"It worked."

Doug finished up. "At the end of your workout, about 5 or 5:30, Mark will handcuff you to him and walk you back, where he will put you back in your cell so you can shower. He'll stay until Bobby or I show up so he can go home for his own shower and dinner. Then someone will get you your supper. Unless you want to just stop at the diner."

Tom looked quizzically at Doug, who quickly said, "Just kidding. You'll be all sweaty."

Tom was not sure what to make of that, so waited for more. There was silence all around.

"We good here?" Doug asked.

Both Tom and Marilyn nodded.

Doug stood. "I have some sheriff work to do. You two enjoy the day. Marilyn, just radio if you need me. Otherwise, I expect to get a call or two right around 3:30 telling me the two of you are walking hand in hand down the street."

Again, both nodded.

Chapter 24

IT WAS A LITTLE awkward the first time. Tom had his sweats on—going with the gold, which he thought would be less conspicuous than the red. He then had to put on his parka, and the handcuff with the cell door open only enough to get his arm out. Marilyn positioned herself to have a fighting chance to slam the heavy door back on him if she thought he was going to attempt a break. She then put the other end of the handcuffs on her left wrist and clamped it tight, putting the key in her right pants pocket. When she did that, Tom had to notice her holstered gun. She was not a large woman, but was probably five foot eight or five foot nine—just a few inches shorter than his own 6-0 even—and with her training in physical defense, she would actually be hard to overpower.

All that aside, Tom's last thought was escape. He was more worried about how he might be treated walking down the street and just what greeting he might get at the gym. He really was hoping to fly under the radar on both counts.

The two of them moved toward the office door. This clearly was better than the shackles. Tom wondered why that protocol had been abandoned for this less secure method of transport. Marilyn opened the office door, kind of dragged Tom out in front of her, then stepped out and closed the door. Tom looked about, dazzled by the direct daylight, even though it was midafternoon. Marilyn turned toward the school, Tom keeping step on the sidewalk: to the corner, then across the street, down another block, across the street to the back of the school and in the door, the whole process taking less than five minutes. As Tom entered the gym, he clearly saw Doug parked in his patrol car across the street. From his vantage point, he could see the entire journey. Tom smiled. Apparently Doug was not as trusting as he had thought. As Tom and Marilyn entered the school, he once again had to adjust from daylight to the artificial light of the gym. Although brightly lit, it was no comparison to the sunlight.

They were both careful to wipe their shoes on the large mat at the door. Once Mark was standing next to him, Marilyn opened Tom's end of the handcuffs, then hers and handed the cuffs and key to Mark. She then nodded to both and went back out the door. Mark actually held Tom's arm until the door closed behind her—not tightly, but firmly enough to detect any movement.

Tom looked around. The gym, even with the bleachers all rolled up, was much smaller than the suburban high school gym of his youth. Probably 80 feet by 80 feet, using the regulation size high school basketball floor as a measuring unit. Not big but functional. On the near end was a stage, and with the curtains open, he saw some basic weightlifting equipment. Mark followed his gaze and noted, "No weight machines really. I'm old-fashioned that way. I like to have the kids use free weights. It builds better core strength, and they all learn the teamwork element of spotting for each other. Besides, we don't have much of a budget for anything fancy."

With that introductory moment passed, Mark let go of Tom's arm and said, "Go ahead and take your parka off."

When he saw the sweatsuit, he said, "Looks like you got the outfitter special."

"That's what I hear, but I do appreciate the clothes and the opportunity to get out of that cell for a while."

"I've got the kids playing volleyball on the far half-court. We do all sorts of things here: volleyball, basketball, relay races, sometimes just free play. I do need to keep an eye on them, though usually once I get them engaged in something, they stay on track pretty well. They're all here voluntarily, and if they get unruly and I can end it quickly, I just show them the door. In your case, I use the radio to call Doug or Bobby, or just shoot you. You can't go out the door, at all, ever, until we link up and walk back to the jail. That clear?"

"Of course. Do you and Marilyn have some kind of side bet on who gets to shoot me first?"

"No side bet, though I could bring that up. I was just trying to remind you that I take my responsibility to get you back to the jail very seriously."

"That's perfectly clear."

Tom was glad that Mark seemed like he hadn't been forced into this arrangement. He was starting to think that it would be best to see if there might be a way to have Mark actually enjoy this time each afternoon—perhaps by being helpful and always cordial and cooperative. Mark continued , "What do you want to do?"

"Can I jog a bit to warm up and maybe just shoot baskets at one of the hoops?"

"Sure. Maybe I'll shoot with you. Helps to not have to shag all your own loose balls. Unless you never miss."

"I haven't played in a long time, so I doubt that's what will happen. I played in high school, then intramurals in college, but even that was a long time ago."

"I'll grab a ball, you do your running, and we can shoot here."

Tom jogged to the far side of the gym, then back, then high-stepped over and back, then backward over and forwards back—just enough to feel loose. Mark threw him a ball, and Tom started close to the basket on the right side, taking a short bank shot. It rimmed out. Next time it went in. Mark grabbed the ball and did the same from the left side. It was clear basketball was not his game. Tom grabbed that rebound and from there it all went like it was normal for both of them: shot, rebound, shot, chasing an errant ball. Within a few minutes, both were lost in the exercise. Mark did keep an eye on the volleyball game, but that was going smoothly, so a half-hour passed pretty quickly.

Mark blew his whistle. Everything stopped. He yelled, "Ethan, Evan, over here." Two of the bigger boys left the volleyball game and trotted over. "This is Tom, boys. He's here to get some exercise. Tom, these are my sons Ethan and Evan."

The larger boy looked Tom over. "I recognize him from the night we stopped at the jail. Mom said she was bringing him over."

Mark spoke next, "How about some half-court two on two. I'll take Evan. Ethan, you and Tom are a team. Ok?"

"Sure, Dad. Is he any good?"

" He's okay. He can handle a ball and move pretty well. Not much of a shot."

Tom matched up with Mark, and the two of them played the post positions. The two boys clearly had the skill advantage, while the two men worked hard in the post. Tom found that Mark was clearly stronger and surprisingly quick. As the first game wore on, he found himself working farther and farther from the basket. Mark and Evan won the first game 10–7. After a brief water break, the second game went the other way, with Tom and Ethan winning 11–9. During a longer water break, with a bit of a chance to rest and cool off, Mark checked over on the volleyball game and repositioned some players to make the sides more even. As he walked back, he said, "If you don't change the sides once in a while, the whole thing turns into a bit of a grudge match."

Then he continued, "Should we have our rubber game?"

Tom wasn't sure how that differed from a grudge match but nodded and walked out to the court. He had a brief conversation with Ethan, and they agreed that on offense, rather than run the point and post offense, they'd work from both sides and try to cut or screen their way to the basket. This pulled Mark out further from the basket, giving Tom relief from the physicality of posting up on him, at least on offense.

Ethan started on the left side, about 20 feet out. Evan gave him some room, so Tom shot across the lane to set a screen. Ethan worked his way around the screen and drove the lane. Mark took the charge, and the ball turned over. On defense, Tom fronted Mark and got a fingertip on Evan's pass. The ball hit the bottom of the rim and bounced down. Ethan picked it up and took it to the left side. Tom moved to the right side and cut to the basket. He managed to get past Evan, took the pass from Ethan, but rather than drive into Mark, he pulled up and dropped a short jumper. He looked at Ethan, who nodded. From there, the game went back and forth, and Tom knew he was running out of gas. With the score tied at 7, Tom cut to the post, took the pass from Ethan, and fired it right back out to Ethan, saying, "Take it!"

Ethan took the jumper from about 12 feet and dropped it. Cheers broke out.

They all looked over, and the volleyball players had stopped their game and were all intently watching the basketball showdown. From there on, it was a grudge match, with Tom and Ethan eventually winning out 12–10. Tom was utterly exhausted. While he had been in excellent shape prior to his arrest, this was a different type of exercise, and he hurt from his Cons to his head. He looked at the clock—it was just about 5:00. All four shook hands and took long drinks of water, then sat down.

"I'll certainly need that shower when I get back. No matter who's watching."

Mark looked at him out of the corner of his eye. "Glad to know Marilyn will be home when you shower."

The volleyball kids were now shooting baskets with Ethan and Evan, so Tom helped Mark take down the volleyball net and pack it away. Bit by bit, the kids started putting on coats and hats and heading out.

"The gym is open until 5:30, but around 5 most of the kids start heading for home. Once they're all gone, I lock up and head out. Today you'll be chained to my wrist."

Tom laughed. "After that workout, I think the risk of me running off is pretty much nonexistent."

"Good," Mark replied. "That was the plan."

Mark didn't laugh.

Parkas on, handcuffs on, Mark followed Tom out the door and turned back to make sure the lock was set. They set out for the jail in silence, Tom looking for a patrol car and readily saw Bobby parked mid-route.

Tom broke the silence. "Your sons can play. Are they on the high school team?"

"Yup. Physically, they take after their mother more than me—more long and lean. Both prefer basketball to wrestling, but I get to coach them in football." Mark continued, "Your rust came off quickly, so you've clearly got some talent."

"I guess. I stayed with basketball and managed to be a starter my senior year, then played intramurals all through college."

"No football?"

"No. I liked playing, but liked hunting more and always had good luck with fall fishing. My dad was an avid outdoorsman, so our time together was in the woods and on the lakes."

"Was?"

"Yeah, he passed away unexpectedly while I was in college. Big loss."

"And your mom?"

"She's doing fine. Still in the house. My sister Marci keeps a close eye on her. I hope my situation isn't taking too much out of her."

"That would be hard on any mother. Marilyn says you are adamant that you didn't do it."

"I didn't. I hope Marci was able to make that clear to Mom."

"Well, here we are."

By the time they reached the jail office door, Bobby had parked in his usual spot and opened the door for them. Mark walked Tom to the cell door, uncuffed him first, and Tom walked into the cell. The door clanged shut behind him. He took off his parka and handed it to Bobby through the bars.

Mark said, "If you get those sweats off, I can take them home for Marilyn to wash. She washes a load or two every evening."

With just the three men in the building, Tom quickly stripped and rolled up all the other clothes in the sweatpants. "Thanks, Mark. That was exhausting, but it really helped to get out of this cell. And thank Marilyn for the laundry service."

"No problem. Besides, with all of Marilyn's extra hours and the laundry bill and the food service, we'll be able to take a nice vacation this summer—or, if you're still locked up, maybe a quick getaway next winter."

That simple comment felt like a blow below the belt. Still locked up all summer? Tom just turned and walked to the shower.

Chapter 25

TOM AWOKE at first light. Still in jail. He rolled over, but it didn't feel right. Moved the other way, then he realized that the basketball had taken a toll. Muscles and joints not stressed in that way for years were protesting loudly. He started some movement exercises in bed, and that helped. He should have taken some aspirin or something when he went to bed. He smiled, though; it had really felt good to be back in a gym. Wonder if I can make it to the gym today? If so, I need to spend the day limbering up .

He saw movement from the other cell, and Marilyn sat up.

"You up for all day?"

"I think so. Your husband and sons really did a number on me yesterday. I hope I can still walk."

"They said you all got a pretty good workout and that you know something about basketball."

"That's nice of them. It was fun. I'd forgotten how much I enjoyed playing."

"Good. I washed and brought back your workout clothes. You were sound asleep when I replaced Bobby, but that wasn't until almost midnight."

Tom looked over at the clock. It was almost 6:30.

"That leaves you with a pretty short night."

"I'll catch a nap sometime today. You've got a busy schedule."

"Really?"

"Yup. Your attorney wants to have a call with you at ten o'clock. He called while you were at the gym. And Pastor Susan will be joining us for lunch."

"That sounds good. I guess everyone wants to eat courtesy of the county."

Tom felt bad the moment the words came out. He felt worse when Marilyn replied.

"Actually, she's bringing the lunch."

"Ouch. I'm not sure who to apologize to."

"Don't worry about it. You're starting to sound like Doug. Well, I'm going to stretch out a little more until Doug gets here, okay? He'll be here fairly soon and is bringing your breakfast. Probably something decadent. He doesn't have the best diet in the world."

"Sounds good. I'll be quiet."

Tom must have drifted back to sleep, which was uncharacteristic, and was awoken again as Doug opened the office door.

"Well, look at you two! I guess jail is relaxing. Maybe I'll have to spend a night here once in a while."

"Sorry, Doug. We were both awake earlier. I didn't get here to relieve Bobby until almost midnight, so it was a short night. I think Tom is worn out from the exercise he demanded."

Tom looked over at her. She was smiling at him. Apparently, her comments were well intended. Marilyn had gotten up and was walking into the office.

"Is it okay if I leave? I can still get home in time to get the kids off to school."

"Sure, but before you go, I need to let you know that I did get a couple of phone calls about the two of you walking over to the school together. Apparently you hid the handcuffs well."

Marilyn stopped in her tracks. Looking hard at Doug, she asked, "What did you say?"

"I told them that a prisoner is entitled to basic rights, including exercise, and that he was under custody the whole time. Double custody for at least part of it. Then it gets a little more complicated."

Tom didn't like the sound of that. As sore and tired as he was, he didn't want to lose his exercise privilege.

"I had a couple of calls from parents whose children told them that Tom had been in the gym with them."

This time Tom had to reply, "And…"

"I told them the same story and that Mark was deputized with full rights and responsibilities and that keeping the town and county safe, including the children, was clearly the key function of his duties. I asked each parent if anything questionable had occurred, and the answer was always no."

Tom waited to see if there was more. There was.

"I also told them that all of us on my staff were dedicated to keeping you in custody and making sure everyone was safe. I also told them that it was incumbent on the town to utilize this jail effectively or we would lose it, and that the cost, danger, and inefficiency of transporting every prisoner, including any minor disturbances, all the way to Thompson Falls is much worse than our current situation. I closed by stating that I was the person they elected as sheriff and that as long as I was in charge, I was going to do what I think is best for the town and the county, including the children."

Tom stared at Doug. He had really given this some thought.

Doug continued. "I also made it clear that this plan had been approved and financed by the county commission, who they had also elected."

Tom couldn't help it. He thanked Doug for his stand and his support.

"Don't take it personally, Tom. We're talking rights that I don't want your attorney poking at in court. And it gets a little bit worse."

Again Tom stared. Where was this headed?

"The DA also got some calls, and guess what? He immediately called me. He and I had a fairly pointed conversation, in which I laid out the points I just made to you, including rights and duties, and in his case, segregation of duties. I had to finally and very specifically ask him just how your exercise plan interfered with his duties. That ended the conversation."

This time it was Marilyn who spoke. "Am I in any trouble, Doug?"

"Absolutely not. I just wanted you to know the buzz around town, in case someone says something to you or to Mark or your kids. You need to give them the heads up, so go ahead and take off. Just make sure you and Tom don't actually hold hands as you walk to the school today. That I cannot explain or justify as department duties."

"If that gets around to Mark, I won't guarantee Tom will live long enough to get to trial."

Tom was a bit concerned now. Is this all supposed to be funny? Marilyn put on her jacket and headed to the door. She turned and blew a kiss to Tom. "See you this afternoon, honey!" And she was gone.

Doug looked over at Tom. "My lips are sealed. I'm trying to get you to trial alive. I'm not sure what she's doing."

"Apparently in their marriage she's the funny one."

"Good observation."

Doug went back to the desk and retrieved a bag he had brought in, unnoticed by Tom. "Here's your breakfast. I'll start the coffee."

Marilyn had been right. Sticky buns with extra caramel and butter. No prisoner complaint on this count.

Doug ate at his desk. Tom took his tray and sat back down on his cot. The roll and coffee were both really good. When he was done, he slid his tray out and took his bathroom break, taking care to wash his sticky hands and brush his teeth. With all the heat Doug had taken over his gym time, he didn't want to have to request an emergency dental visit.

When the phone rang, both Doug and Tom looked at it a moment, then Doug walked over and answered it. "Yup, he's ready. Give me a moment to get him to the phone."

Doug opened the cell door, cuffed Tom's left wrist, then walked him to the phone and attached the other end of the cuff to the ring in the wall. He then went back to his desk.

"Hello ."

"Good morning, Tom, Lionel Levitt here. How are you?"

"Fine, considering…"

"But physically okay? Still being treated well?"

"Yes. Treatment is fine."

"Good. Now listen carefully. I'm going to update you on what I've done and found so far, but since the sheriff is listening in, I want you to keep your responses as brief as possible. Not a lot of Q and A. Understand?"

"Yes."

"Good."

"I found your description of the events around the murder to be quite helpful. It has helped me construct the investigation I need to get you cleared. I still don't know if we will end up at trial, or if we can find a different means to dispose of the accusations, but the investigation is the same, regardless. I spent yesterday putting together investigation steps, including interview scripts for my associate and me, since the firm has afforded me one junior attorney for this matter. I have lists of questions for the motel owner, the former motel owners, the current doctor, and the former doctor, as well as the pastor. I really cannot approach any law enforcement personnel except through formal depositions, but I can and will, in writing, request all their reports, notes, and any other records, which I am entitled to review. You still with me?"

"Yes."

"Good. So what I am saying is that I have created the framework for my investigation, but am just now going to begin the steps. I need you to be patient. I know jail is not the best place to be, but for now it is best for you to stay there."

"I understand. In fact, the sheriff has arranged for me to get some exercise time each weekday, which I much appreciate."

"Excellent. That should help keep you sharp and your spirits up. So with that backdrop, I will come back to Purdy one week from today, so you and I can discuss what I have found, good, bad, or indifferent, including getting a sense of anyone who doesn't seem to want to be all that cooperative. Also, sometimes these interviews are by phone, sometimes they are in person, and sometimes they are circular. For example, we could learn something from the current motel owner that needs to be vetted with the former owners, or stories that don't match, things like that. That is part of the reason an investigation like this can take more time than someone in your situation would like. However, tying up all the loose ends ultimately works in your favor. So, whereas the DA wants to rush to trial, we want to string it along. You never know what thread might be just the lead we need."

"I see."

"So your jail time may extend, but you need to let me do my job, which may not be quick."

"Got it."

"And obviously, the biggest mystery of all: Who is the victim? Where is she from? Criminal record? Why was she in Purdy? Was she in Purdy before? Who did she know in Purdy? And, of course, the coroner's report. Not just cause of death, but was she sexually assaulted, did she have drugs in her system, all the little details. Somebody killed her for some reason, or you wouldn't be in jail."

Tom just listened, so Levitt continued.

"As you can see, this is a lot of work, so again, bide your time and give me time to do this."

"Makes sense, and I appreciate your diligence. I guess my life is in your hands."

"Not quite, since we are not in a death penalty state, but where you spend your life certainly is, and I take that seriously."

Again, Tom decided saying nothing was better than what he wanted to say, with Doug well within earshot.

"I also know time drags a bit for you, so again, I will travel to Purdy one week from today, so we can discuss in private what I have found up to that time. I can justify that as a prisoner well-being check, and I will ask Marci if she wants to ride along, even though she cannot sit in on our actual conversation, which will by necessity be privileged. I will also bring my junior associate, so she can meet you and share directly what she has learned. Talking to an actual accused criminal will be good experience for her."

"She?"

"Yes, a young woman who is attempting to get some experience in litigation. Her name is Monica Simpson. The firm doesn't get much in the way of criminal cases, especially murder, so we all agreed it would be beneficial for her to assist me in this case."

Tom thought a bit. "Just how junior is she?"

"She's been with the firm about a year, but she interned with us before that, so she has some experience."

"I guess I'll meet her then. What time do you think you will arrive? My exercise time is about 3:00 to 5:00 p.m. each day. Would just as soon do that if possible."

"I can work with that. We'll get an early start and can be headed home by 3."

"Sounds good. Again, I appreciate your willingness to take my case."

"No problem. I enjoy the work, and I have a feeling this is going to prove to be an interesting case."

"Is that good?"

"Early to say, but I think yes. Anything else, Tom? Any issues from your end?"

"No, I will wait to see what we have to discuss next Tuesday. Thanks for the call."

"Happy to do it. See you Tuesday."

Levitt hung up, so Tom did as well. Tom looked over at Doug, who came with the handcuff key and put Tom back in his cell.

Chapter 26

TOM DID SOME STRETCHING to loosen his sore muscles. Lying back down on his bunk, he thought, "I really need to find something to read or do. Just waiting all day for 3:00 p.m. is still too boring, and my thoughts from time to time turn very dark. What is prison like? Certainly not like this. Maybe Susan can help me argue for some books or something."

The office door opened: It was Susan! Speak of the devil. Wow, that's an inappropriate expression!

Susan spoke first. "Hi, Doug. May I see the prisoner?"

"Of course. I heard you were bringing lunch. Let me get the table and chair set up for you."

"I brought enough for you, too, if you'd like."

"You know I won't turn that down."

"I also brought Tom a few books to read, or at least pick from. Do you need to preapprove?"

"I do need to make sure there isn't a gun, knife, or file hidden in them, or they're not too racy, or have directions on how to escape from jail. That's about it."

Susan smiled and put the books on Doug's desk. "A pastor delivering racy books. That would get the tongues wagging in town."

The table ready, she pulled a pan of lasagna out of her bag, along with some garlic toast and a Caesar salad.

"No chianti?" Doug asked.

"No, we need that for communion."

"Just kidding. Can't serve that in jail anyway."

"So I figured."

Doug fixed a plate for himself and walked back to his desk. Susan prepared a plate for Tom and slid it through to him on his tray. As she bowed her head to pray, Tom had to drop his fork. Again, a custom he had long forgotten. He attempted to make light of his blunder, saying, "Sorry about that. You know how us hardened prisoners are."

"So I see. Maybe I can reform you. I just have to talk Doug into keeping you here long enough."

"Not what I was going for."

The food was great, but the conversation was pretty mundane. Both knew they couldn't discuss the case, and Tom didn't want it to sound like he was doing a deep dive into Susan's life. Susan did ask if, besides the books, there was anything she could do for him. "No, not really, but I really do enjoy your visits. Even with my new exercise program, the days get pretty long."

"By exercise you mean walking hand in hand down the street with Marilyn?"

Doug laughed. Tom winced. "Wow, that sure got around."

"Just kidding. I did hear some gossip, but figured out it's more handcuffed than hand in hand. If Mark and Marilyn come in for marriage counseling, then I'll take it seriously."

"If it comes to that, I'll be safer in jail than on the street. I've played basketball against Mark, and he is a mass of muscle."

Susan nodded. "Fortunately, he's a really good guy who is dedicated to his family and to the school. He does his best to be a positive role model for the kids in this town."

There was just a little more small talk while Susan started cleaning up. Marilyn came in, and Doug announced he was leaving to go out on patrol. He passed Susan's books to Tom without any comment, then left.

"He's sure been quiet lately," Marilyn said as the door closed behind Doug. "And kind of mysterious about what he's doing. But he's always played his cards close to his vest."

Susan offered a prayer, then put her coat on, took her bag, and left.

"Lasagna, eh?"

"Yup. And it was really good."

"Well, you can nap for a bit before you go to the gym. Mark said you worked him pretty hard yesterday."

"Worked him hard? I thought it was the other way around. Your sons are pretty solid basketball players. It's been a long time since I played, so I got a good workout."

Chapter 27

TOM LOOKED through the three books Susan had left, picked one, and was fully engrossed when Marilyn stood up to rinse out the coffee pot. He got up and took a drink of water, then went in the shower, mostly out of sight, and put on the clean sweats that Marilyn had brought for him. He just couldn't make himself wear red sweatpants out in public.

The whole routine seemed a little more relaxed than the day before. When Mark took the handoff, he said, "I have to admit, I am stiff and sore today. Basketball is not my game, and I've got some aches I haven't felt in years. How about you?"

"The same," Tom replied.

"Then let's let the kids play, and we'll officiate. More jogging, less running, and no jumping."

"Sounds good to me."

Mark handed Tom a whistle, then blew his own.

"Listen up, kids. Today our organized activity will be basketball. Full court, but side to side to side on the far side, as usual. Boys and girls, whoever wants to play. We'll leave the other half court open for free play."

Most of the kids walked over to that side of the court. Several boys and a couple of girls drifted up to the weights. Mark watched them go. "Be sure you know who's spotting for whom up there."

"We got it, coach," one of the kids replied.

That left an even dozen to play basketball. Ethan and Evan were picked as captains and each chose their team quickly. Obviously these kids knew each other well.

"Usual substitution rules. In and out every two minutes. I'll keep the clock." Mark had done this before too.

The skill levels varied and both sides played two-three zones. The game quickly developed a pace of its own, and Tom appreciated Mark's suggestion to officiate. He jogged down one sideline and Mark the other. Anything close to a foul was called. No free throws, just loss of possession, which kept the game moving. Tom was loosening up. Mark also kept an eye on the weight room. An uneventful hour passed, then Mark blew his whistle. "Time for some relays."

Some of the kids groaned but all came to the end line.

"Basketball teams stay as you are. Let's draft the others and get started." Ethan and Evan finished their picks rapidly, then Mark said, "OK, each relay team winner gets a dollar certificate to the diner."

"Coach, the sides aren't even."

'I'll sit out," said one boy .

"No, not an option. Tom, care to participate?"

"Sure, why not ."

"First relay, cross court, so each team has their own basket. Run the length of court, make the layup, then rebound and pass back to the next person. Ready?"

Nods all around and the whistle blew. Tom took the end of the line on his team and watched. Mark was a genius. These kids really went at it hard. The only problem seemed to be missed layups, which led to frantic running to get the ball, try again, then the long pass back. Making that long pass back really tested some of the kids, but it was, Tom knew, a great basketball skill to develop. "Bounce pass back," he said to the girl in front of him. "Easier to control."

She nodded without looking back. She caught the pass coming back and took off, dribbling effortlessly. She made the layup and threw it directly back to Tom. She clearly knew how to play. He dribbled down, made the layup, and passed back to the leader of the line. Virtual tie between the teams, but Tom's team won.

"Again!" Mark yelled from the other side of the gym. "Reverse order."

Both lines rearranged themselves and the whistle blew. Tom drove across the court, a little looser and more confident now. He drove to the rim, elevated, and from just an inch or two below the rim, laid it softly off the boards, landed, picked up the ball, and threw it on one bounce to the teammate next in line.

As Tom jogged back, he noted his team was in the lead. This time they won easily.

"Next relay, same teams. Put the balls away. Run to the other line, do five pushups, and run back ."

Tom smiled. Mark was getting a wrestling workout into the mix. And so it went. A few more relays, then the time was gone. Tom couldn't believe how much he enjoyed this. The kids still wouldn't talk to him, but no one said anything derogatory either. As they put their clothes on to go home, they all talked a bit, as did he and Mark.

"Good workout again. How many different relay games do you know?"

"Enough to get by. It helps to keep kids engaged to always be changing things up."

"Who's the girl in the red shorts?"

"Not sure I should tell you that."

"OK. Then I'll just say she's a pretty good athlete."

"Yeah, she is. She's a junior. Plays volleyball, basketball, and runs track. Good kid, good student, too."

The walk back to the jail was uneventful. Bobby was at the desk. Tom showered and changed back into his orange coveralls. He handed his workout clothes to Mark and sat down on his cot. Feeling pretty good for the moment, he said, "Hey, Bobby, what's for supper."

Bobby looked at him for a moment. "Not sure, Tom. Doug radioed that he'd be here late. I'll have to see if I can find a runner for dinner."

Just then, Marilyn came in, carrying a couple of bags from the diner. "I heard the message from Doug saying he'd be late, so as soon as Mark got home, I swung over to the diner and picked up a couple of the daily dinner specials. I need to get back home, so enjoy. See you tomorrow."

With that, she was gone. Tom was glad for dinner but sorry she was in and out so quickly. He missed getting a little teasing from her. It was kind of like the relationship he used to have with Marci. It would be nice to see Marci again next week. For years he had been happy with his annual summertime visits. He could catch the local shuttle bus from Purdy to Thompson Falls, used mostly by senior citizens heading to medical appointments. From there, he could catch a bus to a suburban stop where Marci could pick him up.

It started with the same routine as his annual midwinter trip: the long walk into Purdy, with an overnight stop at the motel so he could clean up and put on "civilian" clothes. His visit was as long as he could stand it. He did enjoy spending some time with his mom and sister, and usually his brother made the trip up from Chicago for a weekend. He also inevitably ran into some old friends and some of those he enjoyed visiting with a bit.

Bobby put Tom's food on his tray and slid it into Tom's cell. "Thanks, Bobby. Looks good."

"It sure does. Need anything else?"

"No, I'm fine."

"Tom, mind if I ask you a few questions? Not related to your case, of course."

"Sure, go ahead."

"You seem to be a pretty likeable guy. You get along with pretty much everybody you come in contact with. You treated me okay when I was at your cabin. My kids say you are willing to do all the games after school. How did you end up living all alone in the woods?"

Chapter 28

"BOBBY, THAT'S A REALLY GOOD QUESTION. First of all, since you are the one asking, I am not running from the law or any kind of legal problem. It was more of a drift than anything. I had earned my bachelor's degree in biology and conservation, a master's in a similar field, and was working on my doctorate in environmental studies when I just got really tired of the academic environment and the university politics. What I really wanted was to enjoy nature and spend time outdoors instead of more and more time reading and studying about stuff that I thought wasn't as interesting as the real thing—nature.

In fact, I was reading about things I really wanted to experience firsthand. I had always enjoyed hunting and fishing and the great outdoors, so I put my academic career on hold and went out into the woods to live the way I wanted for a while. I ended up buying some land that everyone thought was useless, building my cabin, setting up traplines, hunting and fishing for meat, and planting and tending a small garden for produce. As you know, I came into town a few times a year for the other supplies I need as well as visits to the doctor and dentist. But as I invested more and more in my little homestead, I found I really enjoyed the work, the solitude, and truly being my own boss. I fell into a lifestyle that I found quite comfortable and just kept extending my stay. I also think I am helping nature by taking game that is at risk of overpopulating and clearing brush and helping manage the natural waterways."

Bobby was staring at Tom intently. Since he said nothing, Tom tried to wrap things up.

"I seem to have put you in a trance, so I'll just say, it wasn't ever my intent to stay forever, but I haven't found a reason yet to pull up stakes and move on."

Again, silence before Bobby spoke. "I can see your position, Tom. Even in a small town like this, there are people everywhere all the time. I moved here to get away from the congestion and confusion of a much bigger town, but I traded the masses for a bunch of people who are always wondering what you're up to. And if you don't tell them, they speculate."

"Yeah, nothing beats small-town gossip. I think that's one of the reasons my parents left towns like this and moved to the suburbs to raise us kids."

Bobby seemed satisfied with Tom's explanation. "Thanks for sharing that. It all makes sense to me now. Usually the guys we find living in the woods are sociopaths you really don't want anything to do with. You sure don't fit that mold. Now, tell me about the basketball. Mark says you have some skills."

"That is very kind of him. When I go over and play, all I see is rust. I played in high school. I was good enough to start my senior year. Certainly not the best player on my team, but in a school with over 400 kids in a class, the talent pool was pretty deep. I also played football through middle school and played baseball whenever I could, but when they interfered with hunting in the fall and fishing season in the spring and summer, I decided to concentrate on basketball."

Tom decided he'd revealed enough, and since Bobby told him the town was full of gossip, he knew his story would get around. Bobby didn't seem to be shy about gossiping himself. So Tom tried to turn the focus back to Bobby.

"How long were you on the force in Thompson Falls before you came up here?"

"Just over three years, Tom. I started there right out of my police training course. When I saw the ad for a deputy here, it looked like a good opportunity, so I took a shot. Unlike you, I'm a small-town boy, so I found it pretty easy to fit in."

Tom was, as with most of the other people he met here, amazed at how readily they shared their backgrounds and how comfortable they seemed to be with each other. The DA was an exception, but that may just be job and situation related. Doug was more quiet, but again, he had to maintain some distance from Tom because of the case. He sure had done what he could to make Tom's jail time palatable. Marilyn was great, and Pastor Susan was nicer than her job required. So was Judy, the nurse. How did Doc Bradford and Phil fit into this small-town situation? They both seemed out of place to Tom, but psychological profiling was a little outside his field of study. He was sure glad a handful of people were treating him okay.

After he ate, Doug came in, Bobby went home, and Tom finished the first of his books from Susan, then fell asleep.

Wednesday morning, Tom awoke to find Doug was gone, and Marilyn was at the desk. When he sat up, she immediately walked over and handed him the Purdy Purview. "Our weekly paper is out and you're front-page headline famous."

Sure enough, his mug shot was front and center, and almost the entire front page was about the murder at the motel. His stomach churned as he read the reporter's version of events. Most of it speculative, but enough connection to reality to give it a solid flavor. Quotes from Doug, Bobby, Phil, and a statement from Doc Bradford, as well as a few discreet photos of the crime scene. Which the Sheriff's department would have had to provide.

While the article did not say he killed the girl, it clearly identified him as the only suspect and made it clear that he ran at the first opportunity. "For more on the suspect, see the editorial on page 3."

He turned to page 3. It got much worse. The editorial discussed the "… obviously antisocial suspect, about whom no one in the community knows much—just that he lives alone deep in the woods, kills animals for a living, sells the furs for his cash income, and wanders into town a few times a year, where he does his necessary business and shuns human contact. Clearly the profile of a dangerous man." Again, not a murder accusation, but a smear, nonetheless. The editor either had a good lawyer or knew enough to not directly state that Tom was a murderer. He was certainly painting the picture, though. Then it really took a turn. "As this paper is going to press, it has been learned that this accused murderer is allowed to leave the jail to spend time at the school gym with our children for an 'exercise program.' More on this in next week's editorial."

Could this end Tom's trips to the gym? Without that, this would turn into a pretty bleak existence. He looked up. Marilyn was watching him. She spoke before he could get words out. Which wasn't hard. He could think of nothing to say that he wanted her to hear.

"Even here in bucolic small-town Purdy, the media has to sensationalize everything. And this may be the biggest story they've ever had. I know Aaron and Mattie, who own the paper. They're not bad people. They just want to sell newspapers ."

Tom just nodded. Marilyn continued, "That had to be hard to read. Especially the editorial. The paper came out last night. Doug is meeting with the DA now. He would like to try to get the paper to tone things down a bit—get them to understand that in smearing you, they are actually making the sheriff's department look incompetent and making it more likely any trial would have to move to another county, making the trial tougher for the DA and more expensive for this county. And character assassination may actually jeopardize the county's case against you. More importantly, he wants the DA to help him present a united front on your 'lax treatment.' As the paper says."

Tom was still in shock. He knew the paper would cover the murder. They had to. But to crucify him personally was not what he expected. They stopped short of calling him the murderer, but they made it clear that he had all the attributes of a murderer.

Marilyn interrupted his thoughts. "Your gym time is a right, and Doug will involve your attorney if he needs to. By the way, I mailed him a copy of the paper right away this morning. He needs to see it."

With no response from Tom, she continued, "The biggest risk to your exercise time is that it may have to be shifted to you alone, rather than with the kids."

To this, Tom finally reacted. "I understand, but I really enjoy the games. It makes the exercise so much more enjoyable, and it seems like the kids are getting used to having me around."

"That's good to hear. Mark says the same thing. So hopefully we can keep things as they are."

Tom was struck by her portrayal of so many discussions. "It sounds like a lot of important people spend a great deal of time talking about me and my case."

Marilyn smiled. "You are a new and novel experience for all of us, and we're all trying to figure out how to manage you and the case. It would actually be easier if you were a sullen jerk or a raving lunatic. Then we could lock you up and lose the key. But you seem to be quite decent, which makes us try to make this situation as easy for all of us as we can. Or at least some of us are trying. Others, not so much."

Tom continued to sit on his cot, staring at the newspaper. Who had they talked with to reach these conclusions? It was almost as if they had contacted Randy. Would even Randy give them that much fodder? Or were they just winging it?

"Thanks, Marilyn. I appreciate the information and your candor."

"Well, Doug put me in charge of giving you all the details. Can you handle one more bad twist?"

"Not sure. How bad?"

"Not sure. But you do need to be aware."

"Okay. Shoot."

"While Purdy is an isolated little town, the newspaper has lines of communication into the larger media world. Usually, they use those lines to get stories from the outside world to print here. However, those lines run both ways. This story can be picked up by any newspaper anywhere in the US, or the world, for that matter."

Tom again just sat and stared at Marilyn. "So if it gets picked up by the right media group, my mom could see it, and my sister and brother and nieces and nephews…."

"Unfortunately, yes. You probably need to call your sister right away."

"I guess I do. Let me use the toilet, then let's get me over to the phone. Unless the newspaper story convinced you I am no longer safe to handle outside my cell." Tom figured even a lame joke was better than saying what he was really thinking.

"I'll have to take my chances. Doug gave me orders. You really are turning into a ton of trouble." Marilyn smiled as she spoke.

Marilyn went back to her desk, so Tom had a bit of privacy. He washed his face and hands, dried them, and then went to the front of his cell. Marilyn walked over and cuffed him to the cell door, opened the door, put another set of cuffs between the two of them, uncuffed the cell door, walked him over, and attached that cuff to the ring by the phone. Then she uncuffed herself. "New routine?"

"Yup, Doug figured that when one of us is here all alone with you, it was the best approach we could go with. Helps us claim we always handled you as securely as we could."

"Actually, kind of slick. I'm always cuffed to something or someone."

"Thanks. You are way too cooperative to be an actual murderer, but don't tell Doug I said that. No, wait! Maybe you're a psychopath and you are manipulating all of us. Hadn't thought of that. Now I'm terrified." Marilyn laughed.

Tom was glad for a moment of levity. "Don't be. I'm not a psychopath."

"That's exactly what a psychopath would say!"

"Is that coming from Marilyn the deputy or Marilyn the psychologist?"

"Pure psychology. Maybe I've finally figured you out! Now be a good boy and call your sister."

Chapter 29

TOM CALLED Marci's office number. It rang once, twice, again, then went to voicemail.

"Marci, this is Tom. Please call me as soon as you can. I need to give you a heads-up on something. Thanks, bye."

"Marilyn, since I'm all hooked up here, can I call my lawyer too? I want to let him know what's going on."

"Sure. Go ahead."

Tom dialed Levitt's number and a woman answered. "Lionel Levitt's office, how may I help you?"

"This is Tom Reynolds. Is Mr. Levitt available? I have something I need to share with him. Won't take long."

"I'm sorry, Mr. Levitt is in court. Would you like to talk to Ms. Simpson, the associate assigned to your case?"

"Sure. I've not met her, but I think that she and Mr. Levitt need to know what I have to tell them."

"Just a moment."

Another ring or two. "Monica Simpson. I understand you are Tom Reynolds?"

"Yes. Thanks for taking my call."

"No problem. I understand I will meet you next week."

"That is the plan."

"What can I do for you today?"

Tom proceeded to carefully tell Monica about the front-page article and the editorial in the Purdy Purview. At one point when he was searching for words, Marilyn walked over and handed him a copy of the paper. Monica asked a few clarifying questions, giving Tom the impression she was a bit surprised by the tone of the editorial in particular. She then said, "If I put you on the phone with one of our stenographers, could you read the article to her?" Tom had no experience in a law office or other office, but he did know, through his college experiences, that stenographers were hired by most big organizations to transcribe oral statements and speeches into written documents that could then be reviewed and then published or at least filed with other documents.

"I suppose. One of the deputies here did mail a copy to Mr. Levitt. It should be there in a day or two."

"That is good, but I think we need to get this in front of Mr. Levitt as soon as we can. I'm sorry to make you go through this, but I'm afraid it is necessary. He will probably want to address a letter to the newspaper immediately. Let me connect you."

Another pause, then a ring and a chipper voice said, "This is Becky. I understand you're going to dictate a newspaper article to me ."

"That's correct."

A brief pause, then Becky said, "I'm ready, so go ahead."

Tom read the article word for word, then described the pictures. "And there's an editorial."

"Ok, read that please."

He read the editorial, then said, "That's it."

"Ok, thanks. I'll get this transcribed and over to your attorneys. Do you want me to reconnect you to Monica?"

"Yes, please, just to make sure we're done with our conversation."

Pause, a little hold music played, then Monica came on the line. "Monica again. Have you finished with Becky?"

"Yes. Ok. I'll read the transcript and make sure Mr. Levitt sees it. Then we'll call you if we need to—or if nothing else, see you next week as planned. Ok?"

"Ok. Thanks."

Marilyn walked over and started uncuffing him when the phone rang on her desk. She re-cuffed him to the ring, then walked back and took the call. "It's Marci. Just stay there and redial her."

Tom called and explained it all to Marci. He could tell she was upset. "I don't know what to say. I can't believe they'd smear you like that."

"Me neither. Just so you know, I read the article to a stenographer at Levitt's office who is transcribing it, so they should have a copy soon, if you want to pick one up there. Everything but the pictures, which don't make me or the situation look any better."

"I'm so sorry for you. This doesn't help anything."

"No, but you absolutely need to brace Mom before she picks up a newspaper and sees it. Or if someone down there recognizes my name or face and decides it's a juicy story with a local twist, it could end up on the evening news."

"Oh, no. So, I also need to sit down with the kids and call Tim in Chicago."

"Afraid so."

Marci sighed.

Tom continued, "I am so sorry this is taking up so much of your time. Maybe when I got away the first time, I should have just kept on running."

"No, then you'd be convicted in the media and live your entire life with this hanging over your head. Whoever actually did it would be thrilled that you essentially plead guilty by fleeing. You would have no chance of ever coming back. That would be hell on Mom."

"I guess I know that. I'm just frustrated."

"I'll take care of things here. And Levitt is a good lawyer. He'll have a response. Just continue to be nice to your captors and don't make things worse."

"You're right. Thanks. Love you."

"You too. I'll see you next week."

Marilyn uncuffed him from the phone ring and walked him back to his cell.

"I'd say something snide about the phone bills you are running up while you're here, but that would be low, even for me."

Tom looked at Marilyn. "Thanks for that. I really don't need any more negatives today."

"Understood."

From there, the day settled into the normal routine: breakfast, some reading (including looking through the rest of the Purview), then lunch. Tom had just laid down after he ate when he heard the office door open. "Hi, Marilyn, can I talk to Tom?"

Tom recognized Pastor Susan's voice immediately. "Tom, are you ok to have a visitor?"

"Of course. Come on in. Marilyn, do we have some fresh coffee?"

"I'll make another pot. We could all use some fresh coffee."

As he sat up, Tom noticed that Susan was carrying a copy of the Purview .

"Did you want to visit, or did you just come in for an autograph?"

"I'm not sure I want an autographed copy of this yellow journalism. I do want to see how you're doing, now that you have seen the worst of small-town life."

"It was a shock, I have to admit." Tom paused, listening to the coffee maker in the background. The smell of fresh coffee filled the jailhouse. "Doug said it would be a big story for the local paper. Didn't hint just how bad it would be. I guess I just believed in all that 'innocent until proven guilty' stuff."

"I feel so bad for you and for your family. As we've all discussed, the ripple effect of this horrible murder is painful for so many people, but this is so unnecessary and has to be hard on your family. Have you had a chance to talk to your sister or anyone yet?"

"Yes, I called her this morning. I also read the article to a stenographer in my lawyer's office, so they have it word for word."

"Yeah," Marilyn interjected, walking over with two cups of fresh, hot coffee. "Not only is he eating us out of house and home, now his phone bills look like a line item in the congressional budget."

Tom looked at her. "You just couldn't let that one go, could you? I can see why Mark loves you so much."

"I was thinking the same thing," Susan said. "That's a little rough, Marilyn."

Tom decided to take a shot of his own.

"On the other hand, I thought my congressional duties were mostly to create the Mark and Marilyn Butler Full Employment Act. I understand a nice vacation is in your future, courtesy of my incarceration."

Marilyn seemed a little surprised at Tom's comment. Maybe she didn't know Mark had shared their plans with Tom. Marilyn didn't take long to reply, however.

"Good one, Tom. See, Susan, it can flow both ways. I'm just trying to keep him from dying of self-pity before we get a chance to hang him."

Susan stared at Marilyn. "Wow. This has taken an ugly turn."

Marilyn smiled, then sort of apologized.

"Yes. I guess I went too far with that last comment. I'm sorry, Tom. I'm with Susan, really. You got smeared undeservedly, and I really am trying to keep up your spirits. Whatever I say, I mean in jest. Besides, we're not a death penalty state."

"I was hoping so. I'm walking a pretty fine line here. Model prisoner, a little verbal jousting with you, walking with you down the street, yet not having your husband kill me before I get hung. It's a lot to keep balanced."

Susan studied them both, then seemed to relax a bit.

"I can see you two have reached the equilibrium of an old married couple, or maybe a couple of elderly siblings. I was going to try to bolster Tom's spirits, but I may not be needed. Or it may not be possible in this environment."

Marilyn laughed and said, "Go ahead, Susan. I'll butt out and enjoy my coffee over at my desk."

Susan turned her attention back to Tom. "This treatment in the paper must have hit you pretty hard. I know I felt angry when I read it. So unfair. And as a closet lawyer, I hope Doug or the DA or someone takes them to task for poisoning the atmosphere before you get your day in court."

Tom replied, "Thanks for that perspective. It's hard to imagine being able to use a local jury now. What keeps my spirits up is knowing that I didn't do it and hoping and praying that the truth will come out." Tom threw in the praying, considering his audience. He hoped it didn't sound too self-serving.

"Obviously, Tom, I have a hard time believing you're a killer, but that is not for me to judge. I just want to minister to you as a person. And I think the editorial, in particular, was mean and underhanded, and I will let them know that."

"So you know the newspaper people?"

"I do. But regardless, I plan to write a letter to the editor. Sort of what you said—'innocent until proven guilty.' This is a nice little town, and there is no place for that kind of animosity, especially at that level. Let's let justice grind out the right answer. So, that's all on the table. How are you doing?"

"Just fine. As long as there's no lynch mob. The only thing that I fear is that I will lose my exercise program. Lovely as Marilyn and the guys are, I think that getting over to the gym is the only thing keeping me from going crazy."

"I can imagine. This is pretty confining. Let me think if there is some way I can help. In the meantime, how about some Scrabble?"

"That sounds good. Marilyn, you in?"

"Of course."

The games began.

Chapter 30

MARILYN WON the first game, and Susan was leading in the second game when Doug came in. "Well, isn't this cozy."

"Hi Doug. Anything I need to be doing?"

"No, Marilyn. In fact, I want you go take off and go home. Run errands, whatever. I'll take Tom over to the gym today."

"Good. I was behind in this game anyway, and this way I can retire undefeated."

Doug nodded at Marilyn as she got up from the table and said, "I've got a couple of desk things to do. You kids go ahead and finish your game."

Tom and Susan turned back to the game, and Susan finished him off fairly easily. "You're a little off your game today, Tom."

"Yeah, but I really appreciated the chance to play. Thanks a lot for coming over."

Susan turned her attention to Doug. "Doug, would it bother you if I wrote a rebuttal letter to the editor of the Purview? I don't want to make things worse, but I really feel someone needs to speak up for justice."

"I think that would be fine, Susan. Just don't go too far and proclaim Tom innocent. Be sure you write about justice, not specific people."

"Absolutely. I'll see you both later. Have fun at the gym!"

But Susan didn't leave; instead, she walked over to the desk and had a whispered conversation with Doug. Finally, he looked over at

Tom and said, "I'll think it over. Let's get through the current firestorm first."

Susan nodded and left. Tom wondered what that was all about, but before he could think too much or say anything, Doug said, "Don't be shy, Tom. Put on your workout clothes. Time to go for a walk."

Tom did as he was told, then sat back down on his cot. He looked at the clock and saw it was still a little early to walk over. He wondered what Doug was up to. He played back the day in his mind. What a whirlwind. Punch below the belt, courtesy of the newspaper. Telephone time with Marci and Monica, who he'd never met, reading the whole newspaper diatribe to someone named Becky, then some quiet time before what was clearly some supportive attention from Susan and from Marilyn in her own unique way. Maybe Marilyn was really the Marine. She sure knew how to be one of the guys.

Now, the whispers between Susan and Doug, and Doug escorting him to the gym personally. A lot to take in.

Doug opened the cell door and handcuffed himself to Tom. They made the walk to the gym together. Tom noted that Bobby was on the corner in his patrol car as usual. A few people nodded to Doug, but no one said anything. There were more people than usual watching their little parade, and Tom figured that's why Doug did this walk rather than have Marilyn do it.

When they got to the gym, both went in. Doug uncuffed Tom and handed him over to Mark, then said, "I want to talk to the kids for a minute or two. Ok?"

Mark nodded, then blew his whistle. All activity slowed to a halt. Then he yelled, "Everybody take a seat on the stage. The sheriff wants to say a few words to us."

"Good afternoon. I won't take long, but when I'm done with my comments, I will be happy to take questions. I know your afternoon gym time is probably more fun than listening to me."

Doug paused to look the group over. Boys and girls, middle school through high school—some athletic, some not, all wanting to run around after a day of sitting in classes. Tom watched Doug read the room and was impressed by his management of time and his ability to capture their attention.

"As you know, over the last couple of days, Coach Butler's wife, Marilyn, who is my deputy, has securely walked Tom here over to this gym for some exercise, which he is entitled to under the law. I could go into details of that, but it's really pretty boring, so let's just leave it at that."

He again looked over the group. Point one made, Tom thought.

"Tom is accused of a pretty bad crime, but we all need to focus on the word accused. He says he is innocent, and again, by law, he is innocent until he is found guilty by a jury who listens to and reviews all the available evidence. If he is found guilty, he will be turned over to the state to determine his punishment."

Again, Doug paused. Point two.

"Until then, he has the same rights as all of us, except he is to remain in custody until his trial. As your sheriff, I am in charge of keeping him in custody. Your coach, Butler, here, is deputized to help me maintain that custody. Part of that custody is keeping you and all the people of this town, county, and state safe. I take that very seriously, and so does Coach Butler, or else I wouldn't have deputized him."

Another pause. Point three.

"If at any time Coach Butler or I do not believe it is safe to have Tom exercise here in this gym at this time of day, then this current exercise plan will end, and Coach Butler and I will have to work something else out. In the meantime, this is Tom's exercise program, and I expect everyone involved to respect my office, Coach Butler, and Tom as a person and as a participant in this exercise time."

Pause, point four.

"And at the same time, I expect Tom to be a positive participant in this program and be fully cooperative in all the games and events that Coach Butler asks him to participate in. He has that responsibility to my office and to you. If that changes, his participation in this program will end."

Pause. "Do any of you have any questions ?"

The girl in the red shorts raised her hand—the one Tom and Mark had discussed as one of the best athletes in town. Too bad Tom didn't know her name. "I guess I'll just have to call her Red Shorts," Tom thought. "Hope that doesn't get me in trouble." Anyway, she was clearly taking a leadership role, which was a good sign given her ability.

Doug acknowledged her. "Yes?"

"Is the stuff that was in the newspaper about him true or not?"

"Good question. Some of it is, and some of it is pure speculation and, in my opinion, unjust. Again, Tom is innocent until proven guilty. I want him treated with respect, as long as he continues to earn that respect. If you see him doing anything questionable or disrespectful to you or anyone else in this gym, please let Coach Butler know right away."

A younger boy spoke up. "My dad says that if he shows up today, I won't be allowed to come back for gym time anymore."

A few other heads nodded.

"I don't want that to happen, so Coach Butler has a letter for each of you to take home with you tonight. It is signed by Coach, your principal, and me. The county commission has approved this program, as has the district attorney, who is responsible for bringing the case against Tom, because we all need to respect him and his rights. Before your dad or mom pull you from this program, please tell them to call one of us. Our phone numbers are at the bottom of the letter. OK?"

Nods all around. Looks like the kids didn't want to lose their gym time, any more than Tom did.

Doug moved to close. "Please let Coach or me know if you have any other questions. In the meantime, thank you for listening to me and go have some fun."

Doug walked to the door. Mark pointed to the far half court where volleyball was set up. "Volleyball is our main event today, so let's pick sides and get going."

The girl in the red shorts and one of the older boys immediately called "Captain!"

Mark tossed a coin. Red Shorts called heads and won. She turned and pointed at Tom. "I'll take the prisoner."

The games began.

Chapter 31

AFTER THE NEWSPAPER turmoil settled down, the next few days settled into a pretty static routine. It was not just a bad dream. Tom actually did wake up every morning in a jail cell, eat breakfast, engage in some banter with whomever was on duty, do some reading, and have some lunch. Afternoons consisted of more reading, a trip to the gym and back, then a shower, dinner, and yet another quiet evening. Usually a board game when Marilyn was on duty, and Pastor Susan also stopped by on Thursday for a visit and a game of Scrabble. Now, Tom had to get through the weekend, when there was no gym time available.

Tom had profusely thanked Doug for his speech in the gym. Doug just nodded and said, "It was a teaching moment for the kids and the easiest way to get through to their parents. Those kids love that gym time and don't want to have it taken away."

"Have you had any pushback from the parents?"

"Some questions, but with the principal and the DA and the county commissioners on board, there aren't many other people to question. Next week, if all continues to go well, we'll be back to you and Marilyn walking over, and I can get back to other things."

Tom nodded. The sheriff had handled the situation very well. Tom was impressed with his political skills—all performed quite professionally. Tom was still impressed with how well he'd handled the gym kids. Make a point, let it sink in, then move to the next point. I guess there's more to being sheriff than patrolling and arresting people.

Doug then continued, "In fact, about the only person who can screw this up now is you."

"Point taken. I will behave, because I appreciate all that you and others have done to get me that gym time and make my stay here as tolerable as possible."

Doug nodded and went back to his desk.

Friday evening, Susan and Maggie came in and played a few games of Clue with Bobby and Tom. It took Maggie a game or two to get the hang of it, but they all enjoyed showing her the tricks of the game. Susan dropped off a couple more books, which Bobby looked through and passed on to Tom.

Saturday was by far the slowest day yet. Tom read and paced and did some calisthenics and then read some more. When Bobby had finished his reports for the week, he pulled up the table to Tom's cell, and they played a few games of gin rummy. Then supper, then a little more gin rummy. About 9:00 in the evening, Marilyn replaced Bobby, but after a few words, both retired for the night. Tom had never felt lower energy and was trying not to let it flow over into his thoughts about his prospects. Doing this for the rest of his life would be no life at all.

Sunday started out just as slowly. As soon as Marilyn left, Doug came in. Then the two of them enjoyed some fresh coffee and a sticky bun. Doug also brought in a couple of Sunday papers: Thompson Falls and the Purdy Purview. Tom went through both carefully. The Thompson Falls Press had already covered the murder a few times, so didn't pick anything new up from the Purview. The Sentinel picked up the Purdy article but shortened it to a page two article in the Statewide News section. The biggest relief was in not finding his picture in either paper.

Tom then went back to his latest book from Susan, expecting the day to drift slowly by.

That lasted until about noon when both Mark and Marilyn came in. After the usual greetings, Doug said, "Well, Tom, Marilyn and I have some official police business, so you are here with Mark this afternoon. Tom could not hide his surprise. "This is a change!"

"Don't want to spend the afternoon with me?" Mark asked, sounding as offended as he could.

"No, not at all. Just a change up from the usual."

"We really need to get going. So, if you two are ok, we'll hit the road."

Mark replied to Doug directly, "Go ahead. We'll be fine. Drive carefully and good luck."

Marilyn blew Mark a kiss. "We'll be fine. You two be good. Try not to let him overpower you, Mark."

Tom noticed both Doug and Marilyn had duffel bags with them. He was not sure what to make of that.

The office door closed, and they were gone. Tom looked at Mark.

Mark spoke first. "I guess I can tell you what little I know. The two of them wanted to do some key interviews out of town for your case, and Sunday worked best, so I could cover here and Bobby could still be on patrol. Besides, I don't mind a quiet Sunday afternoon."

"And where are the kids?"

"Ethan and Evan are with some friends of theirs. I think they're going to the movie later. The younger two are with Susan and Maggie. I'm sure Susan has some plan for them. They may even stop over later."

"I've met Ethan and Evan and have been with them at the gym. Remind me about the two younger. Names? Ages?"

"Well, just to backtrack a bit. Ethan is 17 and is a junior. Evan is 15 and a freshman. They're actually about 18 months apart. Next is Elizabeth, who is almost 11, and bringing up the rear is our seven-year-old, Eddie. I have to say, all good kids, at least so far. It's different raising kids here in a small town than it was for me growing up. The school is such a focus. Not much for jobs for teens, or I might say, more teens than jobs. That's why I do extra work at the school. After-school activities are much appreciated. And they help the kids get some exercise, especially in the winter. Another couple of teachers run an afterschool homework program in one of the bigger classrooms. The music instructors make sure the practice rooms are open and monitored both before and after school as well. We all want these small-town kids to have every chance to succeed.”

“That is great,” Tom replied, and he meant it.

“Which is why,” Mark continued, “we all feel so bad for that girl killed in our town motel. I sure hope you are telling the truth when you say you didn’t do it. It really made us all think about our small-town life and values here. She ended up in some kind of really bad situation, and those of us in Purdy feel quite bad that her life ended here, at such a young age.”

Tom gave that some thought. “Is that why the Purview published such a scathing article and crucified me in the editorial?”

“Most likely. It really shook this town, and they see themselves as the public voice of the town. Lashing out at you personally may have been a bit overdone, but you are certainly an easy target at this point.”

“I can see that, but it really hurts to get publicly humiliated like that. I just hope my sister was able to keep my mom from getting too upset over it. No kid wants their parents to have to deal with that.”

“Just like no parent ever wants to get a call that their daughter has been murdered in a motel room in a small, out-of-the-way town.”

“Yeah, that would be worse. My hope is that my attorney does a good job and can prove my innocence. I didn’t kill her and would never do something like that. I certainly don’t want my mom to think for a second that I might. Even if it wasn’t about clearing my name, it is important to find out who did kill her and why.”

“I understand that about your mom. I got into a little trouble when I was younger—just stupid teenager stuff—and I was mortified about the shame I brought to my parents. Lucky for me I was able to join the Marines and straighten my life out before I went further down a bad path. Even luckier when I met Marilyn and found such a good partner.”

“Well, you certainly have made a good life for yourselves here in Purdy, and I know you make a difference for the kids who come to the gym every day.”

"Thanks. I'll assume you really mean that. But enough of our life philosophies. I understand you need some Scrabble lessons."

"That had to have come from Susan. So let's get on with it. I'd hate to let her down."

"But first, let's eat the lunch Marilyn packed for us." Cold tuna sandwiches, potato salad, and some other sides were all put on the table, and both ate in silence.

As soon as the table was cleared, the two men began the World Series of Scrabble. After an afternoon of back-and-forth games, Tom managed to win the decisive game seven, just as the shadows were working across the cell. Tom spoke first as Mark packed up the game.

"I don't know about you, but I'm mentally exhausted."

"I was just going to say that, despite the amount of coffee we consumed."

"Well, if we want to sleep tonight, we should probably switch to something else."

"Or just take a nap."

"Agreed. Any idea when we might expect Doug and Marilyn back in town?"

"Not sure. I know they were going to Thompson Falls, so not too far. Unless their interviews took them further down the road."

"Any idea who they were talking to?"

"Not for sure. I'm the deputy in the dark," Mark said with a smile.

Tom rinsed out his mug and filled it with water. "Maybe I should take a shower while it's just us guys. I skipped yesterday."

"Go ahead. I'll read the papers."

Tom undressed and stepped into the shower. Just as he got good and wet, he heard the office door open.

"Whoa, whoa, whoa, everybody. Tom is having a private moment. You'll have to wait outside for a few minutes."

Tom, tight in the corner of the shower, heard the door close again. "Go ahead and finish up. You have visitors and they brought dinner, so don't take too long."

Tom showered quickly, dried off, and got dressed. Mark opened the office door, and in came Susan and Maggie, along with the two younger Butler children, Elizabeth and Eddie.

"Sorry for the intrusion, Tom. We brought supper and a pan of brownies we baked this afternoon."

"No problem. I can shower fast if it means I get to eat."

"Mark says you beat him at Scrabble."

"It was actually pretty even. I just managed to squeak out a win in game seven."

Susan continued, "Any word from Doug or Marilyn?"

It was Mark who replied, "No, nothing yet."

"Well, then let's eat."

Tom thought it strange that the three adults and three young kids sat down to eat in the jailhouse just like it was the most normal thing in the world. Especially with him, an accused murderer. Though he was behind bars and the others weren't. That was always front of mind for Tom.

As usual, Susan led with a prayer, and then they all dug in, Susan preparing a plate for Tom. Hamburger casserole, fresh warm homemade buns, and a pea and carrot mix for a vegetable. Tom again was struck by the variety and healthiness of the food. And the flavor. The flavor was incredible. Cooking for himself, he focused on flavor only when he had some extra time, which wasn't often. And home alone, he ate because he needed to keep up his energy for the strenuous life he lived. Here, he played Scrabble and ate really good, tasty food.

The kids were clearly comfortable with each other, and the conversation flowed easily until Eddie made a snorting noise while laughing at something Maggie said. Then the kids went all in, trying to mimic him. It took both Mark and Susan to get them settled down again.

Supper dishes cleared, Susan brought out the pan of brownies. She dished them up onto small paper plates. Tom couldn't believe how much he anticipated his brownie. This was not something he made for himself when he was at home in the woods. He was really getting spoiled! In jail!

When they had all finished eating, Maggie came over to Tom's cell and asked, "How long do you have to be in jail?"

Tom looked at Susan and Mark, but neither offered any help, so he replied, "I don't know, Maggie. Hopefully not too much longer. I've hired a lawyer who is working to help me get out. I talk to him again on Tuesday, and I'll see how he's doing."

"How did you hire a lawyer from jail?"

"I get to make a phone call when I need to, and I called my sister, who actually hired a lawyer."

Now all the kids were interested in Tom, and the questions were coming rapidly.

"How old are you?"

"Why do you have a beard?"

"Do you really live in a tent?"

"Do you have a wife? A girlfriend?"

"Did you kill that girl at the motel like the paper said?"

At that point, both Mark and Susan cut things off. Mark went on, "Tom, feel free to answer any or all of those questions. Except the last one. Leave that alone. Ok, kids, one at a time. Tom is a guest of the county, so treat him like a guest."

Tom figured he'd better get some kind of control, so he said, "Let me start with your questions so far and try to take them in order. I live deep in the woods in a log cabin. I hunt for my meat, and I grow a garden for the other food I need, except I come to town a few times a year to buy the things I can't shoot or grow. I don't have a wife or girlfriend. I have a beard because where I live, it is hard to shave every day."

Maggie jumped right in. "My mom doesn't have a husband either."

"So noted." Tom looked over at Susan. Better hope that just drops. Who knew where Maggie was going with that topic.

"Do you really trap animals and sell the furs?"

"Yes, I do. That's how I get the little bit of money I need for the supplies I buy in town and get a haircut once in a while."

"Does it hurt them?"

"I use traps that kill them right away, so they don't suffer."

Tom couldn't help but think about how this conversation would go in any big city or even the suburbs where he grew up. These kids grew up hunting and fishing, so they were well in tune with the realities of nature. The only animals the kids in the cities saw were family pets, and hunting was strictly prohibited, so their view of life in the wild was mostly from movies like *Bambi *.

Tom was a little worried about where the line of questioning would go next, but he was saved by the door opening and Doug and Marilyn stomping in. "It's really snowing out there. Looks like our March blizzard is already moving in."

Chapter 32

DOUG THEN LOOKED AROUND. "This has to be a record for people at this jail. Looks like we've had lots of juvenile offenders today."

"Actually," Susan said, "the juveniles were attacking the lone actual prisoner, bombarding him with questions until Mark and I got them under control. It was brutal."

"Good practice for Tom's time with our DA. Did anyone think to put him under oath?"

Susan laughed. "No, no time for that. But he kept his story straight the whole time."

Doug redirected the conversation. "With this snow moving in, we need to get on the phones and get as many of the country kids into town for the night as we can, so we don't have to cancel school tomorrow." He turned to Tom. "This is a small school district, with Purdy the only real town, but because of the geography of the county—lakes, woods, hills—only a handful of people live outside of Purdy, but those who do are often on roads that are hard to keep open. So, when it storms, and we can get ahead of the weather, we all take in a kid or two. That way, unless it really blows, we can keep the school open, or at least those kids don't have to miss school."

Turning back to the other adults, he returned to the original topic. "You all have your calling assignments, so let's do that. I will call the county commissioners, as usual. Hopefully we can get the kids in before the weather gets too much worse."

It took a few minutes to get everyone bundled up and out the door. Doug turned back to Tom. "I thought they'd never leave. You sure do attract a crowd. Maybe the county could recoup some of the cost of your stay by selling tickets."

Tom wasn't sure how to reply, but he managed a feeble thought. "Susan brought the supper and the kids and the brownies, so no cost there, unless she sends you a bill."

"That does help. And you still owe her for the communion bread."

Tom shook his head. This guy never let up.

"Well, Tom, I hope you're ready for some quiet time. As I said, I've got some phone calls to make."

It took Doug a little over an hour to make his phone calls. Then he settled in at his desk and opened the duffel he'd carried in. He removed file after file and separated them into two piles. He started reading slowly through the files he'd placed on the left side of his desk. The phone rang a few times, always followed by the briefest of conversations, but other than that, it was quiet, and Tom drifted off to sleep.

When he awoke, it was light out, and Doug was still at his desk—or at his desk again. Tom was beginning to wonder when Doug slept, or if he slept. Once he was ready for the day, he asked, "How's the weather?"

"Lots of snow, not too much wind yet. We got almost all of the country kids into town last evening, so school will be open. The forecast is for this to turn to cold and wind by this evening and blow all day tomorrow, so you'll have to reschedule your meeting with your attorney. Probably by just a day or two."

Tom couldn't help but feel a bit down about that. He had high hopes for what his attorney might be able to tell him, and it was always nice to see Marci. "Do I need to call them?"

"If they don't call to cancel by noon or so, I'll make sure you get to call them. Here's the bad news. And you can be glad if this is the worst news you get for a while: no gym time for you today. With the bad weather, the school will be overrun with kids all the way through supper time. Mark will have to get other teachers to help him with the bedlam. All the programs will be packed."

"Sorry to hear that but I understand."

The jailhouse fell silent for the next hour. Doug continued to read through files until Marilyn burst in. "Wow! It is really coming down out there. I need to catch my breath. I had to wait in line at the diner. Apparently, everyone is planning to spend the day there drinking coffee. You'll have to redo a Sunday breakfast. I didn't want to wait for them to cook something up. I'll try to get you a more nutritious lunch, even if I have to run home."

Doug took the food from Marilyn. "That might be tough. Bobby is out patrolling, which in this weather means checking in on accidents and keeping the tow trucks straight on their assignments. He'll be doing that all day, or at least until people get sense enough to stay home. Apparently a 'no travel advised' announcement doesn't cut it for some people."

Marilyn nodded and said, "Then I'll wait an hour or so and phone in an order to the diner, so we can have some lunch."

"Ok. I'm going to go home and take a shower and nap until the phone or radio interrupt me. Did you get your homework done?"

"Most of it. Wasn't able to connect on one of the phone calls."

"Give me that number. I'll try it when I get home."

Tom thought that was odd. Why not just call now from the office? But there was no opportunity to dwell on that, as Marilyn put a sticky bun and a fresh cup of coffee on his tray and handed it through to him. He was getting addicted to the food here. Maybe he could extend this stay through round after round of appeals and by the time he had to go to prison, not only would he get credit for time served, but he'd be too fat to get out of this cell—or into a prison cell.

Tom enjoyed the heavy caramel flavored pastry, making it last as long as he could. This was going to be another long day, so no need to rush anything.

At about 9:00 a.m., Judy trudged in. "Wow! Tough walk over. Lots of cancellations at the clinic today. Which is fine because one of the cancellations was Doc Bradford. He's a no-show and is not answering his home phone either. Hope he's ok, not stuck in a ditch somewhere."

Marilyn said, "I know this is not protocol, but I need to use the restroom. Can I do that while you check his arm? I'll be quick. I'll take my radio so Doug and Bobby can reach me."

"Sure. Ok, Tom, let's see that arm."

Tom was surprised by Marilyn's decision to leave him alone with Judy. He uncovered his arm and stuck his shoulder out between the bars. Maybe they were all beginning to understand he was no threat to anyone.

"It's healing nicely, Tom. It will leave you a very masculine scar. Just a change of bandage and you should be good to go. I'll be back to check next Monday. Keep it clean and put a new bandage on after every shower. You probably won't even need a bandage after that."

Marilyn had come out of the bathroom and said, "Good luck on your walk back, Judy. Hope nobody gets seriously injured with no doctor around."

"Yeah, me too. Take care."

As expected, at about 10:00, the desk phone rang and Marilyn answered.

"Yup, Yup, understand. Thursday early afternoon. No problem. We'll make it work on this end. Thanks for calling."

"Guess who just called."

"Levitt?"

"No, but someone named Monica from his office. As you may have heard, they'll be here right after lunch on Thursday. Guess I'll need to plan for lunch just for the two of us on Thursday. I was looking forward to having company."

"Maybe we can invite them to stay for dinner?"

"Sounds good. I'll plan for something by candlelight. Don't tell Mark."

"Never crossed my mind."

"I'd better call the diner and see what we can get for lunch."

The phone conversation with the diner took a while, back and forth on what they had on hand. From what Tom could hear, the delivery trucks had not come in and weren't likely coming in for a day or two, so the menu was limited. Marilyn hung up. "Looks like fish and chips, with a side of coleslaw. No dessert. Apparently they got cleaned out last night when everyone brought their kids in. They're baking now with the supplies they have on hand, but it's going out the door as fast as they can put it on the counter."

"No problem. If you look over by the coffee pot, there should be part of a pan of brownies from last night."

Marilyn walked over. "Nope. Just an empty pan. Either the kids cleaned them out or Doug had more than one snack overnight."

"Oh well. I think I had dessert for breakfast anyway, since caramel is just sugar when it gets right down to it."

Right at 11:45, the office door opened and a guy Tom had never seen before stomped in, handing Marilyn a bag with the diner's logo.

She turned to Tom. "Can you give him a tip, honey? I'm low on cash."

The man took them both in with a quizzical look. Tom replied, "Sure, dear, but you have my wallet locked in the filing cabinet in the corner. Help yourself."

Marilyn laughed and handed the guy some coins. "Don't worry about us, Ron. We're both a little stir crazy and this weather isn't help-ing."

"I understand. The way we're going through coffee at the diner, I just hope the toilets keep working."

Ron continued, "We've used up a lot of our supplies, and between us and the other people in town, even the grocery store is starting to run short on some things."

With that, Ron left. The lunch was good, but the conversation was sparse. Marilyn was focused on the work on her desk, and the phone rang frequently with reports of car accidents and people not coming home when expected. She managed it all, with frequent radio calls to Bobby and Doug.

After one of the calls, she hung up and said, "Change of plans. The teachers are stretched too thin to cover all the extra after-school activities. Some of the younger teachers have to get home to their own little kids, and some have elderly parents they want to check on, so Mark needs you to come over and help with the gym time."

"That's the best news I've had all day!"

"Get your stuff on. I won't look. The walk over may be all the exercise you need."

Tom was well aware of the toll fighting snow and wind could take, having been caught out on his traplines a handful of times over the years. He had learned to avoid that if at all possible. Though a walk down a couple of sidewalks couldn't be as bad as fighting his way up and down steep hills.

He changed into his workout gear quickly. Marilyn looked him over and said, "It's not brutally cold, but the wind is picking up. She opened a closet. "Here's your coat and hat and mittens. Can't have you freezing to death out there."

The walk over was tougher than he'd thought, both of them wading through the deep snow and taking turns slipping and sliding. At one point, Tom thought that if they weren't handcuffed together, they'd need to hold hands anyway. Despite leaving the jailhouse earlier than usual, they barely made it before the kids began pouring into the gym. Marilyn uncuffed both of them, and Tom put his parka and other winter items on the bench in the corner. Marilyn stayed a few moments to catch her breath.

Mark blew his whistle, then again, then a third time. Finally it was quiet enough for him to talk—or rather, shout above the background noise. "Ok! Everybody on this sideline here." The kids ran over to the line nearest Tom and Marilyn. There was just room for all of them on the official basketball court sideline. "On the whistle, run, fast as you can, to the other sideline." The whistle blew and the kids took off. In a few seconds, they were on the other sideline. "Now line up and back again." The whistle blew and off they went, running back past the line right by Tom and Marilyn. Mark repeated that drill twice more before he said,

"Now, stay on this sideline. I want middle school kids on this half and high schoolers on the other half." It took a minute or two for the kids to sort themselves out. Mark handed Tom a whistle. "Now, we'll break up into relay teams. Looks like we have enough for four middle school teams and three high school teams. Kelly, Ethan, and Steve, you're the high school captains. Pick your teams.

"Aha! The girl in red shorts must be Kelly!" Tom was feeling good about figuring that out but was rapidly pulled back out of his thoughts by Mark. "Tom, do the same with the middle school kids." He proceeded to name four captains, two girls and two boys. The teams were picked quickly, Tom feeling bad for the kids who got picked last. "Ok, first relay, run to the other sideline and back, hard as you can go. You must touch the sideline with your hand or foot."

From there on, the din was unbelievable. Mark was running relays on his side and Tom on his. Again, as they ran, Tom tried to count. Probably forty middle school kids and twenty-five high school kids, all making as much noise as they could—or so it seemed to Tom, missing the quiet of the jail. After three relay runs, Tom grabbed two basketballs and blew his whistle. "Now, two relay teams at a time. We'll have a relay tournament. Down to the other basket, make the layup, then pass back to the next kid on your team."

Mark looked over and said, "Just hold up a minute."

He ran over and opened a panel on the end wall. He hooked up a crank and lowered the basket by about a foot. "We want this to end eventually! Go ahead."

Tom picked two of the relay teams. "Ready?" He blew the whistle, and they took off, one dribbling and one just running with the ball. "Cheating! Cheating! Cheating!" the kids started yelling.

Tom blew his whistle again. "Okay, let's start over. Since you're not all basketball players, you can do whichever you want—dribble or just run with the ball, whichever you think is faster. Let's start again. Ready?"

At his whistle, they were off again. Some of the kids dribbled, pushing the ball out in front of them. Others just put the ball under one arm and ran. Some needed both arms to hold the ball. The bigger problem seemed to be making the layup. Eventually one team won. "Next two teams," Tom yelled.

At his whistle, the mayhem started anew. Again, as soon as one team was done, he declared them a winner. Then he had the two losing teams race each other, then the two winning teams, then the second-place team and the third-place team. By that time, they had settled down a bit. Mark was right to work them hard right at the beginning. They were now willing to sit when Mark pulled them all back together.

He looked at Tom, and to Tom's surprise, said, "What's next , Coach?"

Tom tried not to look as flatfooted as he felt. He said, "Let's break into two groups. Everyone who wants to work on dribbling skills over on this side. Everyone who wants to work on shooting skills over here." Just then a woman Tom had not met, along with a couple of high school girls, walked into the gym. "Welcome, Coach," Mark said. "We're working on basketball skills today ."

The unidentified woman replied, "Good. Can't have too many skills. Did I hear we were splitting into dribbling and shooting? Can I help with the shooting drill?"

"Of course," Mark replied. "Looks like many more shooters than dribblers, so I'll help you. We'll switch after 20 minutes or so ."

Tom got his twenty or so dribblers lined up, broke them into four lines of kids each, and started them down the floor, walking and dribbling. The next round was a little faster, and then again at a speed closer to full speed. Balls were now bouncing everywhere. Once the kids and balls were collected, Tom tried to give them some additional coaching on dribbling at high speed, then ran it again. Some mishaps, but it went better. Mark and the bigger group came over, and Tom's group switched to shooting with the still unidentified woman, and they repeated the exercises.

The rest of the gym time vacillated between high-energy excitement and outright bedlam. Bit by bit, the kids wore down.

After the kids were just busy on the gym floor, shooting baskets and, in some cases, talking in small groups, Mark and the woman walked over. "Tom, this is the girls' basketball and softball coach, Karen Johnson."

"Nice to meet you and thanks for the help. This is a lot of kids."

"I could hear the noise from the hallway, so I figured I'd better come in. I was working with my captains on softball practice prep, but we wrapped up quickly when it sounded like this was a lot more fun."

Tom smiled. "Well, thanks again."

Mark jumped back in. "We need to let them settle down and cool off a bit. We can't send them out into that cold wind all sweaty, so we just need to keep an eye on them. Some parents will come and take them in groups to walk them home." Turning to Tom, he said, "Then I'll walk you home."

Parents began coming in singly or in pairs, and each took a handful of kids with them. It was 5:45 before all the kids had cleared out. Mark and Tom bundled up and headed to the door. "No cuffs?"

"No, I just have my gun handy. Trust me. In this snow and wind, you won't get far."

"That's very reassuring."

"No problem. You go first and break a track. That alone should keep you in check."

Tom put his head down and went out the door. The wind by now was really howling down the streets, and the drifts were getting harder. Some he plowed through, others he just walked over. It never blew this hard at his cabin, because it was protected by miles of forest. This was new, and a couple of times he slipped badly, catching himself with a mittened hand. He could always hear Mark just behind him.

The walk to the jail took a good ten minutes. Tom went through the door. "I never thought I'd be glad to be back at this jailhouse, yet this time I am."

"Me too," Mark said. "Move a little further in so I can close the door."

Tom pulled off his parka, hat, and mittens, laid them over a chair, and walked to his cell, where he pulled off his wet gym shoes and put them in the sink. He sat on his cot for a moment to catch his breath.

Mark sat down in the office chair. "You did a good job with the kids today. Thanks for helping out. I'm also glad you got to meet Karen. She's good at what she does, both as a teacher and a coach."

"That's good to hear. It always helps to have good people on staff. Is the rest of the staff that competent?"

"For the most part. It's very well run for a small district. The parents are very supportive, and we manage our finances and other resources well. If a teacher is not doing a good job, the word gets around quickly and they move on."

"Do you guys have to be so noisy?"

They both looked at the other jail cell, where Doug was curled up under a blanket.

"Just where do I have to go to get a nap? Mark, you can take off. Tom, you can shower if you can do it quietly."

Just then the phone rang. Mark picked it up. "Sorry, Sheriff, it's for you."

Doug walked over and took the phone from Mark. "Yup, yup. Ok. Thanks much. We'll try to get the paperwork started tomorrow, but it's storming like crazy up here, so we'll need to figure out how to track down the judge."

Tom was undressing and Mark was dressing for outdoors while Doug talked. Mark winked at Tom, said, "Thanks again," and went out the door.

Chapter 33

TOM STEPPED out of the shower and dried quickly. It was none too warm in his cell.

"I'm really sorry, Tom, but dinner tonight will be a bit of an adventure—and not in a good way."

Doug continued, "The diner ran out of any decent food, so I raided the pantry at home. All I could find is a loaf of bread, some peanut butter, and some jelly. My wife is stuck in Thompson Falls with her parents, and so I might just as well stay here tonight. I'm sure there's better food somewhere in the fridge or freezer, but I really can't take the time to do any actual meal prep. Besides, this way Marilyn can sleep with Mark like God intended and hopefully everyone in the county has been rescued or found shelter by now. It's times like this I wish I was paid by the hour. I've been at work or on call now since Sunday noon. By tomorrow morning I'll have the 40 hours that would make up a normal workweek."

"I'm sorry I'm adding to your workload."

"No, it's okay. I could have left you in the woods, I guess, with you and Bobby conversing by smoke signals, but this way I know where you are, so it actually relieves a little of the stress."

"What are you and Marilyn up to? The trip to Thompson Falls and all the phone calls and files?"

"All I can say is 'official police business.' Can I trust you enough to hand you a table knife for the peanut butter and jelly, or do I have to make you a sandwich?"

"I will be fine. I won't even try to steal the knife and make it lethal. I am actually quite hungry, though."

Doug made himself a sandwich and passed all the materials through to Tom. Tom took his time making his sandwich. Raspberry jelly was his favorite, and, regardless, it sure beat going hungry—or having nothing but some jerky and a biscuit, which is what he would have had if he were stuck out in the woods in weather like this. Besides, a cot was better than a sleeping bag in a pup tent. Odd that suddenly his situation looked pretty comfortable. And Doug's answer to his question about the files and phone calls was interestingly terse. Maybe it really wasn't any of his business. Then again, maybe it was.

Bobby poured through the door with a blast of snow and cold wind. "Hi, guys. I know I'm on patrol, but needed a cup of coffee and for the moment am not dealing with an emergency."

"Why don't you stretch out on that other cot for a few minutes, Bobby? Tom and I are eating supper, if you want to call it that. If you can catch a nap, that would be great. As long as the phones and the radios are working, we are certainly as available as we need to be ."

"Can I have a sandwich?"

"Sure. You'll have to get the stuff from Tom."

Tom handed the sandwich makings and the knife back through the bars to Bobby, who said, "I must be hungry. This peanut butter actually smells good."

The next several minutes were oddly quiet. Doug sat in his chair and focused on his sandwich. Bobby looked at Doug a couple of times like he might have something to say, but then went back to eating. After a bit, Bobby laid down on the cot and was quickly snoring. That lasted about 45 minutes when the phone rang. Doug took the call, then looked over at Bobby, who had awoken. "Sorry, Bobby, but we have a car in the ditch on the road to Deer Lake. The wrecker wants some assistance, and there may be some frostbite. Take them to the hospital if you need to."

"I'm on it, Doug. Just let me take a coffee with me."

Once Bobby had left, Doug went to the recently vacated cot and laid down.

"Let's see if we can get a little sleep before the phone or the radio wake us up."

Just a minute or two later, the phone rang. Tom jumped. He looked around. Doug was making his way to the desk. It was still fully dark out. "Sheriff's office. Yup. Ok. Thanks. Got it. We'll track down the judge at first light and get the paperwork started."

Doug walked back to his cot without even looking at Tom.

The next time Tom woke up, the light was just beginning to stream into his cell. The wind seemed to have gone down a bit. The desk chair was empty, but the other cot was occupied. Good, Tom thought. Doug can finally get some sleep. Tom rolled over to get more comfortable, and Bobby sat up on the other cot.

"Where's Doug?" Tom asked.

"He actually went out on patrol about three o'clock this morning and then went home. I'm up next, but we're all still on call. The wind is going down, but so is the temperature. We'll all need to stay on the streets to make sure the kids get to school safely. Mark can take their kids, so Marilyn will be in soon to take over. Once the kids are in school, if nothing else comes up, I can go home for a shower and a nap.

"What happened with the call down by Deer Lake last night?"

"The tow truck driver had them located, and the two passengers were waiting inside the truck while he winched it out of the ditch. They apparently had decided that sitting in the supper club down there and drinking until it closed, then driving home in this blizzard, was a good idea. They went off the road and down a short embankment. One of them was able to walk back to the tavern. He called the tow truck, but both of them were pretty drunk. The one who walked back to the tavern is lucky he made it. I had to take them all to the ER to blood test them and treat them for frostbite and hypothermia. We left them there to warm up and dry out. Had to call Mark to babysit them there."

"So a short night for everybody?"

"Yeah, but it should get better today. Once we get the kids to school and the wind dies down, it should be better by the afternoon. The snowplows will be out as soon as it's light enough."

"So the country kids can go home today?"

"Should be able to. Wind's down, roads plowed. We'll be working our way back toward normal operations."

True to Bobby's prediction, the wind continued to drop, and Tom could hear the snowplows working their way up and down the streets before they headed out into the country.

Tom and Bobby enjoyed a breakfast of peanut butter and jelly toast. Marilyn came in midmorning, and the day settled into the usual routine. She brought some sandwich meat, and at lunch, their diet was still sandwiches, but with a little more variety than peanut butter.

Right after lunch, Ron came over from the diner with some freshly baked cookies. The grocery truck had come in, and the diner had started getting caught up. "We should be able to get you a normal supper, depending on what was on the truck."

The walk to the gym that afternoon was much easier, and Marilyn handed him off to Mark right on time. It was pretty much back to the regulars, so Mark set up a full-court basketball game with Kelly and Ethan as captains. Tom and Mark officiated, and Mark kept the subs moving in and out, using his watch to mark off three-minute intervals so everyone got to play. They took a water break every half hour and readjusted the teams once, so the time went quickly.

After the final whistle, Kelly walked over to Tom and said, "You're actually a pretty good official. You've either done this before or you've got a lot of basketball experience. Not to say you were perfect, but you did a pretty good job."

"Thanks. It's more the latter. I played all through high school and intramurals in college, where there are no coaches or plays and you have to wing things constantly. But thanks for the compliment. Officials don't hear that very often."

"No problem. It's just nice to have two officials, or sometimes Coach Butler made me do it. I'd rather play."

"So would most people. And you're pretty good. You have a nice shot. And you handle yourself really well. You play with a lot of poise."

"Thanks. See you tomorrow." And then she was out the door.

"You ready?" It was Mark, who was all set to go.

Tom finished putting on his coat and hat and led Mark out the door, down the street, and into the jailhouse. Mark locked the cell door behind him and dropped the keys on the desk.

Tom stripped and stepped into the shower, finishing quickly. He dried and redressed in the familiar orange coveralls.

Mark was at the desk, reading something, so Tom tried a little conversation. "I hear you had to go to the hospital last night and do some babysitting."

"Yeah. Fortunately, both of them fell asleep, so I got to doze most of the night also."

Tom saw his opening and took it. "Any sign of Doc Bradford?"

"No. No sign of him."

"Any idea where he went?"

"Not me. I've got all I can do to keep track of you and Marilyn. And honestly, you're easier to track these days than she is. All I can do is look forward to that overtime check."

Doug walked in and interrupted any follow-up Tom might have tried. "Sorry to cut this off, but you can take off, Mark. Marilyn is at your house, I think. I'll take over here and I'll get a hot meal out of the deal."

"Thanks, Doug. See you later." As Mark shut the door, Doug opened the bag he'd brought from the diner and said, "Winner! Winner! Chicken dinner!"

And Tom did feel like a winner. A complete chicken dinner with all the trimmings, followed by a couple of the cookies that Ron had brought over earlier, made for a great meal. And the phone didn't ring the whole time he and Doug ate, which gave him time to think. So, he figured he'd take another run at getting some info out of Doug.

"Did you find the judge this morning and get him to sign the documents you needed?"

"Yes, I did. All taken care of."

While that was a direct answer, it certainly didn't provide the illumination Tom was looking for. But rather than pressing that directly, he swerved a bit.

"So, with the weather clearing, do we still expect my attorney to be here Thursday afternoon?"

"I think so, yes. The roads should be just fine by then. Nice thing about a March blizzard. Once the cold front moves through and the sun comes out, the roads clear up pretty quickly."

Perfectly accurate information, but again, not what Tom was hoping to pry out. One more try. Maybe a little more direct.

"Mark said no sign of Doc Bradford last night. Any idea where he went?"

"I know right where he is. But you don't need to."

Doug leaned back in his chair. "I could sure use a nap."

Tom smiled. Hard to give a more obvious hint than that: this conversation is over.

Chapter 34

WHEN TOM AWOKE, it was just beginning to get light outside. He looked over at the desk. No one there. He looked at the cot to see who would be there—a kind of new game for him. How did they come and go in the night so quietly? Were there sleeping pills in his food? Seemed unlikely. As he peered over at the other bunk, he could tell it was Doug. So no stealthy shift changes overnight. Maybe they weren't drugging him after all.

Tom lay quietly on his bunk and thought through the past few days. The weekend had been better than he had anticipated, with a steady flow of visitors, and Sunday afternoon with Mark had gone quickly. They were evenly matched in Scrabble, so that helped. Then the visitors Sunday evening. But what the heck was Doug up to and why take Marilyn with him? Gone all afternoon and into the evening.

Then the greatest mystery: Doug knows exactly where Doc Bradford is but Tom doesn't need to know. What does that mean? Is the doctor dead? Is he just on vacation and Doug tracked him down?

And what did Doug need from the judge? Apparently, he got it. Tom hoped the noose wasn't tightening around his neck. Had Doug found enough evidence to put him away? Was the doctor helping him? That couldn't be good. Still no word on the dead girl. That still seems to be the crux of the issue. Who she was and what she was doing in Purdy was at the heart of the matter. And, of course, who killed her and why. Tom was sure it was Doc Bradford, but still had no idea why. The obvious answer was that he was involved in some drug-running or sex-trafficking scheme. Hard to believe for a small-town doctor.

With all these questions circling again through his head, Tom really wished Levitt was coming to see him today. He needed someone to talk to about his new information and his concerns. Should he ask to call him today? Anything he said would be overheard by whoever was on duty, so no, that wouldn't work. I guess Thursday would have to do. And maybe more will happen before then. Hopefully not bad. Tom's thoughts continued, If I'm being railroaded, the train must be on the tracks, and it might be moving already .

Doug snored one last time and sat up on his bunk. "Wow, I really slept. Hope I wasn't run out of office while I was that disconnected."

Tom felt he had to reply, "Well, no one's sitting at your desk, so that's probably a good sign."

"And no one locked me in my own cell, so that's an indication there was no outright coup."

Tom took a chance on being overly familiar with the sheriff and said, "After what I've seen of your job over the past few days, I'm not sure who would want to take it over."

Doug didn't respond verbally but looked over at Tom and shook his head. Tom took that as an affirmation of Tom's observation.

Tom and Doug both headed to their respective bathrooms. After that, Tom sat back down on his bunk, but Doug walked out of his cell and over to his desk. And therein lay the difference. As subtle as that difference seemed, it was an enormous one. Tom was still locked up in a jail cell. He had to depend on his attorney and the decency and honesty and hard work of Doug and others to set him free. He was, for now, completely dependent on the efforts and intentions of others. Despite his good treatment and the good food and relative freedoms afforded to him, he was still helpless to work on freeing himself. In fact, he had to depend on others just to bring him food. This was as far as he could get from his life of total freedom and self-reliance—and all that was just a couple of weeks and a few miles away. All because of the motel room he was in for one night of his life.

He laid back down and stared at the ceiling. He had taken great pride and comfort in never being under someone else's control, and that was a large reason he had left his PhD program. Too many people had a say in whether he was deemed successful or not. Escaping to the woods was the ultimate freedom. Maybe he should have figured out how to never come into town at all.

Tom made himself sit up. This was not a healthy thinking process. While it was all true, it did not help him move forward with his life and certainly did not help his mental state.

He went back to the bathroom, washed his face and hands, and brushed his teeth—anything to help him feel better about himself and his situation and gather some more positive thoughts.

If Doug was working on framing him, would he really go out of his way to get him gym time and allow so many visitors? Tom's thoughts went back to Monday and Tuesday. The gym time was a lot of fun. Monday was a bit much, with so many kids, but he was really glad Mark had specifically asked him to come over to help. Would that happen, or would Doug agree if they really thought Tom was a murderer? That kind of bedlam and the storm might create the perfect escape opportunity. And the compliment from Kelly on his officiating. That never happened. Ever. Not to any official he'd ever heard of. If he was going to the gallows, why was everyone so nice? Was it all part of some sadistic scheme?

Stir crazy. That's what Marilyn said. Maybe he really had gone stir crazy. Is this what stir crazy actually is?

The office door opened, and Marilyn walked in. That was a relief. Anything to stop these swirling thoughts—even if she picked on him ruthlessly or threatened to shoot him. Anything is better than this!

"Biscuits and gravy, guys."

That sounded really good. Could something as simple as a hot breakfast completely change his attitude?

As he started eating, he decided the answer was definitely yes. Once again, the food was really good!

Marilyn walked back over when he was done, took his tray, and warmed up his coffee. Oddly, she and Doug then stepped outside for a bit. She came back in alone.

Tom couldn't help it. "Marilyn, what is going on? You guys are doing something that's a big secret to me, and frankly it's bugging me."

"Oh, sorry. We're working on skipping the trial and going right to the hanging. I'm on the gallows design committee. We're buying the lumber and the rope and figuring out the trap door and also how to weigh you without you knowing. When you came in, you were too skinny to hang, so we've almost got you up to a good hanging weight. By the way, did you enjoy breakfast?"

How did she come up with this stuff? Suddenly he felt sorry for Mark, but he decided to play along.

"If you're going to hang me, please, let me cooperate. I certainly want it to be quick and effective. No sense hanging around needlessly."

"Good one, Tom. I'll have Mark weigh you in at the gym today."

"Probably not a bad idea. I don't want to have to have my coveralls let out."

"Ok. Go back to sleep. I've got work to do."

Marilyn did indeed turn her attention to the files on her desk, reviewing each one and adding handwritten notes as she went.

"Anything I can help you with?"

"Nice try. I'm trying to get you hung, and you keep interrupting."

"So you are working on my case…"

"Seriously, Tom. You're worse than Eddie. Go to sleep!"

Wow, worse than a eight-year-old. That's a shot. Guess I'd better leave her alone. Tom turned to his reading, but a few minutes later, Bobby came in.

"The paper finally came out. They waited until this morning to deliver it. Here's your copy, Tom. I brought you your very own. Fresh off the press."

"Thanks, Bobby. Hope it's better than last week."

Tom turned to the front page. Pictures of the storm. Some cars in the ditches, usual winter storm stuff. Interviews with Bobby and the tow truck drivers. Article about the two people Bobby helped bring in from the Deer Lake Road.

Nothing about him. Good. Page two. Weddings and funerals, a few ads. Page three—here it is—an article about the motel. Owner out of town, assistant manager on duty 24/7. Rooms were full during the storm, so it had been a busy shift. Hmmm, "Owner out of town." Now both Phil and Doc are gone. What does that mean? Apparently the Purview couldn't cover the motel without a mention of the recent murder and the suspect Thomas Reynolds, still being held without bail in the county jail. That was unnecessary.

Next page: editorials, opinions, and letters to the editor. The first editorial was a positive commentary on how well the school system, the highway maintenance department, and sheriff's department handled the snow emergency. The second one was about Tom. Still in jail, but out interacting with kids, walking around town sometimes not even in handcuffs. Ouch, hope Mark didn't get in trouble for that. Was any progress at all being made in bringing him to justice? Until that happens, this local murder is a black eye to the entire town and county.

First letter to the editor was from the Reverend Susan Andrews. This could be interesting.

"Dear Readers - As you may know, I am the pastor at Purdy Community Church. One of my duties is to provide pastoral services to anyone held at the local jail. In that capacity, I have visited several times with Thomas Reynolds, currently being held without bond in connection with the murder of Sarah Thompson at the Purdy Motel. But then, if you read this paper, you are well aware of that fact. I have no idea if Mr. Reynolds murdered Miss Thompson or not. But in my visits with him, I have found him to be a decent, civilized man—not the sociopathic madman this paper worked so hard to portray him as in the most recent edition. As we all know, the wheels of justice grind slowly, so let's not rush to judgment. Whether guilty or not, I trust the truth will come out, and if Mr. Reynolds is found innocent, I hope he can return to his life, however he chooses, without wearing the horrific brand this paper attempted to sear him with."

Tom almost teared up. While Susan didn't exactly proclaim him a saint, or even innocent, she did make him sound like a human being.

The rest of the paper was made up of the usual ads for local businesses and a few items picked up from the news wires: a man in NYC found to be harboring protected species turtles, a woman in Wyoming shot a record elk, a woman in Wisconsin shot her husband, Congress working on a bill to raise taxes, and hundreds displaced by flooding in Asia. Nothing that mattered to Tom, except that he was now a bit more human thanks to Susan. But reading through the paper did take up some of his time, so it was good enough to fill an hour or so of his morning.

Marilyn had been working at the desk all morning now, and she barely looked up when Bobby came in with lunch. "I got you cheeseburgers and fries. Nothing fancy, but I did get you malts to go with 'em.

"I see your evil plot now. You really are fattening me up to hang me."

Bobby looked over at Tom, but he spoke to Marilyn. "What the heck is he talking about?"

"Nothing, Bobby. He's finally gone over the edge. Been talking to himself all morning. Thanks for lunch."

Bobby shook his head. "I'm off duty the rest of the day, so call Doug if you need anyone. I've pulled the overnight shift again."

"Noted."

Marilyn set up Tom's lunch, then went back to the desk. Tom watched her while he ate. She ate absentmindedly as she worked. Whatever she was doing was sure taking all her attention.

Chapter 35

THE AFTERNOON DRIFTED slowly by, and Tom kept reading to prevent his thoughts from going to a completely dark place. Marilyn spoke abruptly. "Oh! It's time to walk you over to the gym. Get ready. I'll pack up and be ready when you are." Tom changed into his workout clothes and was ready in a couple of minutes. Marilyn cuffed him to herself, and they walked over. "Marilyn, I know something is going on and it's related to me. Can you share anything?"

"No, Tom, not yet, but hopefully in a few days we'll be able to fill you in."

Again, not a great answer, but more positive than the gallows topic.

Marilyn uncuffed him in the gym. There were fewer kids than usual. "Where did the kids go, Mark?"

"It's perfect snowman and snowball fight weather after the storm, so a lot of the younger kids are playing outside. Mostly high schoolers today. Let's play some serious basketball. Full court. We have picked up a few track kids, and they need to run."

Eighteen kids, so nine on each team. Ethan and Kelly volunteered to serve as captains. Sides were picked, and the game began. It became evident early on that this was more intense than any prior games. The speed of the game was incredible, with Ethan and Kelly both prodding their teams to push the ball up the court and then running full-court defenses.

After about 20 minutes, Mark called a water break. He walked over to Tom and said, "I should have warned you. Ethan and Kelly broke up yesterday. Things are a little on edge. Guess they're taking it out on the basketball court."

Another 20 minutes didn't change things much. Apparently it was not an amicable breakup. Another water break and a few kids, unable to keep pace, decided to go home. Maybe a snowman wasn't so childish after all. Another 20, another break, another few defections. Some of these kids were clearly figuring out this was a grudge match. Now down to eight players and Mark and Tom. Ethan looked at his dad. "Guess you'll have to play, coach."

"Good. Then I get the murderer." Kelly was not smiling as she stared at Tom.

"Guess we're in, Tom."

Tom would have thought it impossible, but the intensity ramped up. The pace was incredible, and it took a few trips down the court to get into the flow of the game. Kelly directed him to play point guard, and she crossed the court from wing to wing looking for an open scoring opportunity. It didn't take long before the two of them were working well together. No matter where he crossed the half line, he knew where to look for her, and if she didn't have a good shot, she found a teammate or flung it back to Tom, who looked for his own openings or a good pass to another teammate.

When Mark found his whistle and enough breath, he called another break. Many of the kids just sat down on the floor, exhausted. Tom considered joining them, but he needed water even more.

Finishing his turn at the water fountain, he sat down next to Mark, who said, "You can really play—and you clearly have a solid grasp on the game. Remember, though, that if you get out of jail, you still can't date Kelly, despite the magic between you." Mark laughed.

"That magic was just her using me, and it's obvious I can't keep up with her anyway."

Mark blew his whistle. "We've got about 15 minutes left, and we all need to cool off a bit before we go outside. Pair up for horse. Use four baskets and get going."

Unfortunately, but not unexpectedly, the finals came down to Kelly and Ethan. The shot selection was increasingly ridiculous, and Ethan won with a shot from deep in the corner that Kelly barely missed.

Both just walked off the court, put on their jackets, and went out the door.

Mark shrugged. "Well, that was fun! Teenage romance. A lot of passion, one way or the other."

Tom nodded his agreement. "Intense. I may need two showers."

"I guess I need to cuff you again. The newspaper squealed on us."

"Understand."

The shower never felt so good. Tom ached all over, and he knew it would get worse as he cooled off. He stood in the hot water as long as he felt he could without Mark asking him what he was doing—or just taking a look for himself.

Dried and dressed, Tom sat down on his cot and took another look through his copy of the Purview. Nothing new struck him. He was hungry but didn't mind sitting a bit. Doug came in with dinner, and they both ate in silence, Doug hunched over the desk, reading files and making handwritten notes, just as Marilyn had done all day.

Right at eight o'clock that evening, Susan came in. "Hi, Doug. Can I visit with Tom a bit ?"

"Absolutely."

Susan came over and pulled up the guest chair. "Lenten services just ended, so I thought I'd come over before I went home."

"Where's Maggie? Wait, I'm sorry. First and foremost, thank you for your letter to the editor. I hope everyone read it. It made me seem almost human."

"Glad to do it. You do seem like a decent person, and you may be fooling me and others with your decency, but you do deserve a fair trial and a chance to defend yourself. And Maggie went home with a friend to stay overnight."

Their visit went back and forth about their backgrounds, their families, Tom's situation, his home in the woods, her studies at seminary,

Maggie. The conversation went on and on. Finally, Doug interrupted. "Do you guys realize it's almost midnight?"

Susan turned to look at the clock. "Oh my goodness. I did not. Sorry, Doug. I'll get going. Good night, Tom."

As Susan went out the door, Bobby came in.

"I did one final patrol around town. All quiet. I'm here for the night, Doug. See you tomorrow."

"Thanks, Bobby. See you tomorrow."

"You need anything, Tom?"

"Nope. Good night."

Chapter 36

THURSDAY MORNING. Finally. He would see Marci and talk to his lawyers. Find out what they knew. Tell them what he had been hearing and seeing. Figure out if any of it fit together.

He sat up. Pain. Wow, even the arches of his feet hurt. He was clearly not a high school kid anymore. Which, given the obvious emotional pain between Ethan and Kelly, was probably a good thing. But he really did hurt.

What about Susan? His thoughts went next to her. That was the longest conversation he'd had with anyone ever in his life. They really seemed to hit it off. Was her letter to the editor more than an official missive?

"Breakfast." Marilyn came in with the usual diner bag. Bobby sat up in the other cell. "Wow. Doug said he slept really well here night before last. Now I would have to agree. This is a really comfortable cot."

Marilyn listened to Bobby but looked directly at Tom. "Exhaustion has its rewards. Right, Tom?"

Now what was she talking about? Tom looked back at Marilyn, so she continued, "I hear you and Kelly Adams put on a basketball clinic yesterday. As mad as he was, Ethan was awestruck by her basketball play and said you were incredible. His team never had a chance."

"She can really play. And she has an intensity you don't see often, especially at the high school level."

"I agree. Not sure what came between her and Ethan. He won't talk about that, but it will come out eventually. Anyway, eat up while it's still hot."

Tom dragged himself to the bars of his cell, got his tray, and sat down to eat. Marilyn and Bobby ate at the desk. Bobby started talking, but Marilyn's eyes shut him down. The rest of the morning was silent. Bobby went home, Marilyn worked, and Tom dug into one of the books Susan had brought him the night before. It was a big hardcover, but when Tom opened it, he found no file or gun, so he just started reading.

His thoughts kept straying back to Susan. That was an unbelievably comfortable evening of visiting. Something he had thought he could never do. Those thoughts were interrupted over and over with thoughts of seeing Marci again. Suddenly, he seemed to like being around people. Who'd have thought?

Lunch was good but uneventful. Even Marilyn had quit her usual banter and focused on the growing stack of files. A courier came in with more paperwork, which she sorted and laid out on the desk.

The DA came in and wordlessly, Marilyn handed him a large stack of files. He left and she went back to her work. Tom had never seen anyone make so many notes, and he'd been in a PhD program!

Tom was wondering when Marci would arrive when the phone rang. Marilyn answered. "Ok. Yes, it's ok. He's here, and you can visit right here. No discussion of the case."

A few minutes later, Marci walked in, followed by their mother. "Oh no," Tom thought, "Mom seeing me in the standard orange coveralls and behind bars. This is not good. Why did she have to come along? More importantly, where are Levitt and Monica?"

Marci looked first at the desk and addressed Marilyn. "Hi, we're here to see Tom Reynolds. I'm his sister Marci, and this is his mother, Eileen."

"Welcome. Tom's been expecting you. I'll grab another chair. I don't expect any problems, but please be advised you can't reach through the bars. Some rule about the risk of handing him a gun or something."

"Understand, though a hug would be nice."

Marilyn smiled a bit. "That will have to wait for now. Rules are rules."

"Hi, Mom, Marci. I was hoping you'd never have to see me in a jail cell."

His mom spoke first. "Oh, Tom. Marci says you are innocent, and I believe her. I don't believe you could kill anyone, but I just had to see you. Are they treating you well?"

Marilyn laughed. Both women turned and looked at her. "Sorry. Ladies, this is the only five-star jail in the state, and if he tells you otherwise, he's flat out lying."

"Is that true, Tom?"

"It is. I have quite a few visitors, I eat very well, and I get to go over to the high school and exercise every weekday."

Again, Marilyn chimed in. "And he's kind of got a thing for one of the high school girls ."

"Marilyn, you are not helping. I sometimes play basketball with the kids, and the superstar girls' basketball player picks me for her team when she gets the chance, and we do play well together. My position is that she is ruthlessly using me because I can handle the ball and pass to her when she's open. Besides, she just broke up with Marilyn's son, so I don't want to just get her on the rebound."

Marci and Eileen were both visibly taken aback by the casual back and forth between Tom and his jailer, so Marci tried to take control of the conversation. "Sounds like you are making yourself at home."

Tom replied. "Yes, it's as good as it can be, given that I'm still in jail waiting to see my fate, which is entirely in other people's hands. Speaking of which, where are my attorneys?"

"They drove up with us, but we dropped them at the courthouse in Thompson Falls where some kind of 'case discovery process work' was going on." Marci used air quotes for the term 'case discovery process work.'

Tom was watching Marilyn and for the first time noticed that she was down to just a few file folders on her desk. "Marilyn, where are all your files? And where's Doug?"

"The files and Doug are in Thompson Falls for some 'case discovery process work'." Marilyn used the air quotes as well.

"Can you tell me any more than that?"

"No ."

Tom looked at his mother and sister. "That is the shortest response I've gotten from her since I was brought in here." Marilyn just smiled, then said, "But I do actually have some work to do on the files that are still on my desk, so you folks just visit and I'll butt out."

Marci picked up the thread. "We were told that Lionel and Monica would drive up with the sheriff tonight and be here tomorrow morning. Lionel also said to not worry, the discovery work they were doing in Thompson Falls would most likely prove beneficial to you."

Eileen chimed in. "Marci has told me everything that happened, as you described it to her and Randy. This must be a real ordeal for you."

"It sure has been. I obviously wish it had never happened, but I must say, I've been treated fairly at every step. The second hardest part is being confined this way, after the freedom I've always enjoyed. The hardest part, in reality, is the helplessness. I feel like I'm at the mercy of a whole bunch of people and I just hope they are doing their jobs well and honestly. That's why I was so much hoping to talk with my attorneys again. They're the only ones whose main duty is to look out for me."

"As I said, they'll be here tomorrow, so for today you just have to put up with us." Marci seemed a little perturbed at Tom's remarks.

"I'm sorry. I am very glad you're here. It is good to see you again. Enough about me. What's going on at home?" Even as he said the word 'home,' he realized it had been a long time since he had thought of his boyhood home as home.

From there, the conversation took on a more normal flow, with all three participating. They covered Marci's family, Tim's family and how well he was doing with his career. Tom waited for a comparison of the two, but nothing was said out loud. They covered Eileen's health and the condition of the house and how long she planned to stay in it. At one point, Tom saw the opportunity to do a little probing of his own.

"Has Randy said much about his visit up here?"

"No, not really . Why?"

Tom looked at Marci intently, looking for any hint of deception. Nothing. Good. Apparently Randy had not shared his rant to Tom with his wife. Tom did note that he was not along on this trip.

"Randy decided not to come up with you guys?"

"No, once Lionel told us it would be an overnight, and there were already four of us in the car, he decided to stay home with the kids, get them to school, and go to work as much as he could."

That sounded logical, so Tom let it go.

Marilyn spoke up. "Tom, do you want to go over to the gym today? It's time if you do. Your mom and sister could tag along, and they could see what you've been up to. Besides, then I can go home so I'm there when my little ones get home."

Tom thought for a second. Sitting here was getting old for all of them. "Sure. I'll get changed. You ladies need to turn your backs. One of the issues here is a complete and total lack of privacy."

Marilyn stood up. "They can use the restroom, then wait by the door. Let me know when you're ready."

Tom changed quickly, and Marilyn came over and followed the usual cuffing routine. For Marci and Eileen's benefit, she said, "If Mark, my husband, who you will meet at the gym, hadn't been ratted out for following Tom down the sidewalk during the blizzard, I could skip this, but we can't have that happen again."

All cuffed up, the foursome worked their way over to the gym, Tom and Marilyn appearing to be hand in hand to hide the cuffs, with Marci and Mom following behind.

The four of them paraded through the gym doors, where Marilyn uncuffed Tom and herself and handed the cuffs and key to Mark. "Mark, this is Marci, Tom's sister, and his mother, Eileen."

"Nice to meet you. Tom's been very helpful with our afternoon gym program. And he's quite the basketball player. Most importantly, the kids have accepted him and he fits in very well."

Eileen stared at Mark. "What is your neck size?"

Mark laughed. "I try to never wear a shirt that requires that and certainly not a necktie. I'm an old wrestler, so I built my neck up over many years. Now it just stays that way, with a little ongoing conditioning."

"Mark is deputized in order to take responsibility for Tom and will walk him back to the jail when they're done. This is a small county and smaller town, so Mark has worked as a deputy quite a few times over the years when we've been short-staffed. I'm supposed to be part-time, but with Tom in jail, I've been putting in quite a few hours. We cannot, by state law, leave a prisoner unattended." Marci and Eileen both nodded at Marilyn's remarks.

Just then, the kids poured into the gym and Marilyn said, "I'd better get going if I'm going to be home when my little ones get there. Nice to meet you both."

Mark directed Marci and Eileen to folding chairs on the stage, then pointed to the volleyball net set up on the far court. "Volleyball today, kids. Pick your sides." Turning to Tom, he said, "I couldn't do another round of basketball like yesterday. We need to cool things down for the kids, too."

Tom nodded. "I share your view."

There were plenty of kids for two teams, so Mark and Tom officiated. Outside of a few contested endline calls, the game went smoothly, with kids shuffling in and out. After a couple of games, a couple of boys dropped out to play horse. Mark kept an eye on them as well as the game. Kelly captained one team and Ethan the other as usual.

As the gym time wound down, Mark cooled the kids off with some slower exercises. Then he walked Tom, Marci, and Eileen back to the jail.

"We should probably go over and check into the motel," Marci said, looking at her mother. "Then Tom can shower in privacy."

Eileen nodded. "That makes sense. Can we come back after dinner?"

Tom replied, "Sure. That would be great. See you later."

The women walked with Tom and Mark back to the jail, then got in their car and left.

"They seem really nice," Mark said.

"Yeah, I come from a good family. They haven't given up on me, so I suppose I shouldn't either."

"I wouldn't. This will all work out. That's all I can say. Take your shower. I'll sit and relax a bit."

Tom took his time in the shower, working out the last of the kinks from yesterday and thinking about all these brief, mysterious comments. 'This will all work out'. What did that mean? And Levitt's comments about the case discovery process work going 'most likely in your favor'. Is there some backroom deal cooking? And where is Doc Bradford? Are they going to ask Tom to plead to something less? He didn't do anything else, except break into the church and hold Bobby overnight at his cabin.

He was drying off when Bobby came in. "Chicken pot pies and homemade biscuits. Man, I hope they never let you out."

Mark laughed. "Apparently I'm the only one trying to keep him healthy. Enjoy your dinner. I'm headed home. I'll be back around 10 o'clock tonight, OK?"

Bobby replied, "Yup, unless I get a call. Then you or Marilyn will need to come in right away."

"Got it. See you later."

Bobby set up dinner for Tom, and they both dug in.

Chapter 37

TOM HAD FINISHED dinner and was relaxing on his cot when he decided there was no harm in doing some more probing on his situation. "Bobby, what's going on? Why all the secrecy? Where's Doug?"

Bobby looked over at Tom. "I am the Sergeant Schultz of this operation, Tom. Remember him from Hogan's Heroes? I know nothing."

"That's a lie and you know it."

"That's what I was told was the only answer I was to give to anything you asked. But you'll find out in the morning. I actually don't know what that information will be, but I do know there's a powwow in the a.m."

Well, Tom thought, no answer but at least there's a time frame. Thinking through all the events of the past few days and all the hints he had picked up, he was deep in thought when the office door opened and Marci and his mom walked in again.

"Are you done with dinner? Can we visit a little more?"

"Sure. Come on in. Marci, you've met Bobby. Bobby, this is my mom, Eileen. They came to visit me on death row."

"Oh, Tom, don't say that." Marci was speaking to Tom but looking at her mother. Changing the subject, she went on, "We had dinner at the diner—chicken pot pie. It was very good."

"That's what Bobby and I had too. It was good. The meals here are great. Better than I feed myself when I'm at home in my cabin. Certainly more variety."

"Glad you are eating well. That's one less worry," Marci said, happy to get the conversation on a better track.

"How's the motel?"

Marci replied, "Very basic. Room, bed, bathroom."

"Who checked you in?"

This time Eileen replied. "A younger woman. She said she'd been on duty for days. Kind of whining about it, actually."

So no Phil yet. Interesting. Maybe this was always his vacation week. Who knew? No, really, who knew anything about Phil and his usual habits? He remained a mystery to Tom, but he was more convinced than ever that Phil had something to do with the murder. Or at least knew something.

Just as the three of them settled into more conversation, the door opened again.

Bobby looked up. "Hi, Susan. Tom's already got company. Do you want to join in?"

"Sure. I'd heard he had company and I wanted to meet them ."

Introductions complete, the conversation turned to the town—observations of the two newcomers and insights from Susan. The flow was easy and natural among all four of them, with Bobby occasionally chiming in, showing he was listening to all of it.

Marci asked the group about the newspaper and why it was so hard on Tom.

"Sensationalism, pure and simple," Susan replied. "Did Tom show you the last edition?"

"I neglected to do that. Here it is. Take a look. Skip to the letters to the editor." Tom handed his mom the latest edition.

They quickly found Susan's letter, and Marci handed it to Eileen as soon as she had read it. "Thank you very much. That was very nice of you."

"It simply needed to be said," Susan replied. Besides, it's true. And it's as nice as Doug would let me be."

"Doug?"

"Sheriff Printer. This is small town, in case you hadn't noticed."

Tom's ears perked up. So Doug had previewed the letter. That was interesting. Everything was getting more and more interesting.

"Do you play Scrabble?" Susan was always looking for a game and she now had new victims in her sights.

"Sure."

"Well then let's get set up."

Susan had won two games when the door opened and Doug came in. Tom looked at the clock. 9:30 p.m. Where was Mark?

"Hello, everyone. I always thought we might have to add on to the jail, but I was thinking prisoners, not visitors."

The usual round of introductions followed, Marci recognizing the sheriff from her prior visit.

"Bobby, why don't you do one last evening patrol around town, make sure the kids are off the streets and the bar is quiet. I'll stay here for the night. I canceled Mark. If I pay him and Marilyn any more overtime, they'll retire and move to Florida and I can't afford to lose them."

Bobby left as directed. "It was nice to meet you, Eileen. Nice to see you again, Marci."

Eileen spoke up. "Thank you, Sheriff. Tom says you've treated him with respect for his entire time here."

"That's good to hear. I try. He's been a model prisoner, so he's earned his good treatment. I think Marilyn is a little hard on him from time to time, but we need to keep him alert, too."

Tom wondered if Doug was in on the gallows humor she'd shared with him. Doug had a way of finding out everything, so he'd probably heard about it.

"I'm going to have to call an end to visitors' hours. I've got a little paperwork to finish and need to get some sleep. Tom has a big day tomorrow too. We have a meeting at 8 a.m. and a court appearance at 9 o'clock. Glad to see you cleaned up after gym today, Tom.

Marci looked at Doug. "Are we invited?"

"Not to the meeting. The court is open to the public as long as you behave. Just come over to the courthouse a little before 9:00 and wait in the hallway. Marilyn will meet you there."

"I'll be there too," Susan said. "I'll see you all there."

She slipped out the door, leaving Marci and Eileen at the bars.

"Go ahead and at least shake his hand. If he breaks out of jail now, he'd be in the news as the stupidest criminal ever."

That comment from Doug really made Tom wonder. What will tomorrow bring?

Chapter 38

TOM WAS AWAKE before first light. He could barely make out the clock on the wall—6:15. He couldn't discern for sure who was in the other bunk. He lay quietly on his cot, trying to relax. He sure hoped all the signs pointing to something good were accurate. To have something go wrong now would be devastating. He also hoped it wasn't just some elaborate buildup only to get him to plead to something lower that would still lead to prison time. Innocent people shouldn't go to prison, but he knew it could happen.

He rolled over and checked the clock. 6:17. This was not working. Concentrate on something else. Susan. She was a saint. Not just a pastor but an actual saint—visiting with him, playing Scrabble game after game, writing the letter to the editor, spending time with Marci and his mom. He owed her a lot more than a loaf of communion bread. So many others had also made this all survivable. Bobby, Doug, Mark and Marilyn, even the kids in the gym. Kelly, who pushed him to play basketball at a level he hadn't experienced in a very long time. Ethan and Evan, even Maggie and the other younger kids who asked him such obvious questions without obvious answers.

Tom woke with a start. He had fallen back to sleep and now Doug had come into the office. Bobby sat up from the other bunk. 7:15. He'd managed to put an hour behind him. It was fully light.

"I see you're both up bright and early!" Doug said. Irony or not. You never knew.

"Here's your breakfast, just some pastries today. I'll start the coffee." Bobby sauntered out of the other cell. Tom did not. Subtle difference but still there.

Tom went over to his bathroom area and freshened up, taking more care and time than usual—mostly trying to fill some time. The coffee smelled good. *I guess it's time to wake up and smell the coffee* How appropriate. More today than ever.

The cheese Danish he selected was as good as usual, but for some reason was kind of hard to swallow. The coffee helped a lot. Tom got it all down, but then it lay in the pit of his stomach. He hoped it didn't come back up. *Come on, Tom, all the hints are optimistic Take heart. Just be sure to listen carefully and don't make any rash decisions, no matter what they offer.*

Tom watched the clock tick minute by minute. At 7:55, Doug came over and opened the cell door. "Walk in front of me, down the tunnel and up into the courthouse holding room. I'll cuff you there until we are ready for you. Got it?"

"Ok." The fact that Doug didn't feel the need to cuff him while still in his cell was yet one more promising sign that things might go well for him this morning.

Doug left Tom in the holding room, cuffed to a ring in the wall. Just like by the phone. Someone had given this some thought.

No clock; time dragged by. Tom concentrated on breathing regularly. The door opened. Doug came in, uncuffed him, and walked him to the meeting room where he had first met with Levitt, Marci, and Randy.

"Have a seat, Tom." He took the chair at the end of the table. At the opposite end of the table from him was the DA. On his right side were Levitt and a young woman he took to be Monica. On the other side of the table, Doug sat down next to Marilyn.

Doug said, "I'll kick this off."

The others nodded.

Levitt said, "First let me introduce Monica Simpson, my associate. I believe Tom has not met her."

"Thanks," Doug said. "Sorry to skip that."

Tom nodded to Monica. "We've talked on the phone. It's nice to meet you in person."

Doug went on. "Tom, I'll start by apologizing for keeping you locked up all this time, but it was absolutely necessary. I've known pretty much from the beginning that you did not commit the crime, but I had to keep you locked up."

Tom couldn't hold back. "Why, if you knew…"

"I'll explain. There are three reasons. First, you have an unbelievable ability to disappear into the woods. No one could track you, and unless you had come back to your cabin to meet with Bobby, we may have never seen you again. That grates on people, mostly me. I didn't want to lose track of you completely, regardless of guilt or innocence. The DA did not know for sure you didn't do it, but knew he had what he needed to arraign you, so he did.

"Second, on your own, you were already launching your own investigation. When Bobby told me how much you'd figured out already, I knew I couldn't afford to have you working in the shadows to clear yourself. I needed to keep you out of my way, so I could complete my investigation and get the results to the DA without tripping over your investigation.

"Finally, as you suspected, the real criminals are Phil Jenson and Doctor Gerald Bradford. More on what they were doing later. But for now I'll just say they are dangerous people who might have killed you if they had to. In fact, I'm not sure Doc didn't already take a run at it. I needed to keep you in jail to keep you safe. In fact, I prohibited the doctor from treating you in jail. I didn't want him anywhere near you."

Doug paused, just like he had in the gym that day.

"Here's what happened." Another brief pause, then Doug went on.

"The Doc and Phil met when the doctor was an intern at the prison where Phil was being held for drug dealing and other acts of crime and violence. He'd been in and out of jail his whole life—mostly in. Doc was a bit shady himself. We're not really sure if his Mexican medical degree is valid, but we needed a doctor in this town. So, when Doc Edwards retired, that paved the way for Bradford to take over.

"Bradford and Phil scraped up $25,000 for a down payment on the motel, and Phil bought it from the Rogers on a contract for deed, thus avoiding any type of background check—criminal, credit, or otherwise. They then set up their own little drug-running scheme.

"Phil let the drug runners use the motel to stay overnight. They brought in uncut heroin and gave it to Bradford. He processed it in the lab at the hospital to make it sellable on the street. Then, the next morning—very early, say around 2 a.m.—he dropped it back at the motel to be taken away. The drug runners had no cars, so they were essentially captive. They were stuck in a small town far from anywhere, with no transportation of their own. The drug bosses didn't want them disappearing with the product. They were dropped at the motel with the uncut heroin, too far to walk to run off to anywhere, then were picked up with the street product early the next morning. Using the motel kept the couriers from going to and from the hospital and was Phil's part of the deal. Doing this all in Purdy kept it out of sight of any state police or other law enforcement departments. That's how Phil earned his cut. It also kept the doc at arm's length from the trafficking, at least until the night you were at the motel."

Again, a pause. Tom had a hundred questions, but he knew Doug would cover them if he just let him proceed.

Doug continued.

"This is what we can piece together from the evidence and statements from Phil and the Doc. The night you were unlucky enough to be in the motel, the girl—and we'll get to her later—started fussing about her role and her cut. Doc lost patience and smacked her. According to him, she then pulled a pistol out of her purse and, before she could do anything, he lunged for the gun. In the struggle, the gun went off, the first shot going into the mattress, muffling the sound. Then he got control of the gun, shot her once, missed her once, driving a shot into the wall, then shot her again. He then ran, with the gun and the drugs he was supposed to drop off. That's when you came into the picture, literally. You checked on the girl, heard a car, looked at the car, saw the driver, who took a shot at you and grazed you, then shot again and missed before speeding away."

Another pause.

"In case you weren't counting, that's six shots, so all he had. That might be the only reason you're still alive."

Tom had a hard time taking that in, but it made sense. Logic was not his forte at the moment, and this was a lot of information coming all at once.

"Any corrections, additions, or deletions?" Doug was canvassing the room.

The DA simply said, "Go on."

"The girl who was initially identified as Sarah Thompson is really Teresa Smith, with a Miami address. She had been doing this awhile and had been caught before but had always been released due to her age and her small role. Unfortunately, she went back because of the money or her own drug problem or something. Her autopsy did show a history of heroin use. Apparently small, plain motel rooms in small, remote towns in the dead of winter was not what she thought she had signed up for. Not the glamorous life she wanted or expected."

The DA interrupted. "And you know this because…"

"Phil and Doc both independently stated and put in their written statements that she was getting to be a problem. They were sorry about killing her. It was never intended, let alone to be so sloppy. They were hoping to get this one last delivery out of her and then let her boss in Miami deal with her ."

The DA responded, "I did see that in their written statements. I thought it would be helpful for the whole group to know."

"Good point. Anything else?" Doug continued.

"So I'll try to put a bow on this. Once the net was tightening, Bradford ran, and once Phil knew Doc was gone, he ran, too. We put out APBs and both were arrested before they could disappear. Had them extradited to Thompson Falls, where we spent yesterday finishing up the interviews and got their statements. Phil and Doc are being transported here from Thompson Falls as we speak and will be arraigned at 10:00, right after your final hearing at 9:00, Tom, when the DA will formally drop all charges so that is all on the record."

"So, Tom, I'll give you first shot at questions."

Tom couldn't believe what he had heard. Marilyn was actually tearing up a bit. Tom turned to Levitt. "You knew this?"

"Not until yesterday. The sheriff and I were in communication, and I knew he was pursuing other leads besides you. A couple of times he headed off something I wanted to investigate, sometimes based on the first conversation you and I had, saying he'd cover that and let me know. The good news for you is that you didn't run up much of a bill at all. The better news is having all charges dropped, of course."

Tom turned back to Doug. "How did you get Phil and the Doc to confess to all of this?"

"We'd been watching Phil ever since he came to town—the oddity of guests to Purdy with no car, pickups and drop-offs, Phil's frequent trips out of town, running the motel, spending quite a bit of money despite the fact the Rogers could barely make a go of it (and they were good at it)."

"There was also the odd fact that Ed Rogers suddenly had some serious illness, diagnosed by Doctor Bradford. We talked to Doc Edwards and he said he'd never seen any such symptoms in Ed and had a hard time believing he had that disease—all had been done to grease the motel sale to Phil.

"Mostly it was when we subpoenaed the guest logs and motel accounting records and found they didn't match the guests we saw come and go. Once we put the pressure on Phil, he flipped on Doc Bradford pretty quickly. Once we had Doc in our sights, we got a search warrant for the clinic and found trace evidence of heroin in the lab. Once we threatened long, long prison sentences, they told us everything, with signed statements. They're the ones who begged for some kind of plea deal."

"We had to bring the murder charge down from premeditated to a lesser charge, but all we had to go on was Bradford's story on how the shooting took place. In other words, it started with self-defense. Figured that was all we could get anyway because there were no other witnesses, just some shots fired and the girl was dead—not Doc Bradford.

"The bigger issue is the drug charges. We will let them plead out, the judge will determine some sentences, and then we turn them over to the feds. Their stay in town will be brief. They'll be taken back to Thompson Falls after the hearing.

"What about the motel? Will it close?"

"No, Phil will have to forfeit that back to the Rogers, and the night manager has agreed to run it for now. They are happy to be retired in Thompson Falls, with family, including grandkids, nearby."

"What about the gun?

"Never found it. Doc's statement says he was going to have Phil put it back in your motel room with your fingerprints on it after he'd sedated—or killed—you. Says he dumped it deep in the woods. Can't remember where. It was a .38 special revolver, so no shell casings at the scene."

Tom was still trying to process all the new information. "And I have to ask. All the kind treatment—the food, the gym privileges—would I have been treated that well if you thought I had done it?"

"Not even close."

"And I hope Bobby isn't in trouble for anything…"

"No, in fact he did everything correctly. The last thing I wanted is for some gun battle where one of you ended up dead. He handled things perfectly up at your cabin, though I suspect you thought you were handling him."

Tom shook his head. He turned to the DA. "You certainly seemed determined to get me to trial at my arraignment."

"I wasn't in on the sheriff's plan or knowledge at that time. It was only after the search warrants that I saw what was really going on. I like convictions as well as the next DA, but I want them to be real. This time we got the real perps, so I'm fine. Sorry if you felt I was trying to railroad you."

"Did everyone know I was innocent? Mark and Marilyn, the county commission, Bobby?"

"They all knew what they had to know. To most, I just made it clear that in my extensive experience and judgment, you were not a threat to anyone in this town. Marilyn helped me a great deal on the final stages of interviews and paperwork, so she was the most clued in."

Tom turned to Marilyn. "So there never was a gallows committee?"

At that question, Doug turned to Marilyn with a confused look.

"Doug, I did what I could to keep Tom in check. I'll explain later."

Tom thought for a moment. "Ok, then. What about the day you brought me in, and you said that the doc and Susan were in some kind of relationship. Was that true?"

"Not for a second. I just made it up."

"Why ?"

"Two reasons. One, I wanted to see your reaction, but mostly I needed you to not use her to launch another investigation like you did with Bobby. I figured if you thought she and the doc were tight, you wouldn't share much with her."

Tom shook his head. "Manipulated every step of the way."

"Don't feel bad, Tom," Doug replied. "What you shared with Bobby was very helpful. It fit well with what our investigation was already telling us and moved things along more quickly. Which was good, because the cost of keeping you in jail was about to break my budget."

The room fell silent.

Doug said, "Then I guess we're done here, Tom. Besides, I need to get you out of jail before St. Patrick's Day. We're usually overbooked then for a few days. I honestly don't know if it's the holiday, or the anticipation of spring, or if it's a holiday in anticipation of spring. Regardless, the jail is full, as is the ER."

Again a bit of a pause, then Doug continued, "Tom, why don't you and Marilyn stay here in this conference room until we're ready for you in the courtroom. We'll call that custody. The rest of you are free to go. I'll tell your mom and sister they can come in. You can fill them in."

Tom wasn't sure his legs would work if he had wanted to go. He sat stock still as the others left. A moment later, Eileen and Marci came in, along with Pastor Susan.

"What's going on?" Susan started the conversation.

"I've been cleared of all charges. They have the real perpetrators in custody, and they are on their way here to be arraigned. Sounds like they've made a deal."

"So why are we sitting here?"

"I need to make a court appearance in a little bit so the DA can formally drop all charges against me so that it's in the court record."

Tom stood up and was mobbed with hugs. After a few moments, Marilyn cleared her throat. "Heartwarming as this is, I need to go over a few things."

All of them remained standing but turned their attention to Marilyn, who continued. "When Doug comes to get us, I will walk Tom in in front of me. The rest of you need to be behind us. Take a seat anywhere in the gallery. Susan, you've been here before, so you know the drill. Tom is officially in my custody until the judge rules."

Heads nodded. Marilyn went on. "Of course, Tom would have to be the stupidest person on the planet if he made a break for it now. Escaping custody is a crime. You don't want that."

Smiles, nods, and happy tears all around.

Marilyn then walked over to Tom and gave him a big hug. "I will actually miss you. And you have been so much help to Mark at the school. The kids are better off because you were there. They'll miss you, too. Any chance you'll just stay in town?"

Tom looked at the women in the room. "I have not had a chance to give that a thought."

Eileen looked at him intently. "His first step will be for a stay at my house. I'm not letting him out of my sight for quite a while this time."

They all laughed. Susan said, "I vote for a stay in town."

Tom then had to say, "I never thought that being a murder suspect would make me so popular. I don't have any long-range plans. I do know I need to get back to my cabin. I left my pack there and some furs to clean. Can't wait until it warms up before I get up there. I have experienced so much kindness here in the past few weeks, I really don't know where I'll go from here. My lonesome life in the woods doesn't seem as appealing as it once did. Besides, I can't afford to let my Scrabble skills erode." He was looking directly at Susan for the last part.

The door opened, and Doug summoned them out. The final hearing went just as orchestrated, and in less than 10 minutes, they were all walking back outside to the jail.

"No tunnel?" Tom asked. Marilyn replied, "Nope. You don't want to meet the two guys in the holding room on this end. Besides, fresh air is good for you."

Epilogue

THE CROWD NOISE WAS DEAFENING. Evan Butler cut through the screen, took the pass, pivoted, elevated, and took the shot from about six feet out. The game-ending horn prevented anyone from hearing the ball swoosh cleanly through the net. The crowd fell silent except for the small band of Purdy fans who had made the trek to Thompson Falls to watch Purdy play Thompson Falls Academy, a small private school that Purdy had lost to in December at home. Tom smiled as the boys celebrated. This was indeed a sign of progress for the team he now coached. His decision to give Evan the final shot had played out well, since Evan's older brother, Ethan, was triple-teamed, as Tom expected would happen.

The bus ride back to Purdy started out noisy and happy as the team and cheerleaders celebrated their victory. The team was now above .500 with a few games to go, and optimism abounded after years of losing records. As the bus worked its way homeward, the kids settled down, letting exhaustion take over. It was well after 10 p.m. when the bus pulled up at the Purdy gym door, and Tom let the kids in to drop off their basketball equipment. Within a few minutes, all had dispersed to the diner or to waiting cars, and he was free to lock up. "Want a ride, Coach?"

Tom turned to his assistant coach and replied, "No thanks, I'll walk. I need to stretch my legs."

"OK. See you Monday."

Tom began the walk across the corner of downtown, behind the jail and courthouse, cutting through an alley, past the church, and to the back door of the parsonage. As he walked, he again marveled. A year ago, he had snuck down these streets and alleys, a fugitive on the run from a murder charge and perhaps even fleeing his own death. That was an incredible change.

Now he was the school science teacher and head basketball coach, and was married to the pastor of the church. You can't get any more embedded in a community than that.

He peered through the darkness to the light of the TV.

"Hi! You didn't have to wait up."

"It's Friday night. Besides, Maggie and I sat up to watch the sports. You won! Congratulations!"

"It was close, but Evan made a clutch shot at the end to avoid overtime, or we'd have been even later."

Tom gazed over at Susan. Hard to believe that change in his life as well. They never really dated, but meals together, countless games of Scrabble, and somehow they ended up married. He didn't remember actually proposing, but Susan said he did. Must have been subliminal. At any rate, once it was apparent they were meant to be married, he did propose the judge marry them at the courthouse, but Susan just laughed.

"I'm a pastor, and I am going to have a church wedding. Besides, I have a number of pastor friends who will be happy to perform the ceremony. But most importantly, we need to get married in our church in our town. You know how this town gossips. We want no doubt that everyone knows we are legally married and that you are a solid citizen. It's bad enough that people know that we met while you were being held in jail for murder."

And so it was. Mark and Randy were attendants for Tom.

Tom had wondered if his relationship with Randy would ever heal, or if they had ever even had one, but Randy was quick to offer a private, profuse apology once he heard the full story from Marci.

Marilyn and Marci were attendants for Susan. Eileen was there, and so was Lionel Levitt, who gave a toast, saying he had never reformed a criminal so quickly or easily. That was not taken lightly by the bride, who quickly stood and said,

"Nice try, Mr. Levitt, but I was clearly the one who reformed him. Countless hours sitting outside his jail cell, converting him to Christian and married, all in one shot."

It seemed like most of the town was present, but to Tom, it still didn't take much to look like a crowd. Tim and his family couldn't make it, but Tom had spent some time with them when he was back visiting his mom.

Tom thought back again to the first days of freedom. As much as he wanted to go back home with his mom and Marci for a visit, he knew he had to get back up to his cabin to finish curing his furs and store everything for the summer. As he approached his homestead, he realized it now looked a little dingy. And the inside smelled. A lot. It smelled of him and furs and now some spoiling food.

He cleaned out the coolers and repacked them with the food he'd packed in, and spent about two weeks curing his remaining furs. Eating his own cooking. Bathing not very often. He found himself missing the banter with Marilyn and the gym time with Mark and the kids. And the shower in his jail cell, public though it was. He even missed Bobby. But mostly he missed Susan. Thought about her a lot, in fact.

Once he had everything done that he had come up to do, he took the furs and the last of his food and packed out. His homestead just didn't have its old appeal. He would go back to Purdy, settle up at the fur dealer and the bank, then head to his mom's for a while.

He arrived in Purdy about suppertime and checked into the motel. He really hoped no one was next to him. The next morning, once he had concluded his business, he went to the diner for a bite. The biscuits and gravy were as good as he had remembered. Before he could finish, Susan walked in.

"Did God tell you I was here?"

"No, I just got a phone call. Just like regular people."

"So you have spies?"

"Absolutely. We all are careful to keep an eye out for you." She winked at Ron, who was working behind the counter.

"Well, it's good to see you regardless of your source."

"Thanks, you, too. So what's next?"

"I need to go spend some time with my mom. And see how big my legal bill is."

"How do you plan to get there?"

"Catch the afternoon shuttle to Thompson Falls, then the bus from there."

"Let me drive you as far as Thompson Falls. We can visit, and I don't mind getting out of town for a bit."

And that drive to Thompson Falls was as natural as every other time they had spent together. And now here she was. His wife.

The visit to his mom was very good. He did some projects for her around the house. He also did the spring cleanup in the yard. He enjoyed the time with his nieces and nephews, and even Tim and his family came for a long weekend.

The last Monday he was there, the phone rang and he answered. It was an unfamiliar voice.

"Tom Reynolds?"

"Yes ."

"This is Martin Anderson, the principal at Purdy Schools. I once signed a letter on your behalf."

The rest of the conversation was a long, involved discussion about Tom's academic background, his time in the gym with Mark, and finally ended with a job offer to teach natural sciences at the Purdy school and coach the boys' basketball team.

Tom hung up and stood thinking for quite some time. If he accepted this offer, that answered the question of the next phase of his life, but added more—where to live, what to do with the homestead… Guess there will always be questions. Just have to take them one at a time.

All he could think of to do now was to call Susan. He realized she was his best resource for life decisions. And all the rest played out as naturally as could be.

"Good night, Tom. Come on up when you're ready."

That simple comment jolted him back into the present. Enough reflecting. Time to move forward. Which meant, get some sleep, enjoy the weekend, then prep for his classes on Monday and the Tuesday night home basketball game.